MW00938626

A Dangerous Man
Complete Collection

Awakening
Rebellion
Claim
Surrender

SERENA GREY

Copyright © 2013 Serena Grey
All rights reserved.

Dedication

For MNC

My first, my last, my everything.

Acknowledgments

Writing this story has been an incredible journey for me, every single step of which has been exciting, rewarding, and unbelievable fulfilling. I have received reviews that have made me so happy I felt over the moon, I have received letters from readers that were so touching they made me cry, and I have experienced the joy of having people I don't even know, discover, buy and love my books.

This journey began sometime in May 2013, when I decided to write a romance series. I've always been a voracious reader, and even though I read everything, from encyclopedias and dictionaries to toothpaste packets and drug leaflets, I've always been in love with romance. So, in the course of a few hours, I wrote an outline for Sophie and David's story, and started to develop the characters in my head.

Over the next few weeks, I wrote as much as I could, while drinking copious amounts of coffee. I created a blog, started a Facebook page, contacted beta readers, and did an enormous amount of research - mostly on kboards.com. Then in June 2013, I published the first book in this series.

I want to thank everyone who has been a part of this extraordinary experience, including, but not limited to, the writers who inspired me, the fellow authors at kboards, who make it the best author forum on the internet, the beta-readers who gave me valuable insight, the reviewers who gave my book a chance, the readers who supported me, and the loved ones who stood by me, believing in me through it all.

Thank you all so much.

In This Series

Awakening (A Dangerous Man #1)

His voice is hoarse. "I am going to make love to you now." He says, "So if you want me to stop, tell me."

I shake my head frantically. If he stops at this point, I'll probably die.

Sophie Bennett has virtually no experience with men. Orphaned from birth, she's gone from living with her reclusive spinster aunt, to a sheltered education in boarding school. So nothing prepares her for David Preston. The intensely attractive businessman is entirely out of her league. Can she handle such a dangerous man, or is she in over her head?

Rebellion (A Dangerous Man #2)

Sophie and David's story continues in this Sequel to Awakening!!!

"Don't you want this Sophie? Don't you want me to touch you? To make love to you, over and over again?" His lips make a trail from my neck to my shoulder. "Isn't it enough?"

David Preston came into Sophie's life and changed it in ways she could never have anticipated. Now the intensely sexy, exquisitely beautiful man is hers, or is he really?

Claim (A Dangerous Man #3)

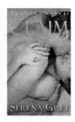

I forget everything but her warmth, her sweetness, and how easy it would be to let everything go, and allow myself to sink into her, body and soul, completely, forever.

Who is David Preston? The mysterious and sexy businessman claimed Sophie Bennett's heart and then broke it. But is that all there is to him?

David Preston likes to be in control, after being neglected as a child, he has his life exactly where he wants. No relationships, no commitments, just sex, no strings attached. Then a chance encounter with a girl in a gift shop changes everything.

Surrender (A Dangerous Man #4)

"Isn't enough that I can't stop thinking about you Sophie?" he says, his voice low and persuasive. "What else do you want from me?"

Sophie chose to be alone rather than be with David Preston, the man who has her heart, and yet refuses to share his. Now she's trying to make a life for herself, a life that will not include him.

But how can she get over a man who refuses to let her go, especially when he can still set fire to her blood with just one touch.

Awakening

A Dangerous Man #1

by

Serena Grey

Chapter One

I LIKE TO LOOK AT THE FRAMED *picture of the young girl that hangs in my room, right by my bed. The girl is smiling, her dark blonde hair ruffled, framing her face in a halo of loose curls. She looks beautiful, happy, and carefree, the only bright spot in my gloomy room. I would do anything to get to know her, to see that smile and hear her laugh, but I can't. She's dead. She died giving birth to me.*

The door opens, and Aunt Josephine walks in. I don't have a lock, and she never knocks. It's her house after all, and I am only twelve. My eyes skip from the picture to her face. She doesn't look mad, but I know she is, she always is. It's never anything I've done or haven't done, although she always makes it seem like it's my fault. She'll always be mad at me. She hates me. She hates that she has to take care of me until I grow up.

I'm glad to be going to boarding school this year, even though

Aunt Josephine says the nuns will 'discipline my mother's faults away from me'. I don't know if the nuns are bad, but I know they can't be as bad as Aunt Josephine. Nobody can.

She comes towards me, her tall, thin frame held straight like a pole.

"What are you doing in here?" She asks. Her voice makes me think of cold, rainy days.

"Nothing," I tell her, shaking my head. I'm just trying to stay out of her way, she tells me off whenever she sees me.

She gives me a long look, as if she can see a sign on my face that I'm lying. I don't want to stare at the layer of shininess on her nose, she hates that, so I look away, and my eyes go back to the picture of my mother.

I can feel Aunt Josephine's disapproval, even though I'm not looking at her.

"So you've shut yourself in here to pine for your precious mother," She sneers. "Well guess what? She's dead, and you killed her." She bends forward, watching my face for my reaction to her words. I'm trying my best not to cry, even though my eyes are filling with tears, even though I know she's saying the truth.

"I don't know why I even bother to try to make something out of you," She snaps, straightening to her full height. "Anybody can see that you're going to end up exactly like her, pregnant with God knows whose child." Her black eyes flash, and I can't stop myself from flinching. "Just don't think I'll be wasting another eighteen years of my life looking after your

bastard."

"Sophie? Are you alright?"

I look up from the spot on the wall where I've been staring while my thoughts wander, and turn towards the front of the small gift shop where I work, to give Stacey Carver a smile. She is sitting at the desk near the entrance, her eyes fixed on me, with a small frown on her face. At the sight of my smile, she relaxes a little. I have perfected the smile that says I'm fine, even though most of the time, I feel far from it.

"I'm fine." I tell her, turning my attention back to cleaning a shelf, which is what I should have been doing in the first place. "I was just thinking." I do have a lot to think about, my life, for instance. Some people have five-year plans, even ten year plans, for me, a two-week plan would be very ambitious. I have no idea where I'll be in two weeks, and the knowledge is frightening.

"You spaced out." Stacey says. "You were staring at the same spot on the wall for a while." She sighs. "You've been doing that a lot lately." At the concern in her voice, I start to feel guilty. She owns the gift shop, which makes her my boss, and she worries about me more than she should. I wish she wouldn't, she has enough things to worry about without adding me to the list.

She's already done too much for me. When my Aunt Josephine died very suddenly, a little more than four months ago, and I found that I had little money, no home, and absolutely no plans, she literally became my guardian angel. While her husband, my aunt's lawyer, took care of discharging the will and settling the estate, which Aunt Josephine bequeathed almost entirely to the local library, Stacey helped me find a small apartment in town, and gave me a job working as an assistant in her gift shop.

"Really, I'm fine." I smile again for good measure. She keeps her eyes on me for a moment, before nodding and turning towards the front of the shop.

I can't see her face anymore, but I can tell that she's still frowning. She raises a slim hand to smoothen her shoulder length brown hair, which is already immaculate, a sure sign that she is still worried. I wish there is something more I can say to put her mind at rest. I wish I had a plan. I hate the fact that I'm the one putting that frown on her face.

The thing is, the gift shop cannot afford to keep me much longer. It's never been particularly profitable, but business is worse than usual. With the recession, fewer people are interested in buying glass sculpture, etchings, and porcelain art, which are the sorts of things we sell. Stacey has to let me go, but she doesn't know how to tell me. For some reason, she feels responsible for me, maybe because she was friends with my mother all those years ago, but it's time for me to be responsible for myself.

I have some money. I've saved a little from the money Stacey insists on paying me for babysitting her kids over the months. I still have the fifteen hundred dollars my aunt left me. Her estate was worth a lot more. Even though she hardly ever left the house, she had been earning an income from indexing textbooks for years. She could have left me enough money so I wouldn't have to worry about my immediate future, but she chose not to. In a way, this makes me glad. If she had shown me any sympathy at the end, I would probably spend the rest of my life wondering if I had misjudged her.

I move my brush to another shelf. The shop is furnished with dark mahogany shelves against the walls, and tables arranged in the center, all covered with a wide variety of items for sale. I run the brush over a miniature porcelain set, admiring it for the umpteenth time. "I've been thinking of moving to Bellevue and finding a job," I tell Stacey. I don't look at her, because I know the expression I'll see on her face. I just think I'm more likely to have some sort of future in Bellevue, population one hundred and thirty two thousand, than in Ashford, population nine thousand and sixty three.

"A job? Are you sure?" I can hear the skepticism in her voice. "That may be harder than it sounds, in this economy." She pauses, "and you don't know anyone in Bellevue, where will you live? How will you find a job?" She is silent for a moment, and I imagine her searching her head for a better alternative. "What about Art school?" She finally asks. "It's what you've always wanted, isn't it?"

It was. I've been drawing for ages, and I have a portfolio full of pencil drawings of things ranging from landscapes to profiles. When I draw I forget everything that's wrong with my life, each stroke of the pencil is like a step towards something beautiful, something that's not tainted with Aunt Josephine's disapproval, my lack of choices for my future, and even my loneliness. My mother was an artist too. There is a watercolor hanging in the local high school gallery that she did when she was seventeen. In a way, drawing makes me feel close to her.

But it's just a hobby. There is no reason to believe that I can make a career out of it even if by some miracle, I somehow found the money to go to art school. Even Aunt Josephine refused outright to pay for Art School, calling it 'a frivolous education'. She insisted that I study something practical, so I applied to City U, UDub, and Bellevue like she wanted. The acceptance letters are gathering dust at the top of the rusty old fridge in my apartment. Now that I have no money, I'm not going to pursue aids and grants to spend four years doing something that's not even close to what I want.

"I didn't apply to any Art schools," I smile ruefully, sorry to disappoint Stacey, "and I can't go if I don't have any money."

"I'm sure you could apply for a loan." She insists hopefully.

I shrug. "Maybe at some point in the future," I'm saying that more for her benefit than mine. At this point, I'm more concerned about surviving than following romantic childhood dreams, "but for now I think I'll just try to find a job and get my life in order." That is if anybody will hire an eighteen-year-old boarding school graduate with zero experience whatsoever.

"Okay." She is still frowning, but she doesn't say anything else.

I move to another table, gently moving my dust brush over the top. It doesn't need the cleaning, but I need something to do. I run the brush over a polished woodcarving of a forest scene, a colorful crystal vase, and a green ceramic piggy bank. As I work, I shut all my worries about my future from my mind, concentrating on the items in front of me, the gleam of the ceramic, the smoothness of the polished wood, the light reflecting in the crystal. It works. For the next few minutes, there are no tough decisions, just me, and the little things that add beauty to my day.

After a while, Stacey gets up and moves from the desk to the front of the store. Through the glass, the tree-lined street is visible. We are in the commercial part of the town. That doesn't mean that the area is busy, only that the mall is just a street away, and opposite us there is a second hand bookstore, a café, and some other small town shops. Stacey peers down the street in the direction of Ashcroft Hills Resort, the only thing that keeps our small town on the map. It has a couple of bungalows, suites, a golf course, a sizeable swimming pool, a spa, a few large conference rooms, and a good bar. It's just a forty-five minute drive from downtown Seattle, which makes it a popular venue for conferences that last a couple of days. On such days, we see a lot of new faces, as the city types sometimes try to get a feel of small town living.

"Lots of cars going to the Hills today," Stacey observes. From the level sound of her voice, I know she's trying not to be too hopeful, but a conference in the Hills can sometimes make a huge difference in sales. She gazes down the street for a few more minutes, and then turns back to me with a sigh. "I'm going to run a few errands," she tells me, picking up her purse from the desk, "You'll be fine, won't you?"

I nod in response. I've learned how to run the shop in the short time I've spent working for Stacey. I actually really like it. The woodcarvings, glass sculptures, etched glass, and vanity items we sell are the closest I've ever been to real art. It's my favorite place in town, and I won't be glad to leave it behind.

I sit at the desk reading a book for a long time after Stacey leaves. Only a few people come into the shop, Doug Randall, who runs the sporting equipment store, stops by every morning to ask how I am, while his eyes explore my chest. A few other people also come in. There are no sales though, but it's too early to lose all hope.

After a while, I retrieve my pencil and sketchpad from my bag and move to the back of the shop, away from the eyes that would see what I'm doing if they look into the shop from the sidewalk. I sit by the small window at the back, and start to draw.

These days, it's always my mother's face, beautifully rendered in the grey lines of the pencil. I draw her the way she looks in my mind, the image formed from all the pictures of her that I've spent hours poring over. Sometimes, I draw her with laughing eyes, at other times, her face is cool and serene, but in each drawing, the jewelry is different. Today it's a pair of oval earrings, with a crystal surrounded by small stones. I draw a matching pendant around her neck, and a bracelet made of ovals. I shade it, frowning in concentration, as I make the crystals glint by leaving some parts white.

When I'm done, I look at the drawing for some time. I have a lot of them. Drawing my mother has always helped to deal with loneliness, and sketching jewelry has become a way of escape for me, a way to create, and dream, of beautiful things. Of course, I have no idea how to make the pieces, but for now, that doesn't matter. It's drawing them that relaxes me.

I close the sketchpad and put it back in my bag. It's already afternoon, and we haven't made any sales. I walk towards the front of the shop, catching a glimpse of my reflection in the old gilt framed mirror that hangs on the wall between two shelves. I pause and study myself for a moment. I'm wearing my red blouse, a gift from Stacey, and the pair of blue jeans that has become my uniform in the last few months. I haven't bought any clothes since I graduated, the week after Aunt Josephine died. In fact I haven't bought anything, only food, and maybe pencils.

I stare at my face in the mirror. I'm not particularly critical of myself, but I am not pretty, at least I don't think I am, though Stacey would argue otherwise. I don't look like any actress or model I've ever seen, and I'm not thin enough to be conventionally good looking.

I adjust my ponytail, tucking the strands that have escaped back into the elastic hair tie. My hair is pale gold and extremely thick. Stacey constantly goes on about how it is my best feature, but I prefer my eyes, they are green, the same color as my mothers' were.

Leaving the mirror, I continue to the door, pausing for only a moment before I step outside. The air is warm and dry, and the wind blows a few dead leaves across the paved street. On the other side of the street, the second-hand bookstore looks sadly empty. The owner, Nina Suarez waves at me from the front of the shop. I wave back, watching as she shuffles back inside. There are only a few other people about. It's a school day, and many of Ashford's grownup residents work in Seattle, which is commuting distance away.

I am about to go back into the shop when a car cruises past, coming from the direction of Ashcroft Hills. It is a black sedan, glossy and obviously expensive. It moves past me with a soft purr of its engines, gliding down the street as I stare curiously at the tinted windows.

I turn around and go into the shop, closing the door behind me as I turn to get another look at the car. I don't know why I am curious, but as I look through the glass front, I see the car stop suddenly, just past the store. I stand unmoving, interested, It's probably only someone from Ashcroft Hills, I tell myself, but there is a feeling of apprehension building in my stomach.

After a short pause, when it stays unmoving on the street, the car glides back to park right in front of me.

The feeling of apprehension intensifies. It's as if my sixth sense can feel a danger in that car, but I ignore it. There is more likely a sale in it.

The back door opens, and as I watch, a man steps out.

Involuntarily, I step back, suddenly hoping that the glass will hide me from him. My heart starts to pound, beating against the front of my ribs with an intensity that makes me dizzy. My blood is rushing in my ears. My skin flushes, suddenly feeling incredibly hot. His eyes meet mine from across the glass, and I am immediately flooded with awareness. The street disappears, the glass, the shop, everything, until the only thing I'm aware of is him. I can't breathe. I'm excited and afraid at the same time, and I don't know why.

Maybe it's because I've never seen anyone who looks like him before.

His face is breathtakingly handsome, almost as if it was lifted directly from one of the classical sculptures or paintings I've seen in art textbooks, and then perfected. His hair is thick and very black, slightly too long and elegantly tousled, framing his exquisite sculpted face. His lips are firm and perfectly shaped. His nose is straight. His eyes, framed by a pair of winged black eyebrows, are the most intense blue I've ever seen.

I'm only looking at him, but I feel as if all the air has been sucked from my lungs. I pray he doesn't come into the shop, and I hope fervently that he does.

I'm staring at him with my mouth hanging slightly open, but I can't stop myself. I can look at him forever. He commands my admiration in a way I've never felt. He is… compelling.

His eyes narrow slightly, as he looks at me. I flush, embarrassed at being caught staring, even though I shouldn't be, since he's been staring at me too. Trying to escape his commanding gaze, I look away from his face, and take in his tall, broad shouldered body in a superbly tailored gray suit. My mouth suddenly feels dry. I swallow.

As I watch, he starts to move towards the door. His movements are graceful and lithe, and yet I can see the strength in the way he carries himself. I've read more than a few romance novels, and I've always thought the phrase 'like a jungle cat' was ridiculous, but it's what comes to my mind as he walks in my direction.

As soon as the obstruction of the door is out of the way, his eyes are on me again, holding me captive. He dwarfs the shop, making everything in it fade to insignificance by his presence alone. His expression is unreadable, but as his eyes hold mine, potent, commanding, powerful, I want to run from him, or to him. I'm totally disoriented.

He doesn't stop walking until he is right in front of me. I am five six, which isn't short by any standards, but I have to look up at him, and when I do, I am hit again by the force of his attractiveness. At such close quarters, it totally floors me. I have a desperate need to lean on something.

We stand there, him looking down at me, and me staring at his face like I've been hypnotized. He doesn't say anything. At first I don't notice because I'm too busy memorizing the contours of his face. I've lost the ability to breathe, which is probably why my mouth is hanging open, trying to get enough air to at least keep me alive.

"Good afternoon." He says at last, interrupting my meditation on his features. His voice is cultured and deep, with a bold inflection that speaks of command.

He is waiting for me to say something, I realize, but there must be something stuck in my throat, because I can't seem to get any words out. *Say something Sophie!* I tell myself desperately, *or he'll think you're an idiot.*

"Good afternoon." I finally manage, my voice, an unfamiliar squeak. His lips move in the beginnings of a smile. I stare at the movement, entranced, and also aware that he's laughing at me. I'm so ridiculous I'm amusing to him, I decide miserably.

"Would you like to buy something?" I ask, knowing that my face is probably a bright red. My voice still sounds unfamiliar. I swallow again.

My question seems to amuse him. I watch, fascinated as a black eyebrow moves up a little higher than the other, "Of course." He replies.

Of course he wants to buy something. Staring at him has obviously made me stupid.

"I'd like ah..." He looks around, his eyes taking in the shop, "a gift for my mother." His gaze swivels back to mine, and I have to bite back a sigh.

I pull in a sharp breath. "Okay." I say, wondering what to recommend. I have to squeeze by him so I can lead him through the shop. As I pass him, my body barely an inch from his, I am careful not to look at him, but I can't stop my nose from breathing in his delicious scent, fresh linen, and soap, with a faint hint of cologne. I have an overwhelming urge to snuggle close and fill my lungs with the scent of him.

I recover myself just in time. "What do you have in mind?" I say instead. "We have um… a selection of items you can consider." As I move ahead of him through the tables where the gifts are displayed, I can feel his eyes on my back, which makes the skin from my neck to the back of my legs tingle with warmth. I have never felt so awkward. I turn to say something to him, and jump when I find that he is right behind me.

I step back quickly, not because I mind being so close to him, but because my heart is beating so loudly I'm sure he can hear it. I swallow and continue talking. "These glass sculptures are all made locally," I say, painfully aware of how breathless my voice sounds. I wonder if he can tell that his presence is affecting me so much. His eyes have not left my face, even for an instant, and I wonder what exactly he is thinking.

"What's your name?" His voice stops me mid-ramble and I blink in surprise. *What is my name again!*

"Sophie." I stammer, "Sophie Bennett."

"Sophie." He repeats. Coming from him, it sounds sensual, not the name I'm used to.

"And how long have you worked here, Sophie?" His voice is soft and fascinating. I want him to keep on talking. I'll tell him anything he wants.

"I… um…" I blink frantically as I try to remember, "a few months."

"Interesting," His eyes are studying my face again, with a curious expression on his face. "College?"

I shake my head. Silently I wonder why he's asking all these questions. I can't imagine any of the boring details of my life being interesting to anyone, let alone someone as beautiful as he is.

He considers me for a long moment, until I feel as if I'm going to drown in his eyes. "How old are you?" He asks suddenly.

Why does he want to know? I frown and lick my lips uncertainly. "Eighteen." I whisper.

His eyes follow the small movement of my lips, and for a moment, and my heart starts to beat wildly again. I'm full of anticipation, though I have no idea what I'm expecting. He looks back up into my eyes, and his eyes are dark and stormy, like the deep blue of the sea turned to a turbulent, chaotic darkness. My insides start to quiver. The feeling is new and delicious, and I don't want it to stop.

He takes a small step back, the storm in his eyes quickly fading to something like regret. "You're very young." He says softly.

I don't know what to say to that. I may be young, but he doesn't look much older than I am. He looks about twenty-five, or perhaps a little older. My eyes drop from his face to his wide chest. I want him to look at me again, the way he did before, I want to feel those quivery feelings inside me again. I feel confused, disappointed somehow.

I look back up at him. His eyes haven't left me. I wonder if I should keep talking about the items we have for sale, but I have a feeling that he is not particularly interested.

We stare at each other. The quivering starts up again, spreading from my belly to my thighs, and getting more insistent. Everything about him reminds me of the things my body has been telling me for months. The things I haven't had the nerve, or the opportunity to explore. I suddenly have a very intense vision of exploring those things with him, and I blush furiously, certain that he knows what I'm thinking.

"I'd like the glass swan."

I have no idea what he just said. "The what?"

He lips twitch in amusement, and he inclines his head towards a smallish figure of a swan on a lake. It's all glass, transparent but with little hints of color. It is very beautiful and costly.

I nod, feeling silly. I pick up the swan and take it to the front desk. He follows closely behind me, and once again, I can feel his eyes on my back. My legs feel strangely boneless, like I have to make an effort to stay steady on my feet. "Do you want it wrapped?" I ask when I reach the desk, doing my best to sound professional, and not like the breathless, discombobulated wreck I am.

"Yes," He is still smiling, "and delivered." He dictates an address in Seattle, which I jot down carefully.

When I'm done with the address, he hands me a card. I reach out to take it, and our hands touch briefly. It's only for a second, but at his touch, something moves through me, taking over my consciousness until the whole world seems centered on his fingers touching mine, and his eyes on my face. I quickly pull my hand away, silently commanding it to stop shaking. I can't look at him. *He only touched your hand, for God's sake!*

David Preston. That's the name on his card. I mouth it silently as I process his payment.

"I want to see you." The words hover in the air between us. I freeze, unable to comprehend what I just heard. For the second time since I saw him, I literally cannot breathe. The strange quivering in my belly moves lower. "What are you doing tonight?" He continues, his eyes never leaving mine.

I manage to find my voice. "Nothing." I tell him.

"Then have dinner with me."

I draw in a shaky breath. I'm unsure, afraid, and feeling rather faint. It is beyond comprehension that this perfect man is asking me out on a date. I want to pinch myself to see if I'm dreaming. I want to dance. I want to run and hide. I have no idea what I want.

He cocks his head, "Please." He says, though he doesn't look as if he is pleading. He is still smiling, his perfect lips curling upwards in a beautiful bow, but his eyes are burning darkly, promising me things I know I want.

"Yes." I accept, wondering what exactly I'm agreeing to.

He has been bending slightly over me, now he straightens, "When do you finish here?" He asks.

"Five."

"I'll be here." His smile widens, revealing perfect white teeth. Mesmerized, I can't take my eyes off him as he backs away from me before turning towards the door. A few moments later, he is gone, with only the slight hint of his cologne in the air, to convince me that I haven't been daydreaming.

Chapter Two

IT'S ALMOST FIVE IN THE EVENING, and I'm still finding it hard to believe that David Preston is not a figment of my imagination. Stacey has gone home already, happy with the sale of the swan, the only sale we have made today. I get ready to close the shop, filled with tension at the thought of my dinner date.

In the bathroom at the back of the shop, I brush my hair, and after debating for a few moments, I pull it back again into a low ponytail. I study my reflection in the mirror, wishing I had some makeup, but I have to make do with applying lip balm and pinching my cheeks a little. I remind myself to buy a few items, maybe lip-gloss, and mascara, as soon as I can. There is no one to disapprove anymore, now that Aunt Josephine is gone.

David is standing outside the shop when I come out of the bathroom. He has changed out of the gray suit, and is now wearing black pants, with a pale blue shirt and a dark jacket. For a moment, I forget everything and just stare at him. He looks effortlessly stylish, and a thousand times more handsome than I remember from this morning… if that's even possible. Next to him, I'll probably look juvenile and plain.

I smooth my hair nervously, trying without success to control my heart rate, which has gone exceedingly high. I have mixed feelings about this. On one hand, I want to go anywhere with him, on the other, I have no idea how I can survive a few hours beside all that gorgeousness. Taking a deep breath, I walk out of the shop and lock the door behind me.

"Hi." I can't believe how nervous I feel. It's cool outside, but my skin feels like I have a fever.

"Hello Sophie." His voice is as beautiful as I remember, and it makes the sound of my name feel like a caress. I try not to look at my feet as his eyes take in my flushed face. "Ready?" He asks.

I nod.

Smiling, he leads me to his car, one hand resting lightly on the lower part of my back. I try not to die from his touch as I follow him, glad that he cannot see my face, which I'm sure is red as scarlet.

The car is not the black sedan of earlier, but a silver BMW convertible that glints in the evening light. He opens the front passenger door, and I step inside. The interior is luxurious, with black leather seats and a sleek dashboard. It smells of leather, with a slight hint of his cologne. I inhale deeply.

He gets into the driver's seat and turns to me. Again, his eyes mesmerize me. What am I doing? There is no way I can survive an evening alone with this man. "So where do you want to go?" He asks.

I have no idea. I wonder if I should have thought of this before. "Where would you like to go?" I reply softly.

His eyebrow lifts, and for a moment I can't help but stare, enchanted. "You know the town," he says, "don't you?"

I shake my head. I really don't. I have never hung out, or done any of the things young people do. My aunt made sure I had no friends while she was alive, and in the months since her death, I have realized that almost everybody thinks that, like her, I'm weird.

He gives me a quizzical look. "You didn't grow up here?"

"I've been away at boarding school." I look out of the window, "and anyway I've never been very outgoing." Luckily, I remember the seafood place Stacey and her husband went to on their anniversary. It's on the other side of town, and I've never been there, but I mention it to him anyway.

He starts the car and enters the name of the restaurant into a GPS system on the dashboard. As he waits for directions, I realize how underdressed I am for where we're going. I should have asked him to pick me up at my apartment, at least then I would have been able to change. I'm not even sure that the only dress I have will be suitable, but I'm sure it's better than jeans.

"Can we stop by my place?" I ask tentatively.

His eyes skip from the road to my face, he looks slightly curious, but he doesn't ask anything. "Of course." He says.

The apartment building is not far from the shop, so I just give him directions. Before long, he is pulling into the parking lot of the old four-storey brick building where I live. It used to be a popular hotel decades ago, but it was converted into apartments when better hotels were built in town.

"I won't be a minute," I tell him as I climb out of the car. He waves a hand, letting me know I can take all the time I need. I almost run upstairs to my apartment, a one bedroom with a tiny kitchen, living room, and bathroom. Everything inside is old, including the furniture that came with it, but it's my place and for a while, it has been home.

The living room windows look out into the parking lot, and further out into the commercial part of town. I can't resist pulling the curtains aside to peek at the silver BMW idling outside, but I can't see David through the tinted windows.

I hurriedly change into the pale blue cotton dress I wore for my graduation. I haven't worn it since then. As I take a quick look at myself in the mirror, I hope desperately that it will do.

When I return to the car, David comes around to open the door for me. I think I can see admiration in his eyes as he takes in my dress, but it could be my imagination. "Nice dress," He says, before closing the door and going around to the driver's seat.

"Thank You." I say, pleased at the compliment.

"You didn't have to change on my account though," he adds as he starts the car, "you already looked great."

He thinks I looked great. The knowledge makes me inordinately happy. "I wanted to." I reply.

He starts to drive towards the restaurant, the car cutting through the roads with a low purr of the engines. We are both silent. I know I should try to make conversation, but I have no idea what to say.

"Were you at a conference at Ashcroft Hills?" I ask finally.

"Yes."

He doesn't offer more. Silently, I search my mind for something else to say. "I hope it went well."

He shrugs, looking over at me. "I went to make a decision about a new software that could be the next big thing, or a complete waste of time."

"What did you decide?" I ask, genuinely interested.

He looks at me again, then turns back to the road. "I bought it." He says. Something in his voice gives me a feeling that he is someone who is used to being able to get whatever he wants, as soon as he decides that he wants it.

"Tell me about yourself." He says, changing the subject. "I already know you're not outgoing," he gives me a teasing smile, "so tell me more."

"There's nothing to tell." I frown at my hands on my lap. "You won't be interested."

"On the contrary, I am very intrigued. I would very

much like to know what you do with your time."

I look up at him, but his eyes are on the road again. I shrug. "I read, sometimes I draw."

He looks interested. "What do you draw?"

"Stuff." I'm definitely not going to tell him that I've been doodling his face on the margins of my book since he left the store.

He chuckles at my answer. "And what do you read? Can I ask, or is it also 'stuff'?"

"No... I read everything." I tell him. "History, classics, popular fiction," I shrug.

A smile curves his lips. "I thought young people never read anymore." He says, making me wonder how old he is.

Maybe he sees the question on my face. "What are you thinking Sophie?" He asks.

"I was just wondering how old you are," I say softly.

He laughs. It's the first time I've heard him laugh. I allow my ears to follow the rich sound. "Oh I'm legal," his voice is full of amusement. "I'm twenty seven."

Legal. The word stays stuck in my head. He is legal and so am I. The thought opens up a whole lot of possibilities. I remember when he asked me my age earlier, and I try to control the shiver of excitement I feel.

At the restaurant, the manager takes one look at

David and immediately puts himself at our service. There is so much deference in his manner that I start to wonder if I'm not missing something. David doesn't seem surprised or bothered. He is used to people serving him, I realize. I don't know what conclusions to draw, I know so little about him.

As the manager leads us to a secluded table with a view of the park, I notice how the women stare openly, while the men look at him with a combination of envy and admiration. They know who he is, I realize. I wonder how soon I will have the opportunity to Google him. I don't own a computer, but there is one at the shop.

The waiter brings the menu, and David orders wine. I take my time studying the food available, trying to decide what to order, and thinking how young and gauche I must seem to him compared to all the sophisticated women he probably knows.

"So you're' not outgoing, you read and you draw." He says, as our food arrives. His eyebrow quirks in that mesmerizing way as I look up at him, "tell me more."

It must be the wine, because I start to feel like there is something to tell. "My mother died giving birth to me," I say suddenly. I don't know why I chose to say that first. It's not something I usually tell people.

"That must have been hard for you." He states,

there is a hint of sympathy in his features.

I think of all the years spent under Aunt Josephine's care, the indescribable ache for the mother I never had a chance to know. "I suppose it was." I say.

He doesn't say anything in reply, so I continue.

"I grew up with my Aunt Josephine, but she died a few months ago." I frown. "She told me that my father was some professor my mother had a 'sordid' affair with during the only semester she spent at college." I pause, looking to see any reaction on his face. There is none. "Unfortunately that is the only thing I know about him."

"Your aunt doesn't sound very nice." He says quietly.

"She was ... different." I'm not eager to speak ill of the dead.

He nods. "So you went to boarding school?"

"Yes, when I was twelve." I shake my head. "I didn't make a lot of friends, but we had a wonderful library."

That makes him chuckle. "Of course." He says.

"That's all there is to me." I finish. "I graduated, Aunt Josephine died, and I started working at the shop."

"So why no college?" He looks curious.

I'm not about to tell him about my financial

troubles. "Maybe it's not for me." I state with wine induced bravado. "I'm moving to Bellevue to find a job."

His lips quirk in a small smile. "Why Bellevue?" he asks.

Good question, I think, but I'm not going to tell him that I'm going to Bellevue because my mother went to college there, and came back pregnant with me. I don't want him to think I am chasing a ghost, so I just shrug.

He is a good listener, which is probably why I haven't noticed that he hasn't said anything about himself. I'm too caught up in the beauty of him to care anyway. I could look at him all day. Everything about him is beautiful, his graceful hands and fingers, the way his eyes seem to penetrate me when he looks at me, and the way his hair frames his face in a soft black wave.

I have a sudden urge to touch his hair, to dig my fingers in the soft black mass and feel the texture in my palms. It's so strong that I have to clasp my fingers in my lap before I make a fool of myself. What is happening to me?

"Sophie?" The voice breaks me out of my admiration of David, and I turn around to see a familiar face, Eddie Newton. His parent's home was right next to Aunt Josephine's house when we were growing up, but I don't know him very well. Aunt Josephine was very good at making sure I wasn't 'negatively influenced' by the other kids around. She didn't like people and she did a good job of making sure they had no chance to like me. I remember Eddie always having a friendly smile and a wave for me when I was a lonely kid, but he's been away at college for a while, and I haven't seen him since long before Aunt Josephine died.

I manage to tear my eyes off David. "Hi Eddie," I say, giving him a smile.

He has an attractive looking brunette with him who can't seem to take her eyes off David. I don't blame her, I know what he looks like.

"It's really nice to see you, Sophie." Eddie says, his eyes moving from my face to David's.

"It's nice to see you too, Eddie." I say, wanting to continue my conversation with David, but I realize that I probably should perform some sort of introductions. "David, this is Eddie," I start. "We were neighbors growing up." David is looking at me intently. Disconcerted, I continue. "Eddie, this is David Preston, he..." It hits me again that I don't know anything about him, and I stop, embarrassed.

"I'm attending a conference here in town," David

adds smoothly, rescuing me, "or I was." He qualifies. "I'm heading back to Seattle in the morning."

I feel my face fall. I haven't thought of him leaving. I try to tell myself that Seattle is less than an hour away, but I'm sure I'll never see him again. The thought is unreasonably painful. I want to see him again, very, very much.

I hardly hear as Eddie introduces his companion, but I can sense almost the same deference in his tone as he talks to David as I had heard earlier in the managers' voice. His companion cannot keep the open flirtation from her voice as she says hello to David, adding that she is very glad to meet him.

"I'm sorry for your loss Sophie," Eddie says to me, after the introductions are done. He gives me an encouraging smile. "I'm sorry I haven't tried to see you before now."

I frown, wondering why he would try to 'see' me. "You were away at school," I tell him, "and I'm okay." I add, "I really am."

He gives me another encouraging smile before he moves away from our table, his companion following behind.

David is still looking intently at me. "Old boyfriend?" He asks. I sense an edge in his voice, and I'm suddenly eager to clear the air.

"No," I deny. "Of course not. I don't have any old boyfriends."

"Young ones then?" He searches my face. I suspect that he is not teasing. The look in his eyes makes my stomach clench. I shake my head.

"You didn't tell me you were leaving," I realize that the question is probably silly. He lives in Seattle, and is only here for a conference after all.

He leans back in his chair and considers me for a moment, his eyes almost fully hidden behind half closed lids. "I was leaving this afternoon," He tells me, "and yet when I saw you, I stopped to ask you to dinner."

I flush with pleasure at the thought that I've kept him in town, even if only for a few hours. "Oh." I manage to say.

He smiles. "But then I left anyway."

I frown, blinking in puzzlement. "I don't understand. You're here."

He shrugs. "I was going to call the shop and apologize to you," he leans forward until I can almost feel his breath on my face, "but I came back, and now here I am, back in little Ashford, on a date with an eighteen year old."

I have a very clear mental image of waiting expectantly at the shop, and being disappointed by a phone call. I would have been miserable.

"I'm glad you changed your mind." I reply hotly.

He seems taken aback by the passion in my reply. His gaze stays on my face for a long moment. "Somebody should have warned you to stay away from men like me." He says finally, his voice low.

I look at him, my eyes devouring his handsome features. I don't believe I could stay away from him, no matter what anybody told me. "What kind of man are you?" I ask anyway.

He gives me a long hard look. "The type that's bad for you."

I hold his gaze. "I wouldn't have listened."

His expression is unreadable, he is looking at me, but he doesn't say anything. He signals for the waiter. "I should take you home."

I don't want to go home, not if I'm never going to see him again. His eyes hold mine from across the table, and I know I want everything those eyes are promising.

"Let's go." He helps me out of my chair and I follow him out, my legs feeling unsteady. He opens the door for me to get in, and I wait until he slides into the driver's seat next to me.

"Will you come back here again?" I can't keep the hitch from my voice. I want to see him again. I need to. I need him in a way that even I don't understand.

"I'm not sure." He shrugs. "You'll be in Bellevue anyway."

I had forgotten about that. I look down at my hands on my lap, and I wish I were older and more beautiful. I wish I were the kind of seductress who could drive him crazy with just one look. It's heartbreaking that I cannot even keep a man like him interested in me for longer than a single date.

"Are you alright?" He asks softly. He places a hand under my chin and lifts my face to his.

He takes in my shiny eyes and the unhappiness on my face. I can't read his expression as he looks at me. I want to say something. I want to tell him that it's not his fault that I'm sad, that I'm just a silly girl who has never been on a real date before.

I'm still trying to form the words when he leans forward and covers my lips with his.

The rush of sensations overwhelms me. His lips are warm and firm, sweet and demanding. I moan softly. He takes advantage of the opening, and his tongue slides into my mouth, stroking mine, and flooding my body with a wonderful sweetness.

He pops my seatbelt in one swift movement, and in the next moment, he pulls me to him, crushing my breasts against his chest. His fingers lightly skim the side of my breast, squeezing it gently, and then softly caressing my nipple through the fabric of my gown.

"Oh!" I moan loudly, my eyes flutter to his face to find him watching me, his eyes dark. His lips are so close to mine, so I raise my head and kiss them. He kisses me back. I could do this forever, I think, my head spinning wildly.

He reaches into my hair and frees it from the ponytail, releasing the waves to fall around my face.

He pulls away to look at me, his chest heaving. "Sophie…" he breathes softly. "I wanted to do that since I saw you outside the shop this afternoon," He runs his fingers through a few strands of my hair, and smiles at me. "You don't know what you've done to me."

I breathe in a lungful of air. My heart is pounding, and I can hear the blood rushing in my ears, I want him to kiss me again.

He sighs and releases me. "I'd better take you home." He says, his voice tinged with frustration

My body stiffens in disappointment, which, I'm sure he can see on my face. He traces a finger over my lip, sending a thrill of pleasure down my spine. "Sweetheart," he says, making my heart sing, "I want you so much."

I know he's not just trying to make me feel better

about the fact that he's rejecting me. I can see the desire in his eyes. He really does want me. My body contracts with a delicious sweetness. "I want you too." I whisper.

He chuckles at my shy words. Then he runs a hand through his hair. He is frustrated, I think, and maybe confused. I, Sophie Bennett, have this incredibly beautiful man confused. I can't wrap my mind around it.

"I can't make any promises, Sophie." His voice pierces my happiness. There is a rueful smile on his face. "You don't deserve someone who will forget about you the moment he's out of town."

My body is aching with longing. While I am dimly aware that he's trying to warn me away, I don't really care. "Will you forget me so quickly?" I ask.

He doesn't look at me. "I don't know."

I swallow hard, confused. My life has changed a lot in the past four months, and will probably keep changing in ways I never expected. Maybe it's time to take a risk. I peek at him form under my lashes. He may be bad for me, as he says, but he may also be the best thing that ever happened to me. If I don't do anything, if I let him go tonight, I'll never know for sure.

"What if I don't care?" I ask softly, my mind made

up. "What if I want you anyway?"

Chapter Three

HIS EYES BORE INTO MINE IN THE semi darkness of the car. I wait for him to say something. He doesn't, instead he turns away from me and starts to drive.

Soon we are at my place. I don't know what he's going to do, and I am reluctant to leave the car. I look up at him, unsure and hopeful. He ignores me, his face unreadable. He steps out of the car and I watch his long legged stride as he comes around the front to open the door at my side.

His fingers wrap around my hand as he helps me out, they feel warm, and strong. I soak in the contact, luxuriating in that slight touch, and wanting more.

I look up at his face. My eyes asking the question I want him to answer. He inclines his head, gesturing for me to lead the way. I can't control the fluttering in my stomach as he follows me towards my apartment. As I climb the stairs, I keep stealing glances at him. My heart is in my mouth, but I know what I want. I want him.

My apartment is thankfully clean. I feel a wave of gratitude towards Aunt Josephine for teaching me to clean up after myself. In the living room, I am suddenly seized with panic and self-doubt. What if my inexperience is too glaring? What if I disappoint him?

As soon as the door closes behind us, he pulls me towards him. He pushes my hair behind my ears and starts to kiss me all over my face, dropping light feathery kisses on my eyes, my nose, and my chin. His lips move to my ear, and he sucks on my earlobe. I moan helplessly, clutching at his arms. It feels so good.

He licks under my ear, making me shudder, then lifts his head and kisses me on my lips, teasing them open, and thrusting his tongue into my mouth.

This kiss is sensual. His tongue explores my mouth, stroking and tasting me, building heat in the deepest recesses of my body.

His hand moves behind me to pull down the zipper

of my dress, his lips never leaving mine. Then his hands are underneath the dress, skimming over my thighs, and moving upwards.

"Your skin is so soft." He tells me softly, kissing my neck.

I don't know what to say. I arch my neck, exposing more of my skin to his lips.

He pulls the dress over my head and tosses it on the floor. Grabbing hold of my thighs, he lifts me, wrapping my legs around his waist. His erection presses against me through my wet panties. The feeling is intensely erotic, and so hot. I press closer, rocking my hips against the hardness, wanting more.

He cups both my breasts in his hands, squeezing gently through my bra, and massaging my nipples with his thumbs until they poke through the thin material of my bra, then he starts to rub them between his thumb and forefinger. I sigh as my whole body weakens with pleasure.

"You like that?" His voice is low.

I nod.

His hands move, with one deft movement he unhooks my bra and pulls it off my shoulders. Under his gaze, my aching nipples pucker up some more, extending towards his mouth. I tremble with pleasure at the look of clear admiration and desire in his eyes.

He bends forward and takes a nipple in his mouth, sucking on it and licking it at the same time. I whimper, straining against the wall at my back, and pressing my body harder against his bulging erection. He grips me, holding me still with his hands on both sides of my ribs, and continues to treat my nipple. His tongue swirls around it, then he bites it gently, before sucking on it. When I'm about to go mad, he moves to the other breast. I lose all my senses to the sweet, sweet fire building between my legs. I rub frantically against him, moaning desperately. I need him to touch me there.

He stops suddenly, and with a finger under my chin, he lifts my face until I am looking up at him. His voice is hoarse. "I am going to make love to you now." He says, "So if you want me to stop, tell me."

I shake my head frantically, if he stops at this point, I'll probably die.

He smiles and covers my lips with his again. I barely notice that he is unbuttoning his shirt. He sets me down so he can pull off his trousers. I lean on the wall, watching him. I can't believe what a beautiful body he has, the muscles of his chest are well defined, and his stomach is flat and firmly muscled, my eyes skip to his erection, poking through his boxer briefs, I feel a mixture of longing and dread.

"Your room?" He asks.

I point in the direction of the door. He picks me up, which is good because I'm not sure I can walk on my unsteady legs. In my room, he sets me on the bed, and presses a hand against the wetness in my panties. I moan and my hips rotate all on their own, rubbing against his hand until he moves it away and slowly starts to pull down my panties.

I lift my hips to help him. As the panties go down, they leave a wet trail on my legs. I look up at him, I don't know where I find the courage, but I reach towards him and pull at his briefs until his erection springs free. I swallow. He is the most beautiful thing I have ever seen.

He pushes me down on the bed and straddles me. I can feel his erection on my thighs. I want to spread my legs wider so that he can touch me. Tentatively, I touch his chest, letting my fingers play with a nipple. I stop in surprise as he closes his eyes and moans my name. Encouraged, I move my fingers over his chest to his other nipple.

He bends over me and kisses me again, making a trail of kisses down to my breasts, then he presses my breasts together and sucks on both nipples at once, teasing them with his tongue and his teeth.

I'm going to die from pleasure, I think, as thousands

of sensations take over my body. He doesn't stop, moving lower, he spreads my legs as his lips move over my belly. I know what he is going to do, but nothing prepares me for it.

At the first touch of his tongue, my body almost vaults off the bed.

"Stay still." The words are a raspy command. He grips my thighs, holding me firmly, and then he licks me again. My body is squirming against his tongue, and I can't stop moaning and shaking. I lift my hips to his mouth. My body is throbbing insistently. I feel like I am going to explode any moment. "Please," I hear myself moan, "Please," I hope he knows what I want, because I don't.

His tongue moves in circles, slow then fast, licking, then sucking. I dig my fingers into his hair. I am so hot, I can't think anymore. "Please," I cry out. He ignores me. His thumb joins his tongue, and he is licking and rubbing me at the same time. My body stiffens, paralyzed by pleasure, then with a groan, I lose all control, bucking and jerking against his lips as waves of pleasure sweep over me. I fall back on the bed, panting, my eyes wide.

His tongue touches me again, and I can't take it, I'm too sensitive. My body jerks away from his touch, and I watch him through glazed eyes as he rises up from between my legs.

I have gone to heaven, I think. My heart is pounding so loudly, I'm sure he can hear it. My body feels unbearably sweet. I reach for him, moving my fingers shyly over his length. There is some moisture at the tip. I rub it and he groans loudly, stiffening. He pulls my hand away and spreads my legs wider, sliding a finger into me, then two. The feeling is strange, but I like it. I can feel my body begin to throb around his fingers. He pulls them out, and I moan in disappointment, which disappears when he presses his tip into me.

"Are you ready?" His voice is rough, and yet tender.

In reply, I press against him hungrily, letting him feel my eagerness for him to fill my throbbing need. He positions himself on his knees between my legs and grabs hold of my thighs. The tip of his erection digs deeper into me. I rotate my hips, and he groans, driving in, and filling me completely. I moan in pain, clutching his arms as a burning sensation tears through me.

He freezes, but the pain is already fading, I can feel a slow pleasure building at the strange sensation of him inside me, it is a different kind of pleasure. I move a little, he groans.

"Are you okay?" His voice is strange, harsh, and his

chest is heaving. I nod, "Please don't stop." I whisper.

My words seem to do something to him. He leans forward on his elbow and starts to move, sliding in and out, slowly at first, and then as I start to moan, faster. I can feel a sweet sensation building up inside me again, growing with each stroke. I run my hands down his back, and over his hard buttocks, his body is slick with sweat, and so is mine. He picks up speed, lifting my leg and rotating his hips as he thrusts into me again and again. I match his movements. Hot pleasure floods my body, spreading from between my legs, to my back, my thighs, and my belly.

I scream his name as my body explodes, he thrusts into me one more time, driving in deep as he groans his release. Then he sighs deeply and collapses on top of me, burying his face in my neck.

"You're beautiful," He says, before pulling me closer as he turns to his side. "You're so damn beautiful."

Chapter Four

THE NEXT MORNING I WAKE UP WITH a start, certain that I have had an erotic dream, but the warmth from the perfect masculine body wrapped around me on the bed tells me that I haven't.

He is lying behind me, his arm over my waist, my back perfectly curved into his body.

We are spooning, I realize in wonder, and I revel in how enjoyable it feels.

I move, turning around until I am facing him. His eyes open slowly, his hair is tousled, and his eyes are groggy, but he is still so hot I want to kiss him again. I stifle a giggle as I wonder what Aunt Josephine would say if she could see me now.

"Good morning," I say shyly. I can't believe all the things I did with him last night. I stretch, reveling in the delicious soreness of my body.

"Good morning," He looks at me for a moment, "How are you feeling?"

"Great." I smile, suppressing the desire to break into song, or something equally ridiculous. "A little sore." I tell him. It doesn't matter though, I feel incredibly happy.

He nods, and I reach out to touch his hair, letting my fingers play with the thick black silkiness. His lips curve a little.

"When do you have to leave for work?"

I frown, I completely forgot about work. "The shop opens at eleven," I tell him, "I usually leave about twenty minutes before then."

He turns to look at the alarm by my bed, it's only eight am.

"When are you leaving?" I'm suddenly filled with dread. Yesterday, I thought I would be satisfied with one night, a first time I would not easily forget, but now, after last night, I know I am not.

"At noon." He shrugs and gets up.

I want to beg him to take me with him, but I stay silent, I don't want to sound like a child. I watch admiringly as he walks towards the bathroom. He has a beautiful body, tight, and firm in all the right places.

I stay in bed for a while, wondering if I have disappointed him in some way. I remember what he said last night, 'You're so damn beautiful.' The words probably meant nothing if he's just going to leave and forget about me.

I get up, put on a robe, and go into the living room. Our clothes are lying around on the floor in a mess. I blush when I see my blue dress crumpled near the door. I pick up all the clothes and place them on the couch.

A weight of sadness descends on me. I try to imagine the next chapter of my life in Bellevue, but I keep seeing his face. I wonder if he cares what happens to me. Maybe he doesn't, maybe he's just eager to leave and forget all about me.

Well I won't forget, and I won't regret anything either. It was the best night of my life, and whether he leaves or stays won't change that.

I am still deep in thought when the doorbell rings, startling me. For a moment, I can only wonder who it is. Nobody ever comes to my apartment. Aside from Stacey Carver, I may well be an island. It's a good thing, I decide, there will be fewer people to miss when I'm gone.

I walk to the door and peer through the peephole. Eddie Newton is standing there looking impatient. As I watch, he presses the bell again. What does he want?

"Are you going to get that?" I turn around, surprised to find that David has joined me in the living room. He is pulling on his clothes. I ignore the doorbell and watch him. In a few moments, he is dressed.

The bell rings again. I realize that David's not going to go back to my room, so I sigh in resignation and open the door just a crack.

"Hey Sophie." Eddie looks relieved to see me. His face relaxes from the frown it was wearing.

"Hey Eddie." I am frowning. I have no idea why he is here.

"I hope I'm not intruding," His words come out in a rush. "It's just, with everything that's happened, I've been a little worried about you, and my mom told me where you live now. I just came by because I wanted to be sure you are all right.

"I'm fine." I tell him, certain that he is taking this worrying about me thing a little too far.

He shifts from one foot to another, and I think for a moment that he still looks like a child, which is ridiculous, as he is older than I am. I wonder what he is waiting for, I start to say thank you and goodbye, but his eyes skip over my head to something behind me in the living room.

His face hardens. "I see you have a guest." He says, his voice suddenly bitter, making his words sound like an accusation.

I turn around, but I already know that David is behind me. His eyes are locked with Eddie's over my head, and as I turn back towards Eddie, he looks away from David, his eyes skipping to mine, and then to the floor.

"I'm all right, Eddie," Something in his expression makes me pity him, "You have no reason to be worried."

"Are you sure?" His jaw is working, and he keeps his eyes on my face, totally ignoring David's presence. "Because if there's anything you need, you should know that I would help."

I have to resist the urge to roll my eyes. I'm not a charity case. Before I can reply, David cuts in.

"She said she's fine," His voice is clipped, and there's a note of annoyance underneath. "She doesn't need you to take care of her."

"And she needs you?" Eddie's words come out in an angry torrent, and my face goes red with embarrassment. I want to tell them both to stop talking about me as if I'm not here. I don't know what's happening, but I want it to stop.

"Eddie..." I start, but he doesn't even seem to hear me.

"Don't pretend that you give a damn about her." He challenges David. "We all know what happens now that you've had your fun, don't we?" He gives a sneering laugh. "The rich playboy strikes again, too bad you couldn't find someone your own age."

David smiles tightly. He is not looking at me, but his smile scares me. The smile freezes Eddie too, whose accusing words have now ceased. "You should go now," David tells him. "And try to remember that from now on nothing about Sophie is any of your concern or your responsibility."

For a moment, I'm sure Eddie is going to cry. He gives me one last look, and then he turns and leaves. I shut the door quickly. As if by doing so, I can make it as if the last few minutes didn't happen.

I'm still trying to understand what has just happened. "I've never seen him like that before."

David's eyes are on my face. "Really?"

I stare at him, feeling uncertain, there is an edge to his voice that I don't understand. "Really." I reply.

"Really?" He's moving towards me, I move back, but after just one step I'm already backed up against the door. He tips my chin up until I'm looking up into his eyes, "because anybody can see that he's in love with you."

"Why would he be in love with me?"

"You really have no idea, do you?" He sighs. "Somebody should have told you how beautiful you are." He drops his hand from my chin. "I promise you that as soon as I'm gone he'll be back to offer you his 'help' again."

"I don't want his help." I whisper.

His eyes hold mine, and I can't look away. As I watch him, his hand moves into my robe, parting the thick material. His fingers stroke my thighs, moving up between my legs, he massages me softly. I part my legs, letting him touch me.

I am so wet already, his fingers stroke me easily, I moan softly, moving my hips to meet them. I grab hold of his shoulders, breathless. He doesn't stop, a finger slides into me, slowly massaging me inside. He finds an unbelievably sensitive spot inside me, and applies more pressure. I groan, and he puts a finger in my mouth. I start to suck on it, spreading my legs wider, opening myself to him. As he drives me crazy inside, his thumb plays with me outside. Finally, I can't take it anymore. My body stiffens, and then I let out a thin cry as it shatters, leaving me trembling.

His lips descend on mine, swallowing my cry. I

gasp, because the kiss is almost painful. It's possessive, as if he is stamping me with his ownership, but I don't care, I want to be owned.

He presses me against the wall, and I can feel the firm push of his arousal. I moan softly. His voice is harsh against my ear. "Don't forget who made you feel like this."

I'll never forget. "Take me with you." I don't consciously form the words, they just come out from somewhere deep within me. Somewhere where there is no shame, only desperation.

He doesn't reply. I wonder what he's thinking. I feel a sense of shame at the thought of his rejection. His hands tighten around my waist, and he pulls me close. I relax against him as he kisses my hair. He is so tender, I brace myself for whatever he is going to say.

He chuckles suddenly. I wonder why, but I don't want to leave his embrace. "There's one way you can come with me." He sounds amused.

"How?" I'm ready to explore any options.

He considers for a moment. "How long does it take to get a marriage license in the town of Ashford?"

Chapter Five

THE NEXT FEW HOURS PASS IN A BLUR. I am happy and excited, but I'm also afraid in a way that I cannot explain. Maybe I am afraid of change, or maybe I am afraid of David Preston. I don't really know.

First, he goes with me to the shop, where I haltingly tell Stacey that I'm getting married and going to Seattle with David. I ask her to witness the ceremony. She agrees, even though I can see from her face that she is worried, and probably convinced that I'm making a mistake.

Am I making a mistake? I am happy, I always dreamed of falling in love, maybe this is it, but even if it is not, I'm sure that if David leaves for Seattle without me, I wouldn't be able to bear it.

Back in my apartment, after his shocking proposal,

he called his assistant in Seattle, Linda Mays. She arrives a few hours later, while we are at the shop, a glamorous looking black-haired woman in her early thirties, wearing a pencil skirt and an incredibly tailored jacket. She takes one look at me and tries not to show her surprise. I try not to show how cowed I am by her obvious sophistication, as I give her the information she needs to get us a marriage license from the courthouse.

After she leaves, David seems reluctant to leave me alone with Stacey. She's grilled him a little already, asking what he does and how we met, all the while unable to hide her suspicion and worry. After answering her questions patiently, he leaves for the Ashford Fairview hotel, where he's staying, and where I'll join him for lunch.

As soon as he's gone, Stacey sits me down for a talk.

"Are you sure of what you are doing?" Her face is a study in worry. In fact, she looks more worried than she did yesterday. "Marriage is not something to jump into, especially with someone you hardly know, you only met him yesterday."

I nod, how do I explain to her that I understand her fears, but I am more afraid of not leaving with him than of anything else?

"If you're worried about moving to Bellevue and

finding a job, you don't have to, you know," She continues. "I spoke with Trevor Beak." Trevor Beak is the manager at the local grocery store, and I wonder what this will have to do with me. "He says there may be a position for you as an assistant trainee manager," She continues, "You may not have to leave town after all."

I smile. "I'm glad you're looking out for me," I tell her, touched by her concern, "but I'll be fine, I promise."

She sighs, and there are tears in her eyes. She draws me into her arms and hugs me tightly, surprising me, and making me want to cry. For a moment, I think I can feel what it may have been like to have a mother.

At lunchtime, the black sedan comes for me. The driver is a strong looking, clean-cut man, who tells me that his name is Steve. His head is totally bald, reminding me of a character in an action movie, but he looks pleasant. He barely says a word to throughout the short drive. At the Fairview, David is waiting for me in the restaurant. Even though this morning I tried to make an effort with my clothes, wearing a gray skirt and a white blouse, I still feel out of place and shabbily dressed.

He is sitting alone at a table close to the windows. When I enter, he turns to look at me, and my stomach twists. The memories of last night engulf me and I want him in a way that surprises me.

He smiles, standing up to greet me. He is wearing a dark blue suit with a snowy white shirt, and he looks so beautiful I can't catch my breath. "Hello Sophie." He says, as he pulls my chair out for me.

"Hello." I reply, breathing in the scent of him. I want to wrap my arms around him, press myself against his hard body. Instead I sit, contenting myself with just looking at him.

The waiter comes with the menu, and I order distractedly. I am not hungry at all, at least not for something that can be served on a plate.

When the waiter leaves, David turns back to me, a teasing glint in the depths of his blue eyes.

"You have to stop looking at me like that." He sounds amused, "or else I will have to take you up to my suite right now, and have you for lunch"

I sigh at the image, "Why don't you?" I whisper. It's exactly what I want.

He leans back in his chair and smiles. I stare at him, I don't think I'll ever get used to how incredible he is to look at. "Linda will be here to pick you up after lunch, to shop for a dress." He shrugs. "We'll be married by tonight." His eyes are full of promise, "and then I'll show you everything I'm thinking of doing to you right now.

There is no way I'm going to be able to eat now, I think, trying and failing to stop the throbbing between my legs. I press my thighs together. I can't wait for tonight.

"So when did you two meet?" Linda asks me later, as we browse the racks for a good dress, me hesitantly, she, rapidly, as if she knows exactly what she is looking for. She ignored me throughout the drive in the car to the dress shop, making phone calls and typing rapid messages on her phone.

"Yesterday." I reply. I know it sounds ridiculous, but I try to say it as if it means nothing, as if people get married all the time a day after they meet.

Her brows go up in a gesture of surprise, which she quickly hides as she continues browsing the rack. I prickle with irritation at her expression, but I don't say anything. I start to look through the clothes on the racks too, suddenly determined to choose my own dress.

Luckily, I find an off-white dress, sleeveless with a wide neck. It's simple but elegant, the kind of dress I've always dreamed of wearing, but have never owned. I pick it off the rack and tell Linda that I've found what I want.

We buy other things, lingerie that makes me blush,

while Linda stares at my reddening face as if she has never seen a blush before, shoes, a few other dresses, and then we go to the hair salon to fix up my hair and makeup. By the time I'm all dressed up, I don't recognize myself. I don't look my age, that's for sure. I look grown-up and stylish.

Stacey meets us at the courthouse with Brett, her husband, who looks confused by the whole situation. They both witness the ceremony, which for me, is only a blur. All I can see is David looking perfect in his dark blue suit, promising to cherish me as long as we both shall live. I know it's probably silly to imagine that I love him, but as I watch his lips say my name, I'm very sure that I do.

The official says something and David lifts my hand to slide the rings onto my finger, two rings, a sparkling engagement ring, and a plain wedding band. I know his assistant has picked them out, but I don't care, because I am happy, and for the moment, I know that everything is going to be all right.

Rebellion

A Dangerous Man #2

by

Serena Grey

Chapter One

THE JOURNEY TO SEATTLE IS SILENT. Steve, the chauffeur, keeps his eyes on the road, and David, my husband - I still can't believe he's my husband - studies some papers on his lap, totally ignoring me.

I can't stop looking at his face in profile, his straight nose, firm jaw and thick, wavy hair. He really is perfect, I think, captivated.

It's still hard to believe that this man, who I only met three days ago, is my husband, and that I am leaving the life I have always known to go with him to his home, his city, his life, of which I know nothing. I don't care though, I feel as if I've been trapped in a box for years, and he has shown me what it means to fly.

Between his reading and the brief, authoritative phone calls he's made, he hasn't looked at me at all. It's unfair, especially since I can't take my eyes off him. I don't understand how he can make such wonderful love to me, tease me until I'm blushing, and in the next moment, act as if I don't even exist.

Feeling suddenly insecure, I look away from him. I can almost hear Aunt Josephine's voice, telling me how foolish I am. 'Have you stopped to ask yourself why a man like him would marry a girl like you? Don't you think he has an ulterior motive?'

I push the doubting thoughts away. What ulterior motive could he possibly have? I'm neither rich nor successful, nor exceptionally beautiful. In fact, I was the one who begged him not to leave me.

Turning back to look at him, I see that he's still engrossed in his reading. As I watch his strong fingers flip through his papers, my mind drifts to last night, our wedding night, and I feel my skin heat up. Last night, I was the one he was engrossed in.

After the short ceremony, we all went back to the hotel where he was staying for drinks and dinner. Halfway through dinner, which I was too tense to eat, he suddenly stood up, and announced to our few guests that he was retiring for the night with his new wife.

The look in his eyes had filled me with such want that I almost couldn't stand. The next thing I knew, he picked me up and carried me out of the restaurant and into the elevator, amidst self-conscious cheers from our guests.

We were alone in the elevator, and as soon as the doors closed, he claimed my lips, his tongue delving hungrily in my mouth. His hands found their way under my dress and started to knead me gently through my new lace panties. I was whimpering with pleasure by the time we reached his floor.

Then he lifted me again and carried me to his room. Someone, probably his assistant, Linda, had arranged for wine in an ice bucket, and strawberries. He ignored those. He dropped me, barely able to stand, at the foot of the bed and pulled down the zipper of my dress, pulling it off my shoulder along with the straps of my bra.

When my breasts were free, he covered them with his hands. I moaned softly as he massaged them gently, arousing me until I fell against him, and he had to guide me unto the bed.

He pulled my dress up around my waist and pushed my panties aside, then his tongue was between my legs, and I was moaning and whimpering, my fingers clutching his hair. In only a few moments, my body was pulsing uncontrollably, shattering around his mouth. Then he stopped suddenly. While I was still wondering why, he pulled down his pants and in the next moment, he had filled me completely.

I came immediately, crying out as the warm sweetness shattered my body into a million pieces, then as he continued to move, I felt the pleasure build up again, heat starting up in my core and spreading until even my fingertips were filled with pleasure. I screamed my release the same moment as he groaned loudly and collapsed on top of me.

Then I said it. I love you.

And he didn't say anything.

The pleasure of my memories fades into a faint heartache. No matter how I think about it, I can't find a way to convince myself that I shouldn't be worried about his silence after I said those words.

How does he feel about me?

I have no answer to my question. It's scary, especially because my own feelings have taken over every part of me. It's as if I've stepped off the edge of a cliff, and even though my heart's in my mouth and my stomach is in knots, I'm the most excited I've ever been in my life. I'm totally enthralled by him. I want him, every part of him, and I desperately want him to feel the same way about me.

"If you keep staring at me like that I'm going to think you're having second thoughts already." His deep voice cuts into my thoughts. He is looking at me, his blue eyes probing into mine, and his perfect lips curved into a faint smile.

I stare helplessly at him for a moment, my skin flushing. He is so insanely beautiful to look at. Will I ever get used to being around all that perfection? It doesn't seem likely. Right now, he looks enticing, dangerous, and incredibly sexy. His snowy white shirt is open at the collar, exposing the strong column of his throat. His dark hair curls softly into the back of his collar, making me want to run my fingers through it, and his dark blue pants stretch over the long length of his legs. Just from looking at him, my fingers are itching to touch him. I want him so much. I don't think I'll ever stop wanting him.

"I'm not having second thoughts." I deny softly. Second thoughts are the farthest thing from my mind. I just wish I knew how he felt about me. If I did, then maybe I wouldn't feel so out of my depth. Next to his perfection, his obvious wealth, his incredibly good looks, I can't help feeling extremely ordinary.

His eyes linger on my face for a moment, as if he's reading my thoughts in my expression. He puts a hand on my thigh and strokes it lightly, in a gesture that should be reassuring but only fills my mind with images of the things those hands have done to me.

"Don't worry," He says, turning back to his work, his hand still on my thigh. He sounds relaxed, his voice faintly teasing. "I promise I don't have a firing squad waiting for you."

"That's not what I was thinking." I reply with a self-conscious laugh.

"Then what are you so afraid of? An underground torture chamber?"

"No." I protest. "Of course not, I was just thinking that I know so little about you."

He chuckles as he turns back to me, and one of his eyebrows rises just a little higher than the other. "Really," His eyes dip to my lips, and stay there for a second before rising back to my eyes, with a teasing and unmistakably sensual look. "I would say you know a lot about me, Sophie."

I don't miss his meaning, and I blush fiercely. We've spent the last twenty-four hours more naked in bed than out of it. The memories are enough to make my body clench with helpless desire. I cast an embarrassed glance towards Steve, but he is totally occupied with driving, his eyes straight ahead.

"I meant… about your life, your work…" I can't stop stammering. I look up at David in despair. Around him, I've obviously lost the ability to be coherent.

He studies me as I trip over my tongue. "You're charming." He says, amusement dancing on his lips. The compliment only makes me blush harder, and I bend my face to hide my flaming cheeks.

He puts a hand under my chin and lifts up my face, so I'm looking at him. "Don't hide your face when you blush," His voice is soft and compelling. "I like it."

I nod helplessly. With his fingers under my chin and his blue eyes doing things to my heart, it's not as if I can refuse him anything.

I'm still thinking of what to say when he bends over to brush his lips across mine in the lightest of kisses. I lean into it, as pleasure flutters through my body. By the time he lifts his head, my whole body is shaking with anticipation. I can't believe how much I want him. Nobody told me it would be like this. My body feels as if it's in a permanent state of sexual hunger.

"We'll be home soon." He says, his eyes dark with desire. It's as if he can read my mind and knows exactly what I want.

I can't wait.

Chapter Two

I FALL ASLEEP SOON AFTER, LULLED by the steady hum of the car engine. When I wake up, my head is resting on David's shoulder, and he is stroking my hair, his fingers gentle and soothing. I realize that the car is no longer moving. I open my eyes and sit up, wondering how long I've been asleep.

"I was beginning to think I would have to kiss you to get you to wake up." His hand leaves my hair. "You were very determined to use me as a pillow." He adds wryly. I wonder if he is teasing me, but I can't tell from his face.

I stretch self-consciously and smooth my hair. Steve is already opening the door on my side, so I step out of the car, looking around to get a feel of my surroundings.

We're parked on a tree-lined street, in front of a towering stone and glass apartment block. I have to crane my neck to try to see all of it. The walls are cream stone, and the glass gleams blue in the sun. It's massive and yet elegantly beautiful.

Right in front of me, a pair of glass double doors stands under a wide curved awning. As I take it in, David comes to my side, slipping his hand around my waist with a touch that is both firm and proprietary. As always, I immediately respond to the contact, my skin tingling where I can feel the pressure of his fingers.

He starts to lead me inside. When we reach the entrance, a doorman holds the door open.

"Good afternoon, Mrs. Preston, Mr. Preston." The man greets me with a smile as David and I step inside the building. I look at him in surprise, and smile back. "Good afternoon." I reply, inexplicably pleased at being addressed by my new name.

"Thank you Jimmy." David's voice is curt. He doesn't pause. His hand on my waist urges me forward, and I follow him into the spacious lobby.

I take a second to look around, taking in the magnificent space. The floors are perfect gleaming marble, so well-polished that I can see my reflection when I look down. The walls are richly detailed and paneled, and the ceiling is at least two-storeys high, and adorned with a sparkling crystal chandelier. Everything carries an air of unmistakable luxury.

I would stand and admire, but David's hand at my waist is firm and insistent, and I have no choice but to follow him. I turn a questioning glance at him, wondering at his haste, but his face is impassive. I assume he has no time to watch me appreciate the beauty that's probably commonplace to him.

The man at the front desk gives us a greeting too, also calling me Mrs. Preston, and making me wonder if Linda has been passing a picture of me around. We acknowledge him without stopping as David leads me further towards the elevators. In only a matter of moments, we've crossed the lobby and are in the private elevator that leads to his penthouse apartment.

As the doors close, he turns to me, and using his body, presses me against the wall, pinning my arms at my sides. His face is only inches from mine, and the desire in his eyes turns my bones to liquid. I swallow hard as my body heats up from the close contact with his. Then his lips dip, and he claims my senses in a scorching kiss.

I open my lips to him, hungry for him, and hungry for more.

"I'm going to make love to you until your voice is hoarse from screaming my name." He promises softly when we come up for air, making my heart pound with excitement, his sudden passion erasing any doubts I have had in the past hour. He kisses me again. "Your lips are so soft." He whispers huskily. He continues to kiss me, his lips tracing a path from the sensitive spot below my ear, down to where the neckline of my blouse covers the top of my breasts, which are heavy and aching with need. My breath starts to come in short moans. I want him here, now.

He straightens with a low chuckle. "Don't be in such a rush, sweetheart," His voice is gently teasing, "We're almost there."

I don't understand how he can be so calm, when the torrent of need flowing through me has made me almost incapable of speech. My hands are shaking with the need to touch him, even the sound of his voice is like an aphrodisiac, stirring me on. I take a deep breath to steady myself.

The bell dings and the doors open into an immaculate foyer, which is bigger than the living room of my apartment back in Ashford. The honey-toned wall paneling complements the perfectly finished dark wood floors, and lovely paintings of subjects ranging from wildflowers to waterfalls add definition to the walls. At one end of the room, a set of polished wood double doors lead out into a large living room.

It's exceptionally beautiful. On two sides, the walls are windows, with exquisite views of the Sound, the city, the Mountains beyond, and many landmarks I can't yet identify. A couple of artfully placed rugs cover the polished wood floors. In the perfectly arranged lounge area, there are two comfortable looking couches and a window seat, where I can instantly see myself curled up and reading. Further inside, in another carpeted area, there is a large dining table, with a vase of beautifully arranged flowers sitting on top of the gleaming wood surface.

Everything is perfect. "Wow." I breathe, entranced. "It's so beautiful."

He nuzzles my neck, sending a quiver of pleasure flowing across my body, reminding me of our unfinished business in the elevator, my body responds immediately, but then he straightens, leaving me feeling a little disappointed.

I don't notice the smallish, middle-aged woman until I hear her voice. "Good afternoon." She says. Startled at the intrusion, I turn around, and see her standing behind us. "Welcome to Seattle, Mrs. Preston." She continues.

She is smiling at me, her face open and friendly. I

smile back. "Thank you."

"Sophie, this is Mrs. Daniels, your housekeeper." David introduces us as the elevator bell dings and Steve comes in, carrying David's suitcase and my luggage as if they weigh nothing.

"Come on," David turns to me, "let me show you the rest of the apartment. Mrs. Daniels will unpack your things."

I nod, wondering as Steve carries my luggage further into the apartment, if I'll ever get used to people doing things for me that I've always done by myself.

I let David lead me through the rest of his home, my new home. I can't help being excited that I'm going to live in this insanely beautiful place. Beyond the dining area is a modern kitchen, with equipment I can't even identify, let alone use. It has a marble-topped island in the middle, and a comfortable looking breakfast nook for four.

There is more. David's study, with dark wood wall paneling and a soft dark rug, bookshelves filled with books, and another set of floor to ceiling windows, which provide more spectacular views of the city, Two guest bedrooms that look beautiful, if unused, and a staircase that leads to a private terrace with a sparkling blue swimming pool.

I already know that he is rich, but this is luxury. "It's

more beautiful than I imagined." I tell him, enchanted with it all.

He doesn't reply, instead he leads me down the hall to the last door, the door to the master suite. He places his hand on the door handle and smiles at me. "Are you ready to see your room, Mrs. Preston?"

My heart quickens. "I believe I am, Mr. Preston."

He chuckles and opens the door into a huge bedroom.

A soft rug covers the entire floor, and the windows are hung from floor to ceiling with long white drapes. There are two armchairs and a coffee table in a corner, and a dressing table with a wide mirror. But it's the bed that catches my attention. It is huge, perfectly made and very inviting, taking up most of the space on one side of the room. It's a bed to roll around in, a bed to make love in. I step towards it, moving almost involuntarily.

At the foot of the bed, I stop and run my hands along the soft linen bedspread. I turn to see if David is following me, and find that he is right behind me.

His face dips to the back of my neck, moving my hair out of the way, as he uses his lips to tease the sensitive skin. "Do you like it?" He whispers, his voice is unmistakably sensual.

I arch my neck, exposing more of my skin to his lips. "Yes." I whisper.

He pulls me to him, his hands circling my waist, and molding my body against his. Sighing softly, I lean back, pressing myself against his hard body. I feel his erection against the back of my thighs and my body clenches in sweet need. I moan softly.

"You're an aphrodisiac." He murmurs in my ear, his voice husky. "I want you every minute," His hands finds my breasts through my clothes and start to rub them gently from behind.

I close my eyes, luxuriating in the feel of his hands and the sound of his voice. His hands roam down from my breasts to my thighs. Gripping the hem of my skirt, he pulls it up until it's around my waist. I feel the cool air on my exposed flesh, then his hands, warm, strong, caressing the softness of my butt, until the heat building between my legs is a pulsing, raging fire, and I want so much more.

We're still standing, and my legs are so weak that I have to lean back against him. He unbuttons my blouse and undoes my bra, pushing it up until my breasts spill naked into his hands.

I sigh with pleasure when he grabs them, massaging them with a slow, rhythmic motion while playing with my aching nipples. I moan and press harder against him, wet and aching, desperate for him to give me what I need.

Still standing, he pulls my panties down and spreads my legs, stroking me with his fingers. I am so wet, they slip into me very easily, I hear him groan, and the sound fires my blood. I reach back for his belt, but he's faster than I am. He releases me for a moment while he undoes his pants, the next moment I can feel him, rock hard, pressing insistently against my thighs.

I shimmy until my panties fall all the way down, and then step out of them, leaving them discarded on the floor. I spread my legs, aching for him to fill me. His fingers start to stroke me again, I hear myself panting as he rubs back and forth, in and out, pleasuring me. I groan loudly, moving my hips to his rhythm. He strokes me until my hips are jerking uncontrollably, then he pulls his fingers away and replaces them with his thick, hard length.

I press backward, and he pushes into me, making me whimper uncontrollably as he fills me. I can't stop myself from crying out again and again as he thrusts, still gripping my hips. I match his strokes, pushing him deeper into my core. I feel out of balance, like any moment I'll fall, but I don't care, the only thing that matters is each sure thrust, each sweet burst of pleasure. My whole body is heating up, and getting slick with sweat, but I don't care, I only want more. He groans and grips my waist tighter, thrusting harder and faster. I can't feel my fingers or my toes, I can't feel anything, only him and the devastating pleasure he is giving me. I cry hoarsely as my brain reduces to nothing but sweetness. My body stiffens and I lose myself, falling against him with a moan, as he groans and comes in a hot rush inside me.

I can't catch my breath. I can feel his heart beating against my back, and his breath coming in deep gasps.

He slips out of me and my body shivers with residual pleasure. My legs give way, and we both collapse on the soft rug.

When I catch my breath, I turn to look at him, unable to suppress a giggle at how ridiculous we both look, half-undressed, and lying on the floor.

David follows my gaze, and chuckles. He kicks off his pants, then gets up and, lifting me as easily as if I weigh nothing, he carries me over to the bed, collapsing on top of me on the soft mattress.

"Welcome home, Mrs. Preston."

"Thank you, Mr. Preston."

I am still giggling. He gets up and starts to take off the rest of his clothing. As I watch him undress, my body starts to throb again. He is so magnificent.

I sit up and pull off my half-discarded blouse. My bra and skirt follow. He starts to watch me, and I revel in the pleasure of seeing him grow hard again. By the time I am completely undressed, I know we're not leaving the bed anytime soon.

"What are you trying to do to me?" He growls as he kneels on the bed, right between my spread legs.

I can't hide my pleasure. "Have I done something wrong? I ask, mock contrite.

He chuckles, "No sweetheart," he says, as he enters me slowly. "You're doing everything right."

Chapter Three

HOURS LATER, I FINALLY DRIFT off, exhausted. I can't remember how many times David has brought me to a brain-shattering climax. I feel boneless and liquid, aching sweetly. He's made love to me slowly, then fast, then slowly again, each time until I cry out his name in senseless surrender.

When I wake up, the room is dimmer, telling me I've slept until evening. I'm alone on the bed. I stretch luxuriously. My body feels delicious.

I'm completely naked underneath the covers, so I take them with me as I get off the bed. My clothes are no longer on the floor where I dropped them earlier. Baffled, I wonder if Mrs. Daniels has been in to tidy up while I was asleep.

Apart from the door we came in, another door leads off the bedroom. I open it and step into a huge, brightly lit closet. On one side, rows upon rows of suits hang side by side, with shirts, pants, shoes and a vast array of all sorts of men's clothing. On the opposite side from the suits, the racks are almost bare, sparsely populated with my few clothes, which Mrs. Daniels has unpacked. My underwear is neatly arranged in a drawer, my shoes tidily placed.

On the far wall, there's a full-length mirror. I walk forward, staring at my mussed hair and wide eyes. My skin is still flushed from all the lovemaking, with a smooth healthy glow. Making love suits me, I decide, giggling, I look far better than I remember.

A frosted glass door leads off the dressing room into a luxurious bathroom. I step inside, admiring the gleaming cream tile walls and the clear marble floors. A deep sunken bath sits in the middle of the room, with solid looking gold taps. A marble-topped sink stands below a wide, mirrored wall cabinet, frosted glass hides a shower stall, and a door leads off to what must be the toilet.

At the sink, I splash some water on my face. Opening the cabinet above, I notice that my toiletries have been arranged inside. I'm impressed. I make my way back to the dressing room to look for something to wear. My jeans and blouses feel like too much of a bother, and the few dresses I bought while shopping for my wedding seem too dressy. An impulse makes me put on one of David's shirts. It's soft, and feels heavenly on my skin. It's probably insanely expensive, I think, walking out of the room to look for him.

At first, the apartment seems remarkably silent, then I hear David's voice coming from the direction of his study, I follow the sound, then pause at the door to eat him up with my eyes.

He is standing with his back to me, looking towards the view of the city from the windows. He's wearing only sweatpants, and his back is bare, showing me his defined muscles up to where they curve into his firm ass. As I watch him, I can't help thinking of a colossus, bestriding the world. He looks magnificent, powerful, and potent.

And he's mine.

I have to try very hard to resist the urge to go to him and run my hands all over his glorious body.

He says something again and I realize that he is talking into a small earpiece attached to his ear.

"How many percent total?" I hear him say, his voice is terse and commanding. He pauses and listens for a while, "Everything hinges on Carole," He says finally,

"Leave her to me, I know exactly how to deal with her."

Even though it's not me he's talking to, I'm hit by the steely hardness in his voice. There is something ruthless in the sound. Vaguely, I wonder who Carole is. The sound of another woman's name on his lips is enough to make my heart constrict with jealousy.

I stay where I am at the door, not sure whether to go in to him. I don't want to interrupt if he's busy. However, as if he can feel me standing there, he turns around. I step back at the coldness I see in his eyes, the blue is faded almost to grey, and his face seems almost cruel.

"Sophie." He smiles, his expression softening as he removes the earpiece and comes around the desk to meet me. I shiver slightly, the fear I felt only moments before, melting as he runs his hand over my arm, draped in the soft material of his shirt. "This looks very good on you." He says, his eyes travelling down to my bare legs, then back to my face.

"Thank you." I say shyly. Outside the windows, it's already dark. I must have slept for hours. "I didn't mean to sleep for so long."

David shrugs. "You were tired." He raises his hand and runs a finger along my lower lip, making me shiver again. "I'm sure I had something to do with that." He says tenderly.

I blush, and he chuckles, pulling me to him, and running his hands over my body, which is naked under the shirt. "You should wear this all the time with nothing underneath." He suggests, the teasing light in his eyes making him look his age, with none of the steeliness I saw in his face earlier.

I laugh. "I would never be able to go out." I point out.

"Hmm...mm," His eyes are on my lips, "you'd always be here, half naked and ready for me." He growls softly and gives me a quick kiss on my lips. "I'd like to show you what that thought does to me," He says, "But I'm sure you are hungry."

My stomach rumbles loudly, reminding me that I haven't eaten all day. "I am."

"Good." He is already pulling me out of the study, his hand gentle on my elbow. "Let's eat."

Dinner is a home cooked feast Mrs. Daniels must have prepared before she left for the day. In the kitchen, David fills our plates from the silver chafing dishes, his fingers moving with superb grace. Is there anything he doesn't do perfectly well? I help him load the plates unto a tray and follow him as he takes them to the living room.

The food is delicious, as is the red wine David pours

for me. We eat, seated on the rug, the couch at our backs, and the gleaming lights of the city laid out at our feet.

There's something about the intimacy of the moment. I feel close to him somehow. "Tell me about yourself." I whisper.

He leans back on the couch, watching me through hooded eyes. "What do you want to know?"

"Everything." I say hopefully.

"My life isn't half as interesting as yours," he states coolly. "My father died when I was young, my mother remarried almost immediately and lived happily ever after till her husband died last year." He shrugs, his voice sounding detached.

Something in his tone gets to me. "Didn't you get along with your step-father?" I ask, concerned. He doesn't sound too happy about his mother's marriage.

"I have no idea." He says cryptically. "I never saw either of them."

"How come?"

He looks at me over the top of his glass. "He was very rich, and he liked to travel, my mother followed him everywhere because that was what he wanted."

My heart goes out to him as I imagine him growing up without the attention of his mother. At least my mother didn't abandon me. She died.

"They never took you with them?" I ask, a small frown on my face.

He shakes his head. "No, they didn't." He says, looking a little bored. "My step-father had a house not very far from here. I lived there."

"Oh." I watch as he leans back on the couch, his face relaxed, his eyes hooded by half closed lids. His lashes are incredibly long, I think, momentarily distracted. "Does your mother still live there?"

"When she's in town, yes."

He doesn't seem eager to talk about his mother, so I decide to switch subjects.

"Tell me about your work." I say, leaning forward. I already know that his company is called Preston Corp and that it has something to do with software, but I'm curious to know more.

"I invest in developing computer software." He says. "There are a lot of products out there with the ability to provide enormous user satisfaction. Some of them never get to reach their target market. I make it possible for them to do so."

I'm impressed, and even more so by the confidence in his tone. "How did you get started?"

"A videogame." He grins boyishly, again looking his age. I have a sudden urge to wrap my arms around him and hold him close, to soothe the lonely little boy my imagination has conjured out of his words.

"Did you miss her?" the question pops out of my mouth before I have the time to consider it. I'm thinking of my own mother, how I've spent my whole life with the faint ache of missing her, even though I never knew her.

"Who?"

"Your mother."

He is silent for a moment, but only a single moment.

"Never." He states finally, his voice cool. He gets up and picks up the tray, and taking it to the kitchen. He loads the dishwasher while I dump the empty bottle of wine in the chrome bin with the 'recycle' icon. It seems our moment of intimacy has passed. We clean up in silence. He works quickly, efficiently, and self-sufficiently. I may as well not even be there. As soon as we're done, he goes back to his study.

I sit at the window seat in the living room, alternately admiring the view, and thumbing through a glossy magazine on interior design. I can't really concentrate though. My thoughts are full of David as I piece the things I now know about him together. I know more than I did when I married him, but he is still a mystery in so many ways.

After a while, I'm filled with a longing to recapture

the feeling of intimacy I had earlier while we were talking, so I drift towards the study, hoping that David would be finished with whatever he is doing.

I find him seated at the desk, his face lit by the glow from a desk lamp and his computer screen. He looks hard as he sits there alone, the planes and angles of his face made pronounced by the dim light. Watching him, I get the feeling that he is someone that's used to being on his own. I imagine him as a solemn, dark haired little boy, left alone while his mother chose to spend her time with her new husband. It makes me sad.

Reluctant to disturb him, I walk on to our room, and lie waiting in bed. I don't sleep until much later, when he comes to join me and makes love to me until I fall asleep in his arms.

The next morning when I wake up, my body is sweet and tender from another night of intense lovemaking. I move, wanting to snuggle close to David, but he's not in bed with me. Disappointed, I get up. The bed feels incredibly empty with me as its sole occupant.

On my way to the bathroom, I see the note propped upright on the dressing table. 'Gone to the office.' It says, in a firm elegant scrawl. I'm already missing him as I go into the bathroom and take a warm shower.

Afterwards, I dress and find my way to the kitchen, following the unmistakable smell of breakfast cooking. I find Mrs. Daniels making pancakes. Still feeling let down that David has already left, I say a friendly hello to her, silently telling myself that it's unrealistic to expect that David and I would spend all our time together, making love. Of course, he has to go to work, he has a business to run after all.

Mrs. Daniels pours me some tea and places a large plate of pancakes dripping with maple syrup in front of me. I'm not particularly hungry, but the pancakes are light, fluffy, and delicious. As I eat, we talk about the apartment, and she tells me the things I need to know, like the names of some of the building staff and all the security codes and emergency numbers I might need. She seems to vibrate with warmth as she talks, and I soon relax in her company.

After my breakfast, she has other work to do, and I'm left on my own again. I find myself missing Stacey and her constant concern. I imagine her sitting at her desk with a frown on her face, wondering if David has turned out to be Bluebeard. I don't have a mobile, I'm sure that if I did she would be calling me every hour. I decide to put her mind at rest.

"Sophie honey," I can hear the relief in her voice that I've finally called, "How are you?" It's so like her to keep fretting about me, even though I've assured her that I'm happy.

"I'm fine." I say, laughing.

"Are you sure?"

"Yes," I insist. "I'm perfectly happy."

"Okay." I try not to hear the skepticism in her voice. Thankfully, she starts to tell me about the reactions to my sudden marriage. I listen silently, but I don't really care. Ashford seems like a very long time ago.

"Mrs. Newton seems to think you broke poor Eddie's heart," She says, catching my attention, "Apparently he was always sweet on you."

"He wasn't." I say defensively, trying to forget the look on Eddie's face when he confronted David at my apartment. Good thing Stacey doesn't know about that. I think, relieved.

"Oh well," She sighs. "Don't hesitate to let me know if you need anything." She says finally.

"I won't," I assure her, "but don't worry about me Stacey, I promise I'll be fine."

The rest of the day passes slowly. Mrs. Daniels clucks in disapproval when I tell her not to bother about lunch. She disappears again, leaving me by myself. I swim laps in the pool, lie on the lounger in the terrace reading magazines, and watching the city from the height of the penthouse. I can't help feeling as if I'm on a solo vacation instead of a honeymoon.

I wander through the apartment, exploring on my own. In David's study, I look through the numerous books on business, and philosophy. Thankfully, there are also some literary classics, Charles Dickens, Thackeray, and even Fitzgerald. They are all sturdy looking, leather bound volumes. Probably very expensive, I think, wondering if he reads them.

I spend the rest of the day drawing. The sound of my pencil scratching the paper of my sketchbook is soothing and familiar. I draw until it gets a little dark outside. As I put my sketchpad away, I realize with a vague feeling of sadness that it's the third day of my marriage, and I have been alone all day.

I'm at the window seat reading a book when David returns. He steps into the living room, filling the space with his striking presence. I spring up from my seat, unable to contain how happy and relieved I am to see him. At the back of my mind, I berate myself for being so pathetically dependent on him, but I forget those thoughts when he drops his briefcase and claims my lips in a soul-searing kiss.

I forget that I have been alone all day, I forget the gloominess of my feelings earlier. Surrounded by the taste and feel of him, I can't think of anything besides how he makes me feel.

"Are you hungry?" I ask when he finally releases me.

The smile spreads slowly across his lips. "I am." He says, his eyes devouring me.

I take a deep breath. "Mrs. Daniels left something for dinner."

"Oh that." He chuckles, his eyes telling me that his hunger was for something else. "I'll be out in a minute." He says, picking up his briefcase and going to our room to change out of his suit.

I set the table in the kitchen. After we eat, David gives me another long kiss before disappearing into his study. Confused, I wonder if all my days are going to be spent like this, waiting for him to come home to make love to me, and staying out of his way when he wants to work. I may not have a lot of experience, but I'm sure there should be a lot more intimacy in a marriage.

It's not as if I blame him for working, but we're supposed to be on our honeymoon. I understand that with the rushed wedding, there would have been little time to arrange his schedule to put a trip together. But it's not even a trip I want. I want him. I want him to be mine the way I've surrendered to being his. I don't want to be like Psyche, wandering all day around a beautiful house, with a husband I don't know, who only comes to make love to me in the dark.

I'm still awake when he comes into our bedroom. I watch him as he comes to sit on the bed. I'm trying to find the words to tell him how I feel without seeming needy. I've told him my feelings once, and the only answer he gave me was silence. I don't know if I can expect anything better this time.

"You left so early this morning." I say finally, when the silence becomes too much.

"I always leave early." His tone is dismissive.

That was before you had a wife. I want to say, but I bite the words back. I understand that he has to work hard. You don't get to have the things he does at his age by being laid back, but I need to know that I'm not just a warm body he comes to at night. I think of all the things I want to tell him. That I was lonely without him, bored, wishing he was here. That we're newlyweds, supposed to be spending this time together.

"You were gone all day." I say instead, my voice low.

He sighs tiredly, "Sophie, maybe in your

imagination being married means spending every single moment together, but real life isn't a fantasy, I have a business to run." His voice is harsh, and I flinch, unable to hide my pain and surprise.

"I was just…" I stop, unsure what to say.

He turns to look at me. Something in my face seems to get to him. "I had a hard day Sophie, I was incredibly busy." He explains, before getting up and going to the bathroom.

I frown at my hands on my lap. I've told him that I loved him, and he said nothing. I'm telling him I'd like to spent more time with him, and his response is to treat me as if I don't know what I'm talking about. Hurt, I lie back on the bed and turn on my stomach. I hate that I feel like crying. I've lied to Stacey, I realize, I'm not happy. I'm afraid. I have a husband who can set my body on fire with just one look, and who is everything to me, but has no desire to be close to me, or to let me get close to him.

I feel him return and slide into the bed beside me, but I don't look up. I try not to react to the warmth of his skin as it touches mine. I try to stay still as he runs a hand gently down my back. When he raises the thigh length t-shirt I'm wearing and spreads my legs, I bite my lip to keep from moaning. The thought that this is all he wants from me is painful. I want to be angry with him, not to respond to what he's doing, but already I'm eager, wanting him so much that it's an intense throbbing ache that needs to be filled.

My resistance lasts until he dips his head between my legs, and starts to lick me, his tongue moving rapidly, swirling round and round my sensitive core until I am breathless and gasping, moaning his name. At the back of my mind, I accept that I need more than this from him, but for now, I don't care. I'm too lost in the pleasure.

I let out a long moan, and he grips my thighs tightly so that I can't move. My fingers dig into the pillow. Imprisoned between his hands and his tongue, I surrender myself to the exquisite pleasure. He teases me to a frenzy until I reach a shattering climax, crying out my pleasure as my hips jerk wildly against his delicious tongue.

Afterwards, while my body is still shuddering with the aftershocks of my climax, I run my fingers down his chest. He lies back on the bed, watching me through half closed eyes as I explore his body. I watch his face, eager to see the signs that I'm pleasing him.

My fingers travel down over his belly, until they close around him. I marvel at the hardness encased in the soft skin, like steel under silk. He feels warm, strong and powerful, I stroke him with eager fingers, loving the feeling. His breathing changes, becoming faster and more ragged, encouraged, I bend my head and take him into my mouth.

He groans, and his hips move, grinding a little. Instinctively, I take him deeper, running my tongue over his swollen tip, and then allowing him to slide further inside my mouth. He tastes of skin, of salt, and a flavor that is all him. I steal a look at his face. His eyes are closed, his lips parted. He likes it. I purse my lips and suck on him, moving my head, so he goes slowly in and out of my mouth.

"Sophie." His groan is deep and raspy, the pleasure in his voice makes me feel powerful and sexy... all woman. I suck harder, feeling him grow harder in my mouth as his hands run feverishly through my hair, but I don't stop. In every other way, I already feel powerless, but in this, I want to see him lose control of himself.

He doesn't give me the chance. He rises from the bed, moving faster than I could have anticipated, and lifts me, pulling me forward until my hips are poised over his erection. Then, with his hands on my waist, he guides me down slowly until I'm completely filled with him. I moan at the exquisite sensation of him inside me. My whole body is tingling. I forget everything but what he's doing to me. I want this, I want this so much.

Even though I am on top, he defines our movements, guiding my hips as he grinds his, stroking my sensitive insides with each deep thrust.

My body starts to shake. I'm moaning incoherently, crying out his name over and over. He quickens his pace, thrusting faster, until his body stiffens, and he groans, exploding into me in a warm surge. At the same moment, I shout his name one final time, and then collapse onto his chest.

Chapter Four

THE NEXT MORNING, WHEN I WAKE up to find myself alone on the bed, my first thought is that David has left for work again. I feel a little depressed until I hear him in the dressing room. It's embarrassing how relieved I am when I see him standing there almost fully dressed, putting on his cufflinks. I lean on the doorframe, watching him as he concentrates on fastening the links.

"Good morning." I say softly, my heart constricting with longing as I look at him. Watching him makes me feel happy and sad at the same time, happy that he's mine, and sad because, somehow, I know he doesn't truly belong to me.

He looks up at me, "Good morning Sophie." He says, finishing with the links. There's a tie hanging loosely around his neck, and his fingers move to knot it.

I don't want to rehash our conversation of last night, but I don't want to spend the whole day missing him either. "I wish you wouldn't leave so early," I say.

He walks away from me, towards the mirror. In the face of his silence, I start to wish I hadn't said anything. I watch as he starts to knot his tie.

"I know you're really busy..." I start.

He turns to me. The expression on his face is one of sincere apology. "I'm sorry Sophie," he says, "Yes, I've been busy. I've had to deal with certain issues at work which were there even before I met you." He stops, "but that's no excuse."

I walk across the room to him, "I understand, really. I'm not complaining, I just wish we had a little more time for us." I look at his face as I say the word, 'Us'. That's what's important to me. I want us to be a success. I want this to last. I don't want to be a short statistic in his life. The thought of not being with him fills me with a sad sort of desperation.

He raises one of his hands, tracing a finger across my lips. "Things will clear up soon," he assures me, "and then I'll make it up to you, I promise. We'll go somewhere that will blow your mind."

I smile, excited as much by his promise as his touch.

"You blow my mind." I whisper.

He smiles and moves his finger from my lips to my chin, lifting it up, so I'm looking into his eyes. My lips tingle, waiting for his kiss, but he doesn't make any move to touch me.

I lift myself unto my toes and touch my lips to his. He kisses me back, his brow furrowing in surprise when I gently push him away, running my hands down the front of his shirt. He watches me as my hands move down. I'm not sure what I'm doing, but I want to show him how much I want him. I want to finish what I started last night.

I drop to my knees on the soft carpet in front of him, stroking him through his trousers, and feeling him harden and push against my palm. I loosen his belt and undo his zipper, reaching in to pull down his briefs just enough for him to spring free, hard, rigid, and eager.

Immediately I cover the head with my lips. I feel him stiffen, but I don't look up. I suck on the tip, pulling him deeper with my lips and stroking him with my tongue. His fingers tangle in my hair, and I hear him groan softly.

I love this. I love the feel, the smell, the warmth of him. I move my head slowly, letting him go in and out of my mouth while I suck deeply. He groans again, and the sound of his arousal causes a warm, insistent need to start in my core, and spread till my whole body is suffused with my desire for him.

I take him in as deeply as I can, he moans, and his hands stiffen in my hair, moving my head in the rhythm that he wants, as he starts to grind into my mouth. I tighten my lips around him, sucking him in as he grinds faster. There is something so erotic about what we're doing. A small moan escapes my lips. The sound does something to him, and his whole body stiffens, the muscles of his hips tightening under my hands, then he jerks forward and with a loud groan, comes into my mouth.

I swallow quickly, I can't believe what I've just done, but I'd do it again and again. He slips out of my mouth, his body shuddering. His breathing is deep and heavy as he comes down on his knees beside me.

"You're a bag of surprises, aren't you?" he says huskily, moments before his lips descend on mine as his fingers find my wet arousal under my t-shirt.

I'm already so hot for him, I moan as his fingers stroke me.

"You're ready for me." His whisper is warm against my mouth.

"Hmm." I nod, I'm so ready.

His fingers rub me until I have to hold on to him to steady myself, but he doesn't stop slipping them in and out of me until I'm squirming wildly, begging him to give me more. Suddenly, he turns me around and enters me from behind.

I bend forward, my hands on the floor as he thrusts into me. He is so incredibly hard, so sweet, so fast. I can't catch my breath. I'm already so far gone when his fingers find my nipples under my shirt, and start to tease them, I explode into a million pieces of pure pleasure, screaming my release in a garbled version of his name.

He pulls out of me, still hard, and turns me around until I am lying on my back and he is still kneeling, poised in front of me. He lifts my legs, raising them around his hips, and enters me again. My body tightens around him, unraveling as he starts to move again. He doesn't stop until we both climax, and he collapses on the rug beside me.

Later, while I'm still trying to catch my breath, he gets up and starts to adjust his clothes.

I watch him through a haze of sexual fulfillment. "Have I made you late for work?"

"Not really." His movements are swift as he knots his tie and pulls his trousers back up. It looks like he has already pushed me to the back of his mind. I watch him silently.

"I've asked Linda to make a few appointments for

you." He says suddenly.

"What kind of appointments?" I frown, I would never admit it to him, but Linda Mays, his assistant, with her glossy black hair, and her skirts that put the 'p' in pencil, intimidates me to heaven and back.

"Things to do with clothes, and shopping, and other stuff you need." He gives me a hand up, dropping a kiss on my nose. "Linda will tell you all about it." His eyes go to my side of the dressing room, which is still sadly sparse.

"Okay." I'm sure I should be more excited about shopping, but there are things I want more than new clothes, to be closer to him, for one.

My day progresses much better than the day before. The new tablet and smartphone arrive only about an hour after David leaves. The note in the package says 'Some toys you can play with while I'm gone.' Even though I find it unsatisfactory that he's trying to take away my loneliness at his absence by buying me electronic gadgets, I fall in love with them immediately.

They're both already programmed, the phone with David's mobile and office numbers, and the tablet with a couple of apps, books, and internet access. At first, I stumble a little with the tablet, but then I find that it's much like using a computer.

Linda has arranged multiple appointments. She calls

me in the morning, sounding incredibly busy and efficient as she tells me she had sent my schedule to my new phone. It would be funny if not that as soon as I cut the connection I see the updates to my calendar. There's a hairdresser, in fact, a beauty team, with hairs, nails, and makeup people, and a personal shopper too. I'm stupefied.

The beauty team arrives before noon. I get my hair cut and styled by a hilariously funny French man called Jasper, who calls Mrs. Daniels 'my love', causing her to blush to the roots of her silver hair. My nails are fixed to perfection, and the makeup artist, a fierce looking girl with purple hair and a lip ring, spends nearly an hour making me up to look as if I'm not wearing any makeup. She leads me through it, finally leaving me with the products that 'fit my complexion'.

After they leave, I get a visit from the personal shopper, a petite but lively girl in her twenties. Her name is Reiko Nakano, she tells me, eagerly shaking my hand. I can't help staring at her. She's incredibly beautiful in an unusual, exotic way, with grey almond eyes, tilted upwards at the corners, pale skin, and straight, waist-length black hair with deep scarlet streaks.

She talks non-stop as she shows me the samples she's brought based on Linda's description of me. I soon discover that her father is a Japanese-American heart surgeon, and her mother is a Spanish jewelry designer. She chatters without pause for almost thirty minutes, but I don't mind, in fact, I like it.

"My father wanted me to be a doctor," She tells me, as she shows me another beautiful outfit, "so I went to pre-med and got accepted to medical school." She shudders, "but I decided I liked clothes more."

I laugh, "Your father must have hated that."

"Yes he did, especially since I'm such a genius," she sighs, "I'm a great loss to the profession of medicine." She smiles impishly, "but a great gain to women who love the way I dress them, right?"

I have to agree. From what I can see, she does know what she is doing. Based on what she has shown me, my new style is part casual, part classy, innocent, and sexy. I flatter myself that she's clothing me in my own personality. "Seattle is not really a dressy city," She tells me with a grimace, "But we do have a little fashion." She winks at me, promising to deliver all my new clothes over the course of the week.

David is still extremely busy, so over the next few days, we fall into a routine. We have breakfast together before he leaves for work. Afterwards, I read on my tablet, mostly books, but I also read the news, especially news about software companies, eager to learn more about what David does when he's not with me.

The little news I find about Preston Corp is mostly what I already know. It's a top-notch software entrepreneurial and investment company, with David as the CEO. There is some information about their investments, but it's mostly abstract. David is as much of an enigma to the public as he is to me, I soon decide. There's nothing about his personal life, only a little about his charity work supporting educational programs all over the world.

When I'm not reading, I draw, filling my sketchbook with more and more pages of jewelry. Sometimes Mrs. Daniels comes to watch me, exclaiming about how talented I am.

The day Reiko delivers the first batch of my clothes, I've been in Seattle for a little less than a week. As soon as Mrs. Daniel's lets her in, she fills the apartment with her chatter.

"Wait till you see your new clothes." She tells me, as Mrs. Daniels wheels the full clothes rack into the apartment.

I've been sitting in the living room, sketching at the window seat. As I get up to join them, Reiko comes over to me. "I didn't know you were an artist." She remarks, her eyes on the sketchpad I just abandoned on the coffee table.

"I'm not." I deny, suddenly a little shy of my work. "I just like to draw jewelry.

"May I?" She looks closer, thumbing through a few pages, "These are really good." She looks up at me, her eyes shining, "Why are you keeping them hidden?"

I laugh, "Please don't spare my feelings."

"No, really!" She nods, "I know what I'm talking about. My mother designs jewelry."

I vaguely remember, her mentioning something like that.

She sound excited. "I'd totally rock these." She turns to me "Have you made any of them?"

"No." I shake my head. "I haven't been to art school or anything."

Reiko's curtain of black and scarlet hair moves as she shrugs, "My mother didn't go either. She took a private course and learned how to smith herself."

"Really!" I'm impressed.

"Do you have any plans to make them?" she asks. Mrs. Daniels is wheeling the rack of clothes towards the door that leads to my dressing room from the hallway while we follow her behind.

I give a little grimace. "Not really, no." I say, "at least, not for now. I just like to draw."

She gives me a look. "You should though, with your

talent, you could make a name for yourself." She sounds serious. "I wish I could talk to my mother about you," she says, "but I'm sure that would violate the NDA."

Mrs. Daniels is already inside the dressing room. I stop at the door. What NDA? I think.

"What NDA?" I ask, an involuntary frown working its way to my face.

Reiko studies my face. "I…" for the first time since I met her she seems unsure what to say. She frowns, obviously uncomfortable. "I'm just not supposed to tell anyone about you." She says finally.

I swallow, trying to keep my face calm even though my mind is churning. "Of course." I pause outside for a moment while she joins Mrs. Daniels in the dressing room. A Non-Disclosure Agreement! Why? I don't understand.

Is David keeping me a secret?

I think of the beauty team, the only other people I've met. Do they have orders not to mention me to anyone too?

Reiko and Mrs. Daniels are hanging up clothes, talking pleasantly about how to organize the closet. I can't bring myself to join them. The questions are raging in my mind. Why am I a secret?

Why am I such a secret that people have to sign a

contract before they can see me.

My mind goes into overdrive, churning out possibilities.

Is he ashamed of me, ashamed of his spur of the moment decision to tie himself to me? As far as I know, he could be working with his lawyers now trying to find a quiet way to get rid of me.

Is there someone else, someone he would rather be with maybe, someone he wouldn't want to find out about me?

Everything starts to fall into place. Almost a week in Seattle, and I have never been anywhere with him.

Leaving Reiko and Mrs. Daniels in the dressing room, I find my tablet and go to David's study. There is a soft leather sofa near the door, and I sit there, starting the tablet and going straight to the web browser.

I've looked at the web encyclopedia page on him before, but I didn't really read it. I was just psyched that he had one. Now I go through the little summary window at the side. It has all the information, like his date and place of birth, alma mater, etc. but there is no field for spouse.

There would be one if anyone knew about me.

I'm a secret.

Why?

My phone rings, startling me.

I look at the screen and see David's name. I spend a few seconds debating whether I want to talk to him. With all the emotions raging within me, I'll probably get hysterical if I try to ask him what it all means.

I take a deep breath. "Hello." I say quietly.

"Sophie." I try not to get lost in the warmth of his voice, at least not until I understand what's going on.

"I hope you can go out tonight." He says, putting a big hole in all the conclusions I've drawn.

I'm silent for a few moments, confused. "You want us to go out together?"

There is a short pause at his end. "Yes." He says finally.

So apparently, I'm not going to be a secret anymore, but that doesn't change the fact that he's had people sign a document to keep my existence quiet. "Where?" I ask.

"Just dinner." He says, naming one of the more popular restaurants in the city.

"Oh. Okay." I still don't understand any of it, but I decide to wait until he comes home to ask him about the NDA.

When I finally come out of the study, Reiko has already left. I spent a few minutes putting away my sketches, still deep in thought. A few minutes ago, I was convinced that he was keeping our marriage silent because he wants to end it with as little fuss as possible, now I'm not sure of anything. It's frustrating not to know where you stand with someone who means so much to you.

I should select something to wear from my new wardrobe, but my thoughts are in too much of a mess. I think about calling Stacey to pour out my confusions to her, but I know how worried she'll get.

Finally, I return to the living room, still deep in thought, and find myself face to face with a stranger.

She is an older woman, in her late fifties or early sixties, tall and slender, with thick wavy black hair and sparkling blue eyes. There's something vaguely familiar about her straight nose, determined chin and sharp cheekbones. She smiles at me, the expression on her face welcoming and warm, as if we've known each other for a long time, and are on the best of terms. I cast a curious glance at Mrs. Daniels, who's standing by the foyer door, not looking happy at all. I turn back to the woman.

"You must be Sophie." She declares, still smiling, and immediately I know who she is.

She moves towards me, determined and graceful. I'm not expecting the warm hug she gives me.

"I'm Marianne Weber," She coos, stepping back to

take a good look at me, "David's mother."

I've already guessed as much, but I still turn to Mrs. Daniel's for confirmation, which she gives with a small nod, still looking extremely unhappy.

Briefly, I wonder at the misgivings that are so clear on the housekeeper's face, then I turn back to my guest. "I'm pleased to meet you." I say politely.

"I didn't believe it when I heard," She exclaims. She sounds playful and intimate as she leads me to a couch, "and you are so cute." She gives me a smile that is so like her son's. "Won't you tell me about yourself? How did you meet David?" There's something about her that instantly invites confidence, or maybe it's just that I've gone through life desperately wanting a mother. I find myself wanting to talk to her. It makes me feel awkward.

"Well..." I notice Mrs. Daniels disappear into the kitchen. This is really odd. It's obvious that whoever told his mother about me, it wasn't David. I'm sure he has no idea that she's here... and yet as she smiles at me, her sparkling eyes urging me to answer her question, I realize that I want to.

"He came into the gift shop where I was working as an assistant," I say, "he wanted to buy a gift." I pause, "for you actually."

She laughs merrily, as if I've said something terribly funny, "and then it was love at first sight." She states.

For me, it probably was, but I still don't know about David, so I don't say anything

She wants to know everything about me. As we talk,

I try my best not to give away too much, and not to sound evasive either.

"You should go out," she states finally, "make friends, meet people, and discover the city on your own." Her voice is earnest. "I'm only here a few weeks every year these days, but whenever I'm in town we could have lunch, get to know each other better.

"That would be lovely." I mean it.

I hear the elevator bell. Moments later, David walks into the living room, his face hardening to stone when he sees who I'm with.

It's really early for him to come home. I immediately suspect that Mrs. Daniels called him to tell him his mother was with me. I look from him to his mother, and I'm sad to see the longing on her face. She loves him, I realize, and he's shut her out. That's his revenge for all the years she ignored him.

I get up from the couch. "I was just getting to know your mother." I say cheerfully. I'm annoyed that he has kept her from me, but I'm also eager to ease the tension I can sense in the room.

"Isn't that wonderful," His smile seems made of ice, "and now she is leaving."

"David..." her voice is a plea.

"David!" I exclaim at the same time, shocked at his rudeness.

He ignores me. "Why did you come here?" he says to her, the contempt in his voice unrelenting.

She sighs. "David, my son got married, and I had no idea." She looks exasperated, "I just wanted to meet

Sophie."

Her answer doesn't get anywhere with him. "I don't want you here," his voice is steel, "The next time you cajole anyone to let you in I will fire them."

I see her stiffen, and square her shoulders. I hate that he is humiliating her. No matter their history she is still his mother.

"No, you won't." my voice is hesitant, but I can see that he's hurting her, and I don't like it, "and you may not want her here, but I do."

David looks at me in surprise, his expression soon changes to exasperation. "Sophie..." he starts.

"No stop," I interrupt, "Why don't you want her here? Is it because you want to continue keeping me a secret? Why don't you make her sign a non-disclosure agreement?"

His eyes narrow. "You don't know what you're saying."

"Don't I?" I stare at him squarely, "didn't you make the beauty team, the personal shopper, every person I've spoken to in all the days you've kept me hidden in this apartment sign a document to prevent them for saying anything to anyone about me?"

He runs a hand through his hair and glares past me at his mother. She shrugs, the movement of her shoulders saying she knew nothing about it. "You wouldn't understand." He says finally, his eyes meeting mine.

My annoyance turns to pain. It's bad enough that he thinks it's okay to keep me a secret, but to keep things from me because he think I don't have the capacity to understand them is just insulting. Of course, I tell myself. It's already clear that he doesn't have any feelings for me. I'm just a willing body to him, a warm body he doesn't have to tell anything.

I turn away from him and walk out of the room. At that moment, I almost wish that I'd never met him. I'm tired of the feelings that have taken over me, the love, the frustration, the desperation, the deep sadness that comes with knowing I mean nothing to him.

"I hope you're glad." I hear him say to his mother as I step out of the room. His voice is like gravel.

I pause, "I'm sorry," I hear her say apologetically. "I had no idea."

"Well now you do."

There is a short pause, and then I hear her voice again. "An NDA seems rather extreme... Does this have anything to do with Carole Banks?"

I don't hear what he says to her, but I hear her footsteps as she leaves. Carole Banks, I remember I've heard that name before, that first night in his study. Who is she, and what does she have to do with anything?

Chapter Five

MY TABLET IS STILL IN DAVID'S STUDY, so that's where I go, hoping that he won't follow me. I hate that I have to find things out about my husband from the internet.

I start up the tablet again as I settle on the leather sofa, and search for Carole Banks. I sift through all the many profiles until I find one that seems likely. She's a heiress, with a social life that spans New York, Palm Beach and Europe. Born in Seattle, her father was Marshall Banks, a name that's only vaguely familiar until I remember the name of the investor who helped to make David's first fortune by investing in a video game company David started with a couple of his friends while they were still in college.

I search for her name coupled with David's and the articles that come up fill me with dismay. I click on images, and what I see is the story of a long relationship that seems to span several countries and numerous events. There are pictures of them together at gallery openings, benefits, nightclubs, vacations, and even at her father's funeral where she leans on him while he holds her hand.

It wouldn't be so painful if they didn't look so good together, he tall handsome and intense, she with her wavy red hair, deep green eyes and languid smile. A hot stab of jealousy passes through me, coupled with sadness. How could I have thought any of this was real? I can't imagine how even for a moment, he'll prefer me to her.

In all the articles, there's a strong indication that the writers consider them a couple. The latest, which has them together at a book launch, is only a few weeks before I met David in Ashford.

The door opens and David steps into the room, looking worried. His expression changes to relief when he sees me sitting there.

"I've been looking for you."

I shrug, turning back to the tablet, I'm angry, jealous and in love. It's not a very good combination.

He comes closer to me and his eyes take in the search pages I have open on screen of the tablet. "Nothing you find there has anything to do with me and you." He says.

I can feel my heart breaking as I look at him. Is there a 'him' and 'me'? Right now, I'm not so sure. I want to ask him once and for all, how he actually feels about me, but I'm afraid I won't like the answer. I turn back to the pictures on my tablet and stare at them for a long moment.

"Tell me about her." I ask.

"There's nothing to tell."

"Really?" I glare at him, "because it's very clear here that she was your girlfriend only a short time ago."

He shrugs, "Don't believe everything you read in the papers Sophie. We saw each other on and off for a while, but it's been over for a long time."

"Do you love her?" I ask, unable to keep the jealousy I feel from creeping into my voice. "Is that why you're keeping me hidden, so that she won't find out about me?"

He sighs and walks over to me, coming to sit beside me. I try not to be distracted by how beautiful he is, by the intensity in his eyes. I have to try very hard to breathe. "You don't need to concern yourself about Carole." He says, his eyes holding mine and keeping me captive.

I want to believe him so much, even though he hasn't even bothered to answer my question.

"Her father invested a lot in your career." I start, looking away from him.

"In return for a huge profit," He says coaxingly, "It was good business, and he made money from Preston Corp every day we've been in existence."

I close my eyes and take a breath. "All those pictures of the two of you…"

"Mean nothing," he says, "We went to a lot of the same places, and people are used to mentioning our names together."

I sniff, unconvinced. "Why don't you want anyone to know about me?" I ask.

There is a long pause as I wait for him to answer my question. My breath catches in my throat.

He doesn't reply. Abruptly, I get up, abandoning the tablet on the sofa. "Fine, don't tell me." I mutter, making for the door. If I needed any proof that I mean nothing to him, this is it. If he cared about me, he would tell me what I need to know. He wouldn't keep me living in this limbo of not knowing where I stand.

His hand closes around mine before I get to the door.

"Sophie." I turn around, hopeful, waiting for him to

say something, but he stays silent.

I pull my hand from his. "Don't touch me." I say, my voice catching in my throat. "Don't ever touch me again."

He looks annoyed. "Stop being childish Sophie."

His words are more hurtful than his silence, I turn from him and rush towards our room. I need to get away from him. I don't care where I go. I just want to stop feeling as if I'm drowning in emotions I can't control.

"Sophie, for God's sake."

I hear him, but I don't stop. I rush through the bedroom towards the closet. The thought of leaving him fills me with physical pain, but I can't stay with him if he won't even talk to me.

He catches up with me before I get to the closet door. He pulls me into his arms, crushing me to his chest. "Stop," He whispers in my ear, "Stop."

I close my eyes, losing myself in his embrace, realizing, as I breathe in the scent of his skin, and feel the warmth of his arms around me, that I could never leave him, not when he can make me feel like this. I melt into him, so overwhelmed by the depth of my emotions, that I can feel the wetness of tears in my eyes.

He starts to stroke my hair, and I press myself to his

chest. I can hear the rhythm of his heart beating. In this moment, it feels as if he's mine, as if the deep longing I feel for him is being fulfilled. But I can't be sure, I can't be sure until he tells me how he feels.

"Why did you marry me David?" My voice is hardly higher than a whisper.

He pulls back a little, looking down at my face. "Because I wanted you," He says, stroking my arms. My skin tingles where his fingers touch me, and I feel the last of my resistance melting. "I wanted you the moment I saw you standing outside that little shop in that small town, looking so lost and alone. I wanted your innocence, your beauty," he leans over and drops a soft kiss on the sensitive corner of my lips, "I wanted your body Sophie, I wanted to see your face when I make you scream my name."

His words set a desperate fire to my blood. I lean into him, hungry for him. When it comes to this, I can't fight him. I make one last attempt. 'You didn't have to marry me," I whisper, "You already had me."

"And then I wanted no one else to ever have the pleasure. Understand that Sophie," He says, moments before his mouth descends on mine in a scorching kiss. "You are mine."

My body melts and I press myself against him, aching to give him everything I am. I want this. I want him to belong to me, even if only for these few moments.

Soon my clothes are on the floor, and his soon follow. He carried me over to one of the two armchairs in the room and sets me down, kneeling on the floor between my legs. I wrap my legs around his waist and press my body against him, rubbing myself against the hard swell of his erection. I want him so much I'm aching. Impatiently, I use my hand to guide him inside me, moaning as his tip slides into my body.

He grips my ass and lifts me off the chair, pressing me towards him as he enters me all the way. My whole body weakens and I fall against him with a low moan. He moves out and plunges into me again, and I cry out, my body shaking. He continues to move, each stroke of his rock hard shaft driving me to a pleasurable madness.

Later, when I am weak from my climax, he carries me to bed, stroking my hair as we lie side by side on the bed, my head resting on his shoulder. I can't help wishing that we would always be like this.

"You know," He says musingly. "I owe you a honeymoon."

"Yes you do," I agree, "Somewhere that will 'blow my mind'" I tease.

"Is there anywhere in particular you would like to

go?" He doesn't stop stroking my hair.

I sigh. "I would go anywhere with you." I tell him, and I mean it.

He turns over, until he is leaning over me. The kiss he gives me is gentle and undemanding. I close my eyes. I can almost feel my consciousness dissolve into him. I've lost myself, I think. This is how love feels.

"I think I know just the place." He pauses long enough to say before starting to kiss me again."

"I thought we were going out for dinner," I ask breathlessly, when we stop for air.

"Forget dinner." He says, his lips dipping to my breasts, and in a few moments, I have.

In the morning, David is in his study arranging our trip, while Mrs. Daniels and I pack a few clothes.

He has refused to tell me where we're going. Even when I asked him what I should pack. "Just a few things," He'd replied, "You're not going to be dressed most of the time."

I've succeeded in pushing all thoughts of Carole Banks to the back of my mind. I don't want to think about her, or about the NDA. I don't want anything to ruin my happiness.

"Won't you tell me where we're going?" I ask David later, as Steve drives us to the airport.

"I like to keep you guessing." He replies. He's wearing jeans and a white T-shirt, with a black leather jacket, he looks so young and cool, I have to hold myself back from slobbering all over him. We pass through cursory security checks at the airport, after which we go out to his plane, which is waiting for us on the runway. I feel like a star as I stroll to the plane, hands linked with David's, my halter neck dress flowing in the breeze, my eyes covered by wide sunshades.

A pilot and steward greet us as we enter the plane. The interior is luxurious. The main cabin is superbly furnished with comfortable looking couches, and well placed coffee tables. There is also a private bedroom, with a bathroom and closet space.

We take off after an immigration official comes to check our passports. I give him my new passport, still unable to believe how quickly it was prepared. An agent arrived in the apartment in the morning with some forms, and watched me fill and sign them. A few hours later, the passport arrived by courier.

The plane sails smoothly through the air. If not for the puffy white clouds I can see through the windows, I can actually forget that we're flying. I stretch happily, taking sips from the glass of white wine the steward serves me.

"It must be exciting travelling like this all the time."
I tell David.

He looks up from the newspaper he's reading and
shrugs. "Yeah, probably."

I roll my eyes at his nonchalance, and he gives me a
teasing smile.

I spent the next few minutes bugging him about
where we are going. When I finally fall asleep, he still
hasn't given me any clues.

When I wake up a couple of hours later, I'm lying in
David's arms on the bed in the private cabin. He must
have undressed me, because I'm only wearing one of
his t-shirts and my panties. Beside me, he is asleep.

The cabin is dark, but I can see his face in the faint
light of dawn stealing in through the windows. I trace a
finger along his chin, marveling at how handsome he
looks while sleeping, boyish, careless, and relaxed, with
his thick hair tousled and all over the place.

His wakes up and stares at me groggily for a
moment before the film of sleep clears from his eyes.

"I hope I haven't grown horns." He says.

If only he knew. "You're still not going to tell me
where we are going?'

He shakes his head and pulls me toward him until
I'm lying on top of him.

"You'll see when we get there."

I roll my eyes. "I'm getting impatient."

In response, he pulls my face down and kisses me.
"I can distract you." He offers, grabbing my butt and

rolling until he's on top of me. I start to laugh, but he silences me with his lips, kissing me until laughing is the farthest thing from my mind. He makes slow love to me, taking his time as he initiates me to the pleasures of the mile-high club.

A few hours later, the plane lands in Italy. We shower in the small but well equipped private bathroom, and get ready to disembark. As we go through customs, I discover that David speaks flawless Italian. He'll probably never stop surprising me. I decide.

"How many languages do you speak?" I ask him, curious.

He grimaces slightly. "A few," He tells me. "French, Italian, enough of Russian and Spanish to have a sensible conversation."

I'm staring at him, mouth open, "and that's a few?"

He winks. "I know, I'm incredible."

I giggle at his words, allowing him to lead me out of the airport.

We've landed in Florence. It's very early in the morning, so the city is still asleep as the black SUV that picks us at the airport drives through it. We travel through the countryside with me dozing on David's shoulder. It's just getting light when we arrive at our destination.

The car drives through a pair of wrought iron gates, and down a paved driveway, which ends in a circular cul-de-sac, with a stone fountain in the middle. The house beyond the driveway is a stunningly beautiful villa. In the early light, I can see the tiled terracotta colored walls, elegant white-painted stone arches, and the lawns that surround it, bounded by groves of trees.

I step out of the car, marveling. I turn to David. "Do you own this place?" I ask.

"We own this place." He replies, making my heart expand. He takes my hand, and we walk inside the house hand in hand.

Inside, it is charmingly furnished and spacious, with French windows leading to outside terraces from almost every room on the ground floor. Upstairs, our bedroom has a marble bathroom and an attached study. I gaze out of the windows at the countryside as the orange light of morning comes over the hills. It's too beautiful for words.

"You are too rich." I accuse him.

"I think that's an oxymoron." I turn to him and see that he is teasing. I laugh softly, and he joins in my merriment. Suddenly I feel so incredibly happy.

I go into the circle of his arms. "I hope you're not tired."

"I'm not." His eyes twinkle, as he leans back to look into my face. "Why?"

"Because I have a burning desire to make love to my husband, in our beautiful villa in Italy."

"I'm never too tired to fulfill your desires." He says capturing my lips in a lush kiss. We sink unto the bed, oblivious to anything else but the pleasure we know we can give each other.

Chapter Six

THE NEXT TWO WEEKS ARE THE height of bliss. The villa is fully staffed and stocked for our arrival. There is a cook, a maid, and a gardener, all Italian. They don't speak a word of English between them, so David does most of the talking. The first evening, we have dinner in the small town closest to us, and attend a Puccini opera about a Japanese girl in the turn of the century Japan, who kills herself out of love for an American soldier. I leave the opera crying even though I didn't understand any of the Italian words.

W We also visit the marble caves where

Michelangelo is supposed to have gotten the stone for his famous sculptures. Some days, we drive to Florence in the Audi Convertible David has in the garage, where we visit galleries, museums, and landmarks, enjoying the experience of being anonymous tourists, as we walk around hand in hand, dressed casually in jeans, t-shirts, and sunglasses.

A few afternoons, David has to take long phone calls from the office. I try not to mind, because I know how busy he is. Luckily, I brought my sketchpad along, so while he works, I draw.

"So I'm going to be one of those men married to famous artists," David teases me one day, looking over my shoulder at my work.

"Maybe I'll be so successful, you'll have to quit your job and let me support you."

He laughs as he looks through my finished drawings. "A life of ease," He says musingly. "I ought to take you up on that."

Towards the end of the first week, we have a visitor, a charming Italian called Carlo Marconi, he lives near Florence, and was at Harvard with David. He arrives for lunch with his wife and two small children, and we eat on the terrace overlooking the lawns and the trees that stretch as far as the nearby town. After lunch, while the children run around playing, David and Carlo exchange stories of their college days, and a summer spent in Italy with Carlo's family. Carlo's wife Gina and I laugh cheerfully at their stories, but I can't take my eyes off my husband, I have never seen this side of him. He looks so relaxed.

"You two look happy." Gina tells me, in lightly accented English. "David especially, I have not seen him like this before." She pauses. "You are good for him."

And he is good for me, I think in silence. "I'm glad you think so." I reply.

She shrugs. "Love can change anyone." She states, smiling at me. The children are demanding to be let into the pool. I smile back at her as we go to prepare them for a swim.

Back in Seattle, David has work to catch up on, I don't mind. My life feels charmed. Even though he still hasn't said anything about love, I feel more secure and happy in our relationship. I feel loved, and that means a lot to me.

I seem to have made a lot of friends in my absence, probably due to the fact that there has finally been an announcement in the newspapers about our wedding. While David leaves immediately for work, Mrs. Daniel's cheerfully hands me my mail, mostly invitations, requesting my presence at a variety of events.

I go through them, wondering which ones to accept and which ones to put under consideration. At times like these, a girl needs her mother or her mother in law. I'm thinking of calling David's mother when my phone rings.

"Hey." It's David. Even after two weeks when I've had him all to myself, the sound of his voice can still turn my insides to liquid.

"Hey." I reply.

"Would you like to go to this charity thing tonight?" He asks, "A dinner to raise money for the alliance for education."

"Oh!" I look through my invites again. "I have an invitation for that." It says black tie, evening dress. Hmm.

"Yes, that makes sense." He pauses. "So, do I get to show you off tonight?"

My heart flutters in my chest. "Of course."

"Good," he chuckles, "see you around seven."

After we talk, I go through my new clothes, trying to choose something to wear. I finally decide on a pale blue strapless gown with a sweetheart neckline, which hugs my figure all the way to my thighs, and then flares softly to my feet. The label has the name of a very famous designer. It's probably insanely expensive, I think, as I lay it out on the bed, but it's also incredibly beautiful.

I shower and blow-dry my hair, brushing it until it is a soft, wavy mass around my shoulders. I use a thick strand to secure it into a loose ponytail at the nape of my neck, and then sweep the mass of hair over my shoulder.

My makeup is simple, mainly because I don't want to make a mistake and end up looking scary. By the time David arrives from work, I'm almost ready, all that's left is to take off my silk dressing robe and put on my underwear and dress.

I revel in the look of appreciation he gives me when he walks into the apartment. He pulls me to him, careful not to mess up my make-up. "How much damage will I do if I kiss you?" He asks, his fingers finding my nipples through the silk dressing gown.

I'm not sure I care, I'd let him damage my make up whenever he wants. "A lot." I murmur, trying to be sensible. We don't have time for this.

He unties the knot holding my dressing gown together. 'Too bad," He murmurs, "because I've been thinking of this all day."

"While you should have been working?" My laugh sounds a little breathless, maybe because his fingers have found my nipples again.

"Who cares?" his voice is husky as he lifts me, wrapping my legs around his waist. I wrap my arms around his neck, reveling in the hardness of his erection pressing against me as he carries me to our room.

He sits on the bed, narrowly avoiding wrinkling my dress. I'm straddling him, my knees on the bed. While he removes his jacket and loosens his tie, I eagerly undo his trousers. When he springs free of the restraint of his clothes, I sigh softly, and wrap my fingers around him, stroking him up and down. He groans and grabs my hips, lifting me until I'm poised over him, wet and ready, then I lower myself unto him, letting out a low moan as he fills me.

He braces his hands on the mattress while I hold on to his shoulders, and starts to thrust into me with an intensity that is both surprising and extremely arousing. It feels so good. I tighten my arms around him, pressing my heaving breasts to his face. He sucks on my nipples, his pace never slowing. My climax is raw and forceful. I scream his name, weak and trembling, as I lose control of my body. Vaguely, I feel him stiffen inside me, and hear his groan as he comes.

I hold on to him, sweaty and satisfied. We're both breathing deeply. Sighing, he lifts me off him and sets me on my shaking legs.

"We still have an event to attend." He says regretfully, his eyes on my exposed body.

I have to fight the urge to climb back onto his lap. "Yes, we do," I try to frown disapprovingly through my haze of pleasure, "and I'm sure you've ruined my makeup.

I go to the bathroom to clean up, and then back to the dressing table to smooth my hair and get my make up back in order. David has disappeared into the dressing room to get ready. While he changes, I retrieve my dress and underwear from the bed and put them on. I'm about to zip the dress up when I feel David's strong hands on my back. He fastens the zip and steps back to look at me.

"You look lovely." He says.

I can see the admiration in his eyes, and it warms me from inside. He looks magnificent, in a black tux, and a dark grey tie. Even though he has just brought me to an earth-shattering climax, I am overwhelmed by the strong wave of desire that passes through me.

"You look wonderful too." I murmur, it's strange how even though we're married he can make me feel like a fifteen year old in the presence of her first crush.

He smiles at the compliment. "I have something for you," he tells me, taking my hand and pulling me towards the dressing table. He gestures for me to sit and as I do, I notice a black velvet box on the table. Before I have time to wonder what's in it, he opens it to reveal a beautiful earring and necklace set.

It looks very familiar. I frown, turning to look at him. "Is this…?"

"Your design?" he interrupts, he is studying my face intently, as if he's wondering if I'll like it. "Yes."

I stare at the sparkling diamond arrangement, mouth open. "But, how did you…?"

I made a copy of one of your sketches and sent it off to a jeweler while we were in Italy." He says, fastening the necklace around my neck as I watch him in the mirror. It's more beautiful than I could have imagined it, even while I drew it. I sigh softly. "It's so beautiful."

"You're a rich man's wife.' He says without conceit, "It's normal for you to have beautiful things."

I would have preferred him to say something more romantic, but I stifle the thought. I don't want to be ungrateful. I put on the earrings, watching them twinkle in the light. They really are gorgeous.

Steve drives us to the event, characteristically silent as he maneuvers the evening traffic. He drops us off in front of the brilliantly lit entrance of an upscale hotel. There are a few pressmen standing outside and one or two flashbulbs go off. I try not to flinch from the sudden bursts of light as David leads me inside, his hand at my back.

At the door to what looks like a grand ballroom, a smiling blonde woman in a flowing, cream silk gown comes to meet us.

"David," She smiles in greeting, kissing both his cheeks, I guess her to be anywhere between her forties and sixties. She looks beautiful, with a well-preserved figure and glowing skin. She turns to me. "You must be the beautiful Sophie." Her eyes sparkle as she looks me over, "I've only recently heard about you, you know. David has been keeping you a terrible secret." She laughs, "Aren't you a pretty thing though."

I turn to David, not sure what to say. He looks faintly amused by the woman's chattering. "Sophie sweetheart," he says with a slight smile, "this exceptionally beautiful lady is the incomparable Peggy Hart."

Her name registers in my head. Her husband was Simon Hart, a recently deceased software billionaire, she is one of the richest women in the country, and a passionate philanthropist.

"I'm very honored to meet you." I say sincerely.

She dimples. "Thank you darling." She says, kissing my cheek. She turns to David and snorts playfully, "I'm not even going to respond to your flattery."

He laughs as she leads the way into the room, which is filled with men in tuxedos and women in evening dresses. A low hum of conversation fills the room, as well as the sound of glasses clinking, and silvery laughter of the women.

"Your table is over there." She says to David, pointing him in the right direction.

We're stopped at least five times before we get to our table. I watch David socialize, feeling the effects of his magnetic personality. He pays attention to people, but always remains somehow aloof. It makes them more eager to get his attention. But it's not their attention he wants, I decide, he really just prefers to stand alone.

Where does that leave me?

Our table seats about twelve. David pulls out a seat for me and takes the one beside it. I feel everybody's eyes on me as we take our seats. They must be curious about me, I realize, I wonder what they're thinking.

The table is almost completely filled, with only two empty seats. We arrived late, so dinner is already being served. As we eat, David converses quietly with the man on his other side, I recognize him as Leon Boise, a website entrepreneur. I've seen his picture while reading the news on my tablet.

As I eat, I play a game of adding names to the faces around me. I only recognize a few, politicians, businessmen, internet pioneers. I have to try not to be intimidated by it all.

After dinner, someone goes up to the podium and after a short applause starts to give a speech about the importance of literacy. As I toy with the program on the table in front of me, I see that one of the sponsors is Preston Corp. I was right, I decide, David will never cease to surprise me.

"I've never been anywhere like this before," the man at my other side whispers to me. I look up at him in surprise.

"I'm Rick Cruzman," he says, proffering his hand, I take it. On closer inspection, I see that he is a boy, really, just a little older than I am.

"Me neither." I respond with a smile.

He grins, revealing a crooked front tooth. For some reason, it makes me warm to him. There is something endearing and boyish about it.

"I keep imagining that someone will come along and ask me what I'm doing on this table." He laughs nervously.

I keep silent, I don't want to tell him that I almost feel the same way. I look over at David. Done with his conversation, he is staring straight ahead, towards the podium. He belongs here, I can see that, with these glamorous people and their sparkling jewelry.

"What do you do?" I ask my new friend.

"Well," His eyes light up, "your husband just acquired a new software I developed. My company is now part of Preston Corp." he grins, "I swear he's totally changed my life in a matter of days."

The expression of gratitude in his eyes as they move to David and back to me fills me with pride. I remember David telling me that he was in Ashford to buy a software. I realize I have this man to thank for the fact that I met David at all. The thought makes me smile at him. "Good for you." I say.

The speech ends, and we all applaud, stopping when someone else takes the podium. I'm trying to pay attention when I notice Rick's eyes skip to something beyond the table and widen discernibly. I turn in the direction he's looking to see a woman approaching our table.

The only way to describe her is extraordinarily beautiful. Her hair is a deep copper, and piled on top of her head in a mass of burnished curls. Her shoulders are slim and pale, and exposed in the scarlet dress that clings to her curves as if she was poured into it. Her only jewelry is a green stone that sits between her breasts, matching the flashing green of her eyes.

She comes straight for our table, a gloved hand lightly resting on the arm of the youngish, handsome man who is escorting her. I stiffen, watching as they take the empty seats. I recognize her from the pictures I've seen. Carole Banks, David's old girlfriend. As she settles into her seat, she looks towards me, and the venom I see in her beautiful eyes almost knocks me off my seat.

I look towards David, he doesn't seem surprised, he was expecting this, I realize, he was expecting her to be here.

"Carole!" The exclamation comes from Leon Boise. "How nice to see you again."

She acknowledges him with a small smile. I notice that she doesn't look at David at all. There's more going on here than I know.

"I had forgotten to congratulate you David," Leon continues, "I read about the attempted takeover," he turns to Carole again. "I hear David has you to thank for retaining his control on the board."

For the first time, Carole looks at David, her eyes absolutely poisonous, but there is something else in them, hurt, desire, I can't say.

"Yes," She says softly. Her voice is as beautiful as the rest of her, "I sold him the shares of his company I got when my father died." She laughs a little, without any merriment. "Which means David Preston will always control Preston Corp."

David's response is a smile. "As he should, Carole," his hand comes to rest on mine on the table, a little gesture of intimacy that's not lost on her. "Have you met my wife?" He asks.

I actually flinch at the look she gives me. Her face tightens, but only for a second, and then her perfect mask is back in place. "No," she says, "I don't believe I have had the pleasure."

The tone of her voice says it will be anything but a pleasure.

"Carole this is Sophie, my wife." He turns to me, "this is Carole Banks." He doesn't offer anything more than that.

I have no idea what's going on between her and David, but I give her a hesitant smile. I can feel her animosity towards me coming in waves, but I decide to be polite even in the face of that. "Nice to meet you." I say.

She chuckles, and it has a mocking ring to it. "The pleasure is mine." She replies, and takes a long sip from her glass of wine.

The second speech ends, and we applaud again. People start to get up from their tables to socialize some more, and to dance to the soft music from the orchestra. Carole is the first to leave our table, taking her companion with her.

I turn as David put a hand on my arm. "Would you like to dance?" he asks.

No, I would like to know what that was all about. But I don't say the words, instead, I allow him to lead me out to the ballroom, where couples of different ages are moving to the live music.

"What was that?" I ask as we start to move. I learned how to dance at school, thankfully, so I don't trip over his feet.

"What was what?" He asks, nuzzling my hair.

He is deliberately avoiding my question. "What just happened at our table, with that woman?" I insist.

He shrugs. "Carole isn't too happy with the price she got for her shares, that's all."

"You didn't pay her as much as she wanted?"

"I couldn't." he says, twirling me.

I frown, puzzled, "Then how did you get her to sell them to you?"

He shrugs again. "I have my ways."

A sneaking suspicion dawns on me. "Wait," I ask,

"what did she want?"

He pauses. "She wanted me," he says without any hint of conceit. "Either me or my destruction," he pulls me close and guides me in a spin. I stare at him open-mouthed.

"I don't understand." I say as the music ends. But he doesn't explain. He kisses me on the forehead as the man he had been talking to at our table, Leon Boise, comes to claim me for the next dance.

David hands me over with a curt smile, "handle with extreme care," he says, before turning around and walking away from us.

"I'm Leon Boise," my new partner tells me as we start to dance.

"I know." I smile.

"You do?" he laughs, his silver hair gleaming in the lights, "I didn't think I was famous."

"I may have read some news articles." I tell him.

He seems surprised, but is happy enough to tell me about his business as we dance.

Afterwards, I excuse myself and go to the ladies room. While I'm checking my makeup, the door opens, and my eyes meet Carole Bank's in the mirror. She pauses at the door, giving me a long hard look.

For a few moments, we just look at each other, her gaze shrewd and assessing, mine puzzled and expecting the worst. She doesn't disappoint.

"Oh look, it's the child bride." She says disparagingly.

I debate whether to reply, then I decide to ignore her, and turn back to the mirror.

"So how's marriage to David treating you?" She asks. "You look happy?"

I turn to look at her, unwilling to be affected by her animosity. "I am, actually." I tell her, not that it's any of her business.

Her expression changes to one of faux concern. "Doesn't it bother you that it won't last?"

I swallow. "Why shouldn't it? Because I didn't try to buy David's love with a couple of shares?"

Her eyes narrow, and then suddenly, she starts to laugh. "You have no idea, do you? You really are as innocent and trusting as you look." She makes the words sound like 'stupid and dumb'. She comes closer to me, as if she has some secret of vital importance to impart. "Sophie, David uses people. That's how he got where he is. He used me, he used my father, and now he's using you."

"You're just saying that because you're..."

"Jealous?" she interrupts, "well maybe I am. But darling the truth is, he married you for a reason, and now that he's got what he wanted, he no longer needs you."

"What are you talking about?"

"Well, he never would have had his company without my father, and he would have lost control of it if I had sold my shares to the wrong person."

"So you told him you would sell your shares to him if he married you?" I mirror her expression of scorn, "That sounds pretty desperate to me."

She ignores me. "So your husband blackmailed me and forced me to do what he wanted. He is a snake, and he always plays dirty." She pauses, "of course it wasn't enough to him to win, he had to marry a green little country rat from the backwater to teach me a lesson."

Her words touch me. Wasn't that the answer to the question I had been asking myself all this time. 'Why did David marry me?'

"You know I'm right," she gives me a measuring look. "Be careful Sophie, David is a dangerous man, he won't hesitate to toss you away as soon he's be done with you."

"I don't believe you." I say with false bravado.

"Believe what you want." She shakes her head "Who cares, just don't get too comfortable in his life, you'll be alone as soon as he gets tired of all that," she gestures in the general direction of my body.

I search my head for a retort, but she has already swung out of the room.

It's only after she has gone that I realize that my fists are clenched so tight, my nails are cutting into the skin of my palms. I don't want to believe the things she's said, but deep down, I know she's telling the truth.

Chapter Seven

WHEN I LEAVE THE LADIES ROOM, all I want to do is find David and make him deny the things Carole said to me. He's not in the ballroom, and the dining room is already empty. I go in the direction of a wide stairway that leads from the ballroom to a mezzanine floor, where there are some chairs and many French doors that lead to a long balcony.

David's not anywhere on the mezzanine floor either, I'm about to turn back down the stairs when I decide to check outside.

The balcony runs along the whole length of the hotel and is filled with different species of potted plants. There are a few people close to the doors, mostly smoking and conversing. I decide to walk a little further, mainly because, there is a cool breeze coming from the sea.

I take only a few steps before I see them.

Carole has her hands on David arm, and she's saying something to him, her expression full of passion. I freeze on the spot, unable to take my eyes off them.

I can only see David's back, but he seems to be listening to her, whatever it is that she's saying. Suddenly she pulls his face down and starts to kiss him.

I stand there waiting for him to push her away, but he doesn't. When I can't look anymore, I turn on my heel and rush back into the hotel. I hurry down the stairs, feeling an actual pain in my chest. It's heavy and aching, and it's spreading all over my body. I need to get away from here. Away from him.

At the lobby, I ask for a cab. It only takes a few minutes before one arrives. I look back only once to see if maybe David has noticed that I'm gone, but I suppose he's too busy reconciling with his old love.

I can't shake the image of them kissing from my head, in my mind it turns to something else, and I can almost see him making love to her. The thoughts fill me with a desperate sadness. I want to go back and pull her off him. I want to do many things, but I know there's only one thing I should do.

When I get to the apartment, I find my bags, the

one that came with me from Ashford. I pack my sketchpad, and my old clothes. I don't want to take anything of his. I don't want to take anything that will remind me of this life. I hear my phone ringing in my purse, but I ignore it, I'm not interested in whatever it is he has to say. I'm zipping the last bag closed when the door bursts open and David walks in.

He looks worried, but then he takes in the bags on the bed, the tears on my face, and his expression changes to steel. "What are you doing?" he asks slowly.

"What does it look like?" I retort without pausing.

"I left you for a few moments at a party, and now you're leaving me?"

"You left me for far longer than a few minutes, to make out with your old girlfriend." I throw the words at him, angry at the tears that are filling my eyes.

"So now you're running off back to Ashford," The hardness in his voice intensifies almost enough to scare me. He comes towards me. "Tell me, is it Eddie Newton who's going to be picking up the pieces of your broken heart, or will it be somebody else?"

"What do you care?" I cry.

"For God's sake Sophie!" the words are harsh.

I try to back away, but the bed is behind me, he is standing so close, I can't see anything but his chest. "Let me go." I whisper, "I don't belong here, in this big apartment, or in your luxurious life, and we both know it."

"You don't know what you're saying," For a moment, I think there is a pleading note in his voice, but it must be my imagination because his expression remains like stone.

The truth is, if I knew how he felt about me, if I thought, even for one moment, that he cared about me, that I'm not just someone he likes to sleep with, I would never think of going anywhere.

I swallow. "David, do you love me?" I ask, looking up into his face. My voice is trembling, maybe because I already know what the answer is.

He looks irritated, "What has come over you?"

"Do you love me, David?" I ask again.

His face freezes again, and I know he has shut me out. "What do you want from me?" he says, turning away.

I stare at his back. Somewhere inside, I still had hope, that maybe he would tell me that he loved me and make me stay with him. "You don't love me do you?" I accuse, shaking my head and feeling all my childish dreams and expectations crumbling around my feet. How could I have thought, even for one moment that he could love me? I am just a means to an end, and he has used me because that's what he does, he uses people. Carole was right.

He turns back towards me. "Love isn't all it's cracked up to be Sophie." His voice is almost gentle, "other people would take what they have and be grateful for it."

Maybe he meant for his words to comfort me, but I feel as if he has just crushed the last of my hopes.

"And what do I have?" I turn back to him. "Tell me the truth David. Why did you marry me?"

His silence tells me what I need to know. I turn away from him, back to my bags on the bed. I'm not looking at him, so I'm not expecting it when he takes hold of my arm.

I turn around and stare up at him, breathing deeply. He looks determined, and I wonder, filled with hope and dread, what he is going to say. He moves closer to me and puts a hand on my cheek, stroking it slowly. I wait, confused. His hand moves down to my neck, and then to my shoulders, his eyes never leaving mine. Despite myself, I stare at him hypnotized.

As his fingers run down my arm, I can't prevent the shiver that runs through my body.

He notices, "Because of that." He says. His expression doesn't change, but his fingers continue their journey, lightly skimming over my body as I stand in front of him.

When my whole body is shivering and aching for him, he leans in closer and whispers in my ear. "Because of this, Sophie. This is what we have between us."

"This is only sex." I whisper helplessly, sadness and sexual arousal fighting for supremacy. "We have nothing."

His fingers skim lightly over a nipple. As I shudder in pleasure, he smiles. "Is this nothing, Sophie?" He has the voice of the devil, tempting and persuasive. I want to throw aside everything I know to be true, and allow him to make love to me.

He leans forwards and whispers in my ear, arousing me with his warm breath on my nape. "Don't you want this Sophie? Don't you want me to touch you? To make love to you, over and over again?" his lips make a trail from my neck to my shoulder. "Isn't it enough?"

I shake my head, tears stinging my eyes. "No."

"Don't lie to yourself? Sophie, what else is there?" His hand slide down over my dress and pull down the zip, making it fall to the ground. His hands skim up over my waist and toward my breasts. He stops just shy of touching them, teasing me.

I look up at him, my eyes pleading. I don't know what I want anymore. I want him to love me, but I also want, more than anything, for him to keep touching me. My breasts are heavy and straining through my bra.

My breath is coming in short gasps.

"What do you want Sophie?"

His fingers move upwards, skimming the lower curve of my breasts. I moan softly.

He cups my breasts, squeezing them until my whole body is aching with desire.

"Isn't this enough?' he asks again, I shake my head.

He sighs and undoes my bra, freeing my breasts. I feel exposed, yet full of expectation. I want this. I want him, despite everything.

He starts to take off his clothes, I stand transfixed as he removes his jacket and tie, his shirt, then his pants. By the time he's totally naked, I'm shaking with arousal, hungry for him.

He guides my hand to his hard length. I touch him, glorying in the stiffness. He wants me as much as I want him. Stroking him, I get down on my knees, trying to pleasure him with my hands and my mouth. Muttering an oath, he pulls me up, turns me around, and bends me over the bed. He starts to stroke me through my panties, and in moments, I'm burning for him. He doesn't make any move to end my torment. His fingers continue to stroke me until my panties are soaked.

"Please." I beg him brokenly. "Please David."

"Tell me what you want." His voice torments me.

"Please."

"Tell me."

"I want you." I cry, grinding my hips against his fingers.

"You want what?"

"I want you to make love to me, David, please."

He pulls my panties down to my knees. Spreading my legs as far as my stretched panties will allow, he enters me, slowly, teasingly, pushing in inch by inch until I'm going crazy and begging him to give me more. I brace my hands on the mattress and push my hips back, urging him further in. He stiffens, then moves, bending over me and grabbing each of my breasts in each hand, and pinning me to his body until I can't move.

Then he starts to thrust into me, His hips slamming into mine while each stroke brings me to screaming, throbbing life.

The pleasure is exquisite. It feels as if I'm going to die. My body explodes over and over, but he doesn't stop. As my body goes limp, I hear him whisper in my ear.

"Isn't this enough?"

When I don't say anything, he starts to thrust again, making me come over and over again until I'm screaming "Yes, yes, yes," to anything he asks.

Later when I'm lying on the bed, unable to move, my body limp with exhaustion and pleasure, he turns to me.

"Don't mistake what we have" he says, his voice like cold water on my skin, "and don't underestimate it either."

I want to cry, to lash out at him, I feel so hurt and humiliated. "And what about Carole?" I ask, "What do you two have?"

"Is that what this is all about? Carole?" He sits up, "Did she say something to you?"

"You used her," I accuse, "just like you're using me." I choke on my words. "You wanted the shares she had in your company."

"And she threatened to sell them to the man who wanted to take over my company if I didn't marry her." he states without feeling, "A man she was sleeping with I might add, along with a few others."

I stare at him, my mouth open. "You're just saying that."

He laughs. "Maybe you should try to get your information accurate before you start throwing accusations."

"It doesn't make any difference." I say. "Even if she did all those things, it doesn't change the fact that you don't love me. I'm just the girl who was foolish enough to marry you so you could teach your ex-girlfriend a lesson." I choke back a sob. "I can't take it David." I get up, filled with resolve.

"What are you doing?" he asks, watching me.

"I am leaving."

"Don't threaten me." The hardness in his voice almost makes me pause. He rises to his feet, towering over me.

"Why not?" I spit at him. "Will you marry someone else to teach me a lesson?"

He takes hold of my arm. "Don't test me Sophie."

I ignore him.

He turns away. "Fine, do whatever you like. Go back to Ashford. I'm sure your little boyfriend will be more than eager to find you a place in his bed. But while you're at it, you might want to ask yourself why you married me."

"I love you." I almost choke on the words, saying them makes me want to burst into tears.

He laughs cruelly, "What love. Did you fall in love with some stranger you hardly knew Sophie, just because he asked you out to dinner. Get real sweetheart, this has always been about sex."

"Not for me."

"Then you're a liar as well as a fool."

I stare at him, tears filling my eyes. I don't care that I've nowhere to go. I can't stay here.

"I hate you," I tell him before I leave the bedroom, "I hope I never have to see you again. Carole was right about you, you use people, and when you're done with them you toss them away like rubbish, you're not worthy of my love."

He flinches, and for a moment, a wounded expression flits over his face, then he turns away from me. "Do whatever you want Sophie."

I spend the night in one of the guest rooms, with my bags for company. Early in the morning, I hear him come into the room. After a few moments, while I pretend to be asleep, he leaves. After he's gone, I take a quick shower and leave the apartment. A few weeks ago, I had a plan to go to Bellevue and find a job, and now, that is exactly what I'm going to do.

Claim

A Dangerous Man #3

by

Serena Grey

David

Chapter One

"MAY I DRIVE NOW?" I ASK STEVE, _as he maneuvers the car through the black, wrought iron gates, and onto the paved driveway of the old brick mansion where I've lived since I was six._

He turns a brief glance in my direction. "Not today." He says, his voice deep and quiet. With his shaved head and permanently severe expression, he could pass for a dangerous mobster, but actually, he's an ex-marine. My stepfather Henry Weber hired him to drive me around and keep me out of "trouble." Whatever that is.

Steve doesn't talk much, but usually, he lets me drive when we get to the house. I still have two years to go before I can get a license, but he says he has extreme confidence in my abilities, after all, he taught me himself.

We get to the end of the driveway, and I see why he didn't let *me drive. The shiny black Bentley that's usually covered up in the garage is parked close to the front door.*

That can only mean one thing.

They're back.

I frown.

Steve stops the car. "See you later kid." He sounds almost sympathetic.

"Yeah." I reply sullenly, climbing out and shouldering my backpack. The thought of running into them makes me reluctant to go into the house. I drag my feet to the door and cautiously push it open.

Inside, all is quiet. Relieved, I let myself breathe. Maybe they're tired from their flight, or sailing trip, or whatever, and have gone to bed already. I move quietly. With any luck, I can hide out in my room until they go out to one of the numerous parties they probably have lined up.

No such luck. When I get upstairs and open the door to my room, I find my mother waiting for me.

She's sitting at my reading desk, her back towards me. Her black hair, which is the same color as mine, is pinned up in a classy looking style, the way Henry prefers it. She never wears her hair down anymore, like she did when I was a kid. She's looking at the picture of my Dad and me that occupies center place on my desk. In the picture, I'm a chubby, toothless baby, and my Dad is carrying me around his shoulders.

She turns around at the sound of the door, and her eyes light up when she sees me. "David!" She exclaims with a wide smile, as if she's spent all the time when she was away waiting to see me again. She gets up and comes to hug me, wrapping me in a cloud of soft perfume. "You've grown so tall!" She continues, still smiling and looking at me expectantly, as if she's waiting for a response.

I mumble something in reply, squashing the instinct to hug her back the way I used to before, in the days when I lived for the moments when she would float back into my life after a long absence, with stories of places they had gone, and parties she'd been to. She'd come with her beauty and her exotic adventures, and my life in her absence would fade to dullness.

Now I just wish she would leave me alone.

She starts to talk about how she missed me, she sounds very sincere, but she can't have missed me very much if she didn't have a problem staying away for nearly six months, I decide resentfully, tuning her out.

I drop my backpack on the floor and go to sit at the edge of my bed. While she talks, I study the picture of my father and me. We're both grinning happily at the camera, or at my mother behind the camera. Of course, that was back when she was still my mom, not Henry Weber's socialite wife.

She's still talking to me, but I can't really hear her. I smile wistfully at my toothless baby grin behind my father's handsome one. He died when I was six, after a drunk driver ran a red light and crushed his car. Almost immediately, my mother married

Henry, an idle millionaire whose only desire is to travel and socialize. She's been travelling and socializing with him for nine years.

"You're starting to look so much like your father." My mother's soft words cut into my thoughts, and I turn towards her. Her eyes are shiny, like she's about to cry.

I don't say anything, even though the comment makes me happy and proud. I ignore her sigh of exasperation at my silence. What's the point of telling her anything? Soon she'll have left for another one of their trips, and my life will go back to normal.

She leaves me alone soon after. They're going out to a dinner party, and she has to prepare. I go downstairs to find Steve, sure that I won't run into Henry while he's locked up in his massive closet trying to decide which one of his hundreds of tuxedos to wear. Steve lives in an apartment over the garage, and sometimes if I plead enough, he relents and teaches me some of his martial arts moves.

It's while I'm walking across the lawn towards the garage that I hear the voices. I turn back towards the house, and through their bedroom window, see my mother and Henry arguing. I'm not surprised. They argue a lot. Henry's a jerk. I can't stand him, he can't stand me, and I have no idea how my mother can stand him.

I'm about to turn away, when I see him raise a hand and strike my mother across the face. I stand there frozen as she holds a hand to her cheek. He turns towards the window, and seeing *me, walks towards it and abruptly pulls the curtains closed.*

Someone is trying to take control of my company.

That's the thought on my mind as Steve drives through the tree-lined streets of Ashford, the small town where I came to do a friend a favor.

The favor is Rick Cruzman, a community college dropout who has developed an innovative software application for managing virtual money, and has been trying to market it for months. He got a few minutes to sell it at a mediocre software conference at Ashcroft Hills, a business resort about thirty minutes from Seattle, and because my friend, who's happily retired from business, asked me to look into him, I took the half hour drive from my office.

I was also curious, restless, and in need of space to think.

It didn't take me long to decide that Rick Cruzman's software had some potential. After his presentation, I approached him and made an offer. He jumped on it, like I knew he would.

I turn to look out of the car windows, my mind going back to my original thoughts. Someone has been stealthily acquiring Preston Corp stock directly from shareholders in the open market, operating behind a group of small companies, which I am sure, are all linked to one person. I shouldn't be worried, I'm the largest shareholder in my company, and I have voting agreements with the majority of the initial investors, giving me total voting control.

Marshall Banks was one of those original investors, and now, Carole owns his substantial shares. As the second largest shareholder, if she sells, I'll lose the shares that make up a large amount of my voting power. I could lose control.

And she knows it.

The memory of our last phone conversation brings a frown to my face. Carole's breathy voice sounded smug and self-satisfied as she invited me to lunch. I accepted because if I were a corporate raider intent of wresting control of Preston Corp, I would approach her, as I'm sure someone already has, hence the smugness. I know Carole well enough to know that she wants something in return for not selling.

I feel a flash of irritation. Carole at her best is selfish and greedy. At her worst, she's calculating and vindictive. I'd rather not have to deal with her at all, and I plan to make it so that in the future, I don't have to.

Steve slows down to take a turn. From the back seat, I can see his smooth shaved head, still the same as when he used to drive me as a teenager. He's a little bulkier now, but still as taciturn as the day we first met. I've stopped trying to imagine what goes on in his head beneath his silence. I know now that there was a time when he was different. He told me himself, in a rare unguarded moment, about his wife and little daughter dying while he was on active duty, when a shooter opened fire in a crowded mall. He's never forgiven himself for not being there to protect them.

Guilt can do worse things to a man than make him reserved, so I don't begrudge Steve his silence.

I'm about to go back to reading the documents I have on my lap when my eyes go to the window again, and I see the girl.

Her hair is pale gold, wavy, and held back in a loose ponytail, with a few escaped tendrils framing her face in delicate wisps. Her figure is slight, yet curvy, and her eyes, as she gazes at the car passing by, are a deep, innocent green. She looks lost. Beautiful and lost.

Something happens to me as I look at her. I forget about takeovers, shares, and software. In the space between dreaming and longing, all I can do is stare. I watch her turn around and walk through a doorway into what looks like a shop. I don't stop looking even as Steve picks up speed and I have to crane my neck.

"Stop." I say the words without thinking.

Immediately the car stops. If Steve is surprised, he

doesn't show it.

"Back." I say, still looking towards the girl. I can still see her through the clear glass front of the shop she entered. I wait impatiently as Steve puts the car on reverse and backs up until I tell him to stop. He parks by the spot where a few seconds before, the girl had been standing.

I only pause for a moment before I follow my instincts and step out of the car.

Through the glass, my eyes meet hers again. She's looking at me, standing as still as a statue. Briefly, I wonder what I'm doing, going to her.

I consider getting back in the car.

But I don't. Instead, I push open the door and walk into the shop, straight towards where she stands staring at me.

Her eyes are bright, her cheeks red, and her soft pink lips gently parted.

I have an insane urge to take her in my arms and kiss those lips until I've tasted every inch of them. It makes no sense.

"Good afternoon." I say quickly, trying to keep a hold of myself. I don't want to do something crazy and scare her.

She is gazing at me, a confused frown on her face, almost as if she has no idea what to say in response. "Good afternoon." When she finally responds, her voice is soft and light, like a gentle breeze on a moonlit night.

The fact that I'm having poetic impulses makes me want to laugh at myself. Any minute now and I'll be writing her sonnets.

"Would you like to buy something?" She asks in that soft voice. There is a very distinct flush staining her cheeks. Is she blushing? I stare at her, fascinated.

I realize that she's waiting for a response. "Of course." I look around, taking in the collection of pretty things in ceramic and glass. "I'd like ah… a gift for my mother." I turn back to her and watch, captivated, as her eyes widen slightly, their green depths darkening.

She has beautiful eyes.

I'm still staring when she suddenly starts to move towards me. My heart nearly stops when she passes right in front of me, our bodies almost brushing against each other as she moves farther into the shop. I take a deep breath, filling my nose with her scent. She smells like shampoo and strawberries, sweet and nice, and yet somehow, extremely sensual.

I follow her through the shop, only half listening as she talks about the items they have for sale. I'm too busy watching her slender waist and the smooth curve of her hips. She stops suddenly and turns around, and I have to look back up at her face.

I don't know what she sees in my expression, but she steps back abruptly, away from me. She looks tense all of a sudden, and I almost feel guilty for checking her out. "We have um… These glass sculptures are all made locally." Her words come out in a rush, and I can tell that she's nervous. Well I'm nervous too, nervous, fascinated, enthralled and so many other things I haven't felt in a long time. It's somewhat gratifying that she's as affected by my presence as I am by hers.

She keeps talking, but I can't tear my eyes away from the lush pinkness of her lips. The hunger to kiss those lips spreads from my brain to my fingers, and straight to my groin.

"What's your name?" I interrupt. I'm more interested in her than in anything stocked in the shop.

At first, she looks bewildered, like she has no idea what I just said. "Sophie." She says, after a short pause. "Sophie Bennett."

"Sophie." I repeat. The name suits her. She looks quite young, I think, studying her face. I find myself desperately hoping that she's not in high school or something else that'll make me feel like a pervert. "And how long have you worked here, Sophie?" I'm trying to play it cool, even though my fingers are itching to touch her, to feel the smoothness of her skin.

"I… um…" She blinks rapidly, "a few months."

"Interesting." I assume she works part time while attending a local college. At least I hope so. That would make me feel less degenerate. "College?" I ask, studying her face.

She shakes her head.

I frown. "How old are you?"

She pauses, licking her lips in a quick movement. I

stare at her moistened lips, unable to look away, or to ignore the sudden and insistent thickening in my pants.

"Eighteen." She says, her voice so low I almost miss it.

Eighteen! I'm lusting after a baby.

I take a small step back, disappointment and common sense piercing through my overwhelming desire for her. "You're very young." I say unnecessarily.

She doesn't reply. I watch as her gaze drops from my face. I'm wondering what she's thinking when she looks back up again, swallowing me with deep green eyes. Lost in the green depths, I can't think clearly, my mind fills of images of all the things I want to do to her, with her.

I am a pervert.

I look away, desperate for a distraction. My eyes catch on a small glass sculpture. "I'd like the glass swan." I tell her.

She looks like I just spoke in Greek. "The what?"

The nonplussed expression on her face brings a chuckle to my lips. I incline my head towards the sculpture, noting her embarrassment as she picks it up. I follow as she takes it to the desk at the front of the shop, trying this time not to ogle her perfect behind.

"Do you want it wrapped?" She asks.

"Yes, and delivered." I give her my address in Seattle, and wait as she jots it down on a notepad, then I hand her my card, and as she takes it, her fingers brush against mine. They're cool and soft, and I suddenly have an urge to take her hand and kiss it. The contact is only for a few moments, but those moments seem to last for a long time.

She's staring up at me like a deer caught in headlamps. She feels it too, whatever this is.

Abruptly, she pulls her hand from mine and swipes my card, not looking at me.

"I want to see you." The words escape my lips without any input from my brain. She stills, and those green eyes find mine again. "What are you doing tonight?"

"Nothing." She says after a pause.

"Then have dinner with me."

She looks as if she's thinking about it, confusion, and a whole lot of other emotions running through her features. "Please." I persist, giving her a smile for good measure. Somehow, I want this very badly.

I watch her expressive face, waiting for her to decide. "Okay." She says finally.

I feel as if I've won a major triumph. I realize that I've been leaning over her, eagerly waiting for her reply. I straighten. "When do you finish here?" I ask.

Her face creases again in a tiny frown. "At five." She tells me, still looking hesitant.

"I'll be here." I give her a reassuring smile, backing slowly towards the door. Outside, Steve is waiting patiently in the car. He doesn't ask me why I'm grinning so widely as I climb into the back seat.

Chapter Two

"LET'S FIND A HOTEL." I SAY to Steve as the car starts to move. Since I've committed myself to remaining in Ashford until evening, I might as well find a place to have lunch, and get some work done. It's not such a big deal. I can work from anywhere, most of the time.

Steve catches my eye in the rearview mirror, then turns to the GPS and begins to search for a hotel.

I have work to do. If I'm going to be fighting a takeover attempt, then I need to be ready. I'm actually excited. This is a challenge, and they don't come often to me. These days, too many things come too easily.

My mind goes back to Sophie Bennett, and my excitement takes a different dimension. I'm incredibly keen to find out what lies beneath that quiet facade, and to explore the silent promises in her eyes. I take a deep breath.

I can't wait to see her tonight.

I don't want to ask myself what the point is. She's little more than a child. If I left Ashford at this very moment, there would be more than enough women, willing, eager even, to help me forget her.

Except I don't want to forget.

There can't be many choices for hotels in Ashford. In a few minutes, Steve is already parked in front of a six-storey building with a sign that says 'The Ashford Fairview'.

It will do, I decide, picking up my phone from the seat beside me. I'm about to step out of the car when I see the reminder flash on the screen.

Lunch with Carole Banks.

I frown. I had forgotten all about Carole. How could I not, when my mind has been, and still is, on Sophie. I can always call Carole and postpone. Right now, what I have is a driving desire to see Sophie again.

I almost step out of the car before the folly of the decision I've just made makes a full impact in my brain.

I'm postponing a meeting that could save my company just so I can see a girl.

An eighteen-year-old girl.

It's insane.

I frown. "Let's go back to Seattle, Steve," I say, a little annoyed with myself. "I have things to do."

Under Steve's guidance, the Jaguar eats up the distance, staying just below the speed limit, and we get to the city in less than half an hour.

He drops me off on the sidewalk, in front of the glass revolving doors of the multi-storey edifice that is Preston Corp. These days, I no longer spend a few seconds just standing outside, relishing the knowledge that it's mine. It just is, and I'm not going to let anyone take it away.

I clear the marble and glass reception area, acknowledging the greetings without pausing. I take the elevator to the penthouse floor, going through the security doors and giving a cursory nod to the receptionist as I walk past her.

My office is at the end of the floor. To get there, I pass by the office where my assistants Linda and Cole are busy at their computers. They both look up when I walk in.

"Good morning Mr. Preston."

"Good morning Linda, Cole." I don't pause in my stride, going directly into my office. Once inside, I ignore the desk and go to stand at the floor to ceiling windows through which I can see the city spread out below me. The office is large, slightly less than a quarter of the entire penthouse floor space, with a bar, seating areas and a very large teleconferencing screen opposite my desk, but it is here, at the windows, that I get most of my work done.

I frown and push images of soft green eyes and wavy gold hair out of my mind. If my suspicions are correct, and Carole has gotten an offer for her shares, my lunch with her will tell me whom I'm going to have to deal with.

I spend a few more minutes at the windows, drawing up, and discarding plans in my head. I'm still there when Linda comes in with a list of all the things I have to attend to.

An hour later, I walk into the hotel restaurant where I'm meeting Carole for lunch. A smiling, middle-aged man in an immaculate suit introduces himself as the host and leads me to a table. As I take my seat, I see Carole walk in through the entrance.

She looks beautiful, as usual, red curls framing her oval face like a high maintenance halo. Today, her lips are deep scarlet against her pale skin, and set in a smug smile.

She pauses at the door, and then, when she's sure that all the eyes in the restaurant are on her, she saunters inside. I watch as she whispers something to the host, leaning towards him - not too close to be indecent, but close enough that he probably loses some of the blood flow to his brain. I watch as he nods, his eyes drinking her in, before he leads to my table.

I get up as he pulls out her chair, after which Carole dismisses him with a light pat on his arm and takes her seat.

"David!" She smiles. Her voice is a whispery, teasing, girlish sound, diligently cultivated and maintained.

"Carole." I settle back into my seat.

"It's been so long since we saw each other, David." She says, giving me her debutante smile. She leans forward, her voice turning intimate. "If I didn't know better, I'd think you were avoiding me."

"Why in the world would I do that?" My sarcasm isn't lost on her. She watches me archly as I pick up a menu and glance through it. After a brief pause, she does the same. When she seems ready to make her order, I signal for the waiter.

"I'm exhausted." She exclaims, after we've ordered.

"I feel like I've been in a plane for years." Her eyes are on my face, looking expectant as she waits for a response. When I don't show any interest, she continues anyway. "I just returned to town." She says. "I've been staying at this lovely villa in the south of France."

The last thing I want is for her to treat me to a story of her aimless globetrotting, or of another poor sucker who has fallen for her charms. I don't say anything. She either takes my silence for interest, or just decides to tell me anyway.

"The Villa belongs to Toby Felt," She pauses, searching my face, "Have you heard of him? The investor? He's a really charming man." She smiles, "and he knows exactly how to treat a lady."

My interest perks up, and not because of her obvious attempt to make me jealous. I couldn't care less who Carole's flavor of the month is, but Toby Felt isn't just an investor, he's a corporate raider, the kind of man who would acquire control of a company and sell off all the assets for his personal gain. If he's behind the attempt on Preston Corp, it would totally explain why he's sweetening Carole up with extended stays at his luxury villa.

"Some women find all men charming as long as they have money to spend." I reply, keeping my face impassive.

"You think I'm one of such women?" She looks affronted. "For your information David, I don't think you're charming, no matter how much you have to spend."

"I am truly heartbroken." I state drily.

Just then, our food arrives, and as we eat, I listen to Carole's small talk with half an ear. I'm determined for her to come out and tell me what she wants without any prompting from me. The moment she senses my apprehension about the takeover, her demands will skyrocket.

"What did you want to discuss, Carole?" I ask lightly, interrupting her chatter. "Why did you ask me to lunch?"

She stops and considers me for a moment. "Why did you accept?" She counters, "Usually you'd just tell me that you're busy."

I shrug. "I usually am."

Her lips form a pout. "Maybe I just wanted to talk about us, David"

I chuckle. "Don't be ridiculous Carole, there is no us."

Her shoulders stiffen, and I can tell that she's not happy with my reply. Then she relaxes and leans back in her chair. "But there used to be," She manages a wistful expression, "and there could be again."

"I wouldn't be too sure about that," I'm amused despite myself. "You can't have run out of men to play games with, Carole. I'm sure if you look around you'd find a couple of eager playthings."

She shrugs, looking up at me from under long lashes in an expression I assume I'm supposed to find sexy, "Maybe I want the one I can't have." She says.

"And that would be?"

"You."

I snort. "Tell me, when was the last time you heard from that fitness guy you used to screw."

"Enrique?" She laughs. "Not recently. He didn't serve his purpose you know. Look at you, not even a little bit jealous that I cheated on you with him."

"Perhaps you didn't serve his purpose either." I tell her. "The last time I saw him he didn't seem very happy with you."

Her eyes narrow. "What do you mean?"

I shrug. I don't intend to tell her of the desperate fitness instructor's attempt to blackmail me with a very explicit video of him and Carole. He hadn't seen her in months, and she wasn't taking his calls. So he came to me, making the mistaken assumption that I and Carole were still together.

She watches me in silence. When I don't offer any

elaboration, she sighs. "I have an offer I thought you might be interested in."

Finally. I let her stew for a bit before I respond. "Which is?"

"I don't know… you're so mean and distant. I'm beginning to think you don't deserve my help." She frowns. "Maybe I'd prefer for you to lose your company." She continues musingly, "I do hate you for leaving me, you know. Plus I've made a lot of silly investments with the money Daddy left me, and I need to sell my shares in Preston Corp to the highest bidder."

"Or maybe you just want something from me Carole." I say wryly, "Tell me what it is."

"David…" She breathes, her voice lowering to an intimate whisper, "You already know what I want."

I raise a brow. "No. I must confess that I don't."

"Don't act obtuse David. Think about it," Her voice is eager. "We were so good together, socially we're a perfect couple. I have a perfect education, a perfect family, friends, and connections. I can navigate any society we ever find ourselves. I would be an asset to you David, and you know it."

While you screw the fitness instructor, and anybody else you choose to play your games with, because every male within panting distance has to be crazy about you and no one else, I think silently. Thanks but no thanks.

"What I'm saying David, is that we should get married." She smiles, as if she hasn't just made the most ridiculous proposal ever. "You know it's what Daddy always wanted. I'd give you my shares then. Think about it, nobody could ever take Preston Corp from you."

I stare coldly at her, "I'd rather just buy your shares Carole. Everything else you're offering means nothing to me."

Her eyes narrow. "Thinks about what I've said, Toby Felt is offering me a lot, and he doesn't have the disadvantage of having dumped me before."

Toby Felt.

She's watching my face for my reaction. When I don't give her any, she shrugs again. "He has a huge vision of adding Preston Corp to his conglomerate. It's like India to his Alexander."

I don't remind her that Alexander died trying to take India. "You're not going to sell him your shares, Carole."

"Why not?"

"Because you're going to sell them to me."

"Well David," She gives me a sidelong glance, "You know exactly how to make me do that." She gets up. "I have to leave now." She says sweetly. "Thanks for lunch."

I watch her leave, my mind on overdrive, I will find a thousand ways to get what I want, but there's no way in hell I'll succumb to anyone's blackmail.

I have to find a way to deal with Carole. I should have known she wouldn't make it easy, but who could have anticipated such an unreasonable demand, even from Carole?

And Toby Felt, I need to find out everything possible about him, the companies he's acquired in the past and his strategies for his acquisitions. Then I'll prepare a new strategy for retaining control of my company.

I could make it easy, I think, as I dismiss the meeting I've called in my office. I could make it easy on myself, save company time and resources, and get the results I want in one easy step.

In the hidden drawer under my desk, there's a flash drive, and it contains one video file.

While Carole's fitness instructor and sometime lover Enrique was in my office trying to convince me to pay him an inordinately large amount of money so he wouldn't release his video of Carole on the internet. I made a few calls. In minutes, there was a team at his apartment retrieving every trace of the file from his computer and tracing every device to which he had ever copied it. Luckily, they'd found everything and brought them to me.

Then I told Enrique that if he brought me every copy he had, I would consider paying him. When he called me an hour later, swearing and cursing, I knew for sure that we had found every copy. I had them all destroyed, except for the copy in the flash drive, the one he'd given me himself. I kept it as proof.

Then I let him know that if he ever tried to blackmail me again, he would die in jail.

That's how much I detest blackmail.

Which is unfortunate, considering that at this moment, blackmail can get me what I want, very easily.

I toss the drive back into the drawer and leave the desk. I walk along the length of the glass walls, staring outside, while my mind works furiously.

There's no way I'm going to lose my company to Toby Felt's need to massage his ego. No damn way.

Carole's terms, of course, are out of the question. I need to get control of the situation on my own terms.

I glance at my watch. It's almost four o clock. I've already asked Linda to find the phone number for the gift shop in Ashford. Efficient as always, she has it printed on a sheet of paper on my desk.

With everything I have on my mind, the sensible thing would be to call Sophie, and tell her how sorry I am that I can't take her to dinner.

And I would do that, if I didn't have this strange compulsion to see her blush again.

Chapter Three

STEVE DRIVES ME OVER TO MY apartment, where I take a shower and change my clothes. I drive myself to Ashford, taking the BMW convertible. I'm not keen to have Steve trailing along on a date.

The image of Sophie's face stays in my mind as I drive. The logical part of my brain keeps asking why the urge to see her again is so incredibly strong. I frown, tapping my fingers on the wheel. I have too much to worry about to be driving out of the city just to have dinner with a girl, and yet, in half an hour, at almost exactly five o clock, I'm pulling into the front of the gift shop.

I step out of the car, looking into the shop through the glass. The lights are on, but it looks empty. At first, I get a sick feeling that she has gone, but then I see her enter the shop through a door at the back, and overwhelming relief floods through me.

What is happening to me?

I like my relationships uncomplicated. I don't do romance, I don't do commitment, and women have learned not to expect those things from me.

What I do is sex. No. Strings. Attached.

A concept which, I'm sure, is alien to the eighteen-year-old girl inside the shop looking at me. This is bound to end in complications. This is something I don't need.

Yet I can't stay away.

I watch her as she runs a hand over her hair, smoothing her ponytail. I wish she would let it hang free. I can imagine the soft waves framing her face and falling to her shoulders. I can imagine a lot of things, and none of them are halfway decent.

She comes towards the front of the shop, locking it up behind her as she steps onto the sidewalk.

"Hi." She says, her soft voice washes over me, reminding me why I've abandoned everything I have to do, to come here, to her.

"Hello Sophie." She's blushing. I don't know why, but I find her flaming cheeks enthralling. "Ready?" I ask.

She nods.

I turn towards the car, placing one hand on her

back to guide her. My fingers are itching to touch her, and just that slight contact causes a distinct heaviness in my groin.

I want her so badly I need a cold shower just thinking about it, and right now, the cold shower seems like the best idea. The alternative is just asking for trouble, and trouble is exactly what I don't need.

"So where do you want to go?" I ask, as I slide into the driver's seat.

She frowns. "Where would you like to go?" She replies.

I pause. I have no idea where anything is in this town. I suppose I should have thought of where to take her, since I made the invitation. I chuckle inwardly as I consider driving to the city, but I doubt she would want that.

She ought to be able to recommend a place though. "You know the town," I ask. "Don't you?"

She shakes her head, silent. I don't know many eighteen year olds, but I doubt there are many left who aren't savvy about everything around them. But then, she's unlike any eighteen year old I have ever seen. She's unlike anyone I've ever met.

"You didn't grow up here?" I ask.

"I've been away at boarding school," She turns her face away, towards the window, "and anyway, I've never been very outgoing."

She has a small frown on her face. I find myself hoping that I haven't made her feel somehow inadequate. I'm about to tell her not to worry, that I'm sure I'll find something, when she turns back to me and tells me about some seafood place.

I start the car and enter the name of the restaurant into the GPS.

"Can we stop by my place?" Her voice is tentative.

I turn to look at her. "Of course." I say, noting that she looks worried. It's only dinner. I don't care if we get burgers and eat in the car. I just want to satisfy this crazy desire to be around her, to indulge the weird excitement that being with her gives me.

I drive, following her directions to a brick walk-up not too far from the shop. "I won't be long," She tells me, climbing out of the car in a rush. I run through scenarios in my mind. Perhaps she has a pet to feed, or maybe she's decided that I'm a serial killer and is now running screaming for the safety of her home.

After a few minutes, she reappears, and I go around to open the door for her, admiring her figure as she walks towards me in a pretty blue dress. She must have been worried about not being properly dressed. As much as I like the dress, I wish she hadn't bothered, I wouldn't have minded if she had been wearing a grass skirt.

"Nice dress." I say, joining her inside the car.

"Thank you." Her perfect lips curve into a small smile.

I start the engine. "You didn't have to change on my account though," I add, "You already looked great."

There is a long pause. "I wanted to." She says finally.

I shrug and start to drive, wondering at her sweetness compared to the brittle sharpness of many of the women I know. But then, if the saying about birds of a feather is true, then perhaps I'm brittle and sharp as well.

Outside, the sun is setting, casting a gold glow into the car, which lights Sophie's face and hair. She looks like a girl in a renaissance painting, beautiful and sensual, yet innocent.

"Were you at a conference at Ashcroft Hills?" Her voice cuts into my thoughts.

"Yes." I reply, remembering self-important, midlevel software company executives and boring conversation.

"I hope it went well."

I shrug. I suppose it did, in a way. "I went to make a decision about a new software application that could be the next big thing, or a complete waste of time."

"What did you decide?"

I turn to look at her, wondering that she is interested. She is looking up at me, her eyes soft and wide. "I bought it." I tell her.

She watches me in silence. I have no idea what she's thinking. I have a feeling that she can see inside me. I don't want her to. Somehow, I fear I won't stand up to the scrutiny.

"Tell me about yourself." I say. "I already know you're not outgoing," I smile to let her know that I'm teasing, "So tell me more."

She turns to look at her hands on her lap, a small frown on her face. "You won't be interested."

I am interested. I want to know her, and not just in the biblical sense. I want to know the feelings behind her expression, the thoughts behind her blushes. I'm confused by my own desires.

"On the contrary, I am very intrigued." I give her an encouraging grin, "I would very much like to know what you do with your time."

"I read," she says, and I'm not surprised. She seems like someone who reads a lot. "Sometimes I draw." She adds.

An artist. "What do you draw?"

"Stuff." She seems embarrassed again.

I chuckle softly. "And what do you read? Can I ask, or is it also 'stuff'?"

"No... I read everything." Her eyes light up as she continues, "History, classics, popular fiction." She stops and shrugs, and I get the impression that she could talk about books for a long time.

I smile. "I thought young people never read anymore."

She gives me a look. It's thoughtful and curious at the same time. I wait for her to say something, but she doesn't.

"What are you thinking, Sophie?"

She looks away, as if she just realized that she was staring. "I was just wondering how old you are." She admits.

I laugh. I would never confess it to anyone, but at that moment, I feel self-conscious about my age. I'm a full-grown man, pursuing someone who is only a little more than a child.

"Oh, I'm legal," I say, laughing at myself. "I'm twenty seven."

She is silent, but she doesn't run out of the car screaming for help, which is a good thing for me. For her own good, maybe she should, maybe she should run away from me.

At the restaurant, we get a table that looks into a

park, it's a little secluded, which is fine by me. I order wine for us and look through the menu. After we've made our orders, I turn back to her.

"So you're not outgoing, you read, and you draw." At this point, that's all I know about her, "that can't be all."

"My mother died giving birth to me," The words are sudden and unexpected. I frown, looking at her face for a clue as to how she feels telling me that.

"That must have been hard for you." I reply. I know a little of how it feels to lose a parent, or both.

"I suppose it was." She looks lost for a moment while I wait for her to go on. "I grew up with my Aunt Josephine," She continues, "but she died a few months ago." Her lips form a sad smile. "Aunt Josephine told me that my father was some professor my mother had a 'sordid' affair with during the only semester she spent at college." She looks up at my face, a small frown on hers. "Unfortunately that's the only thing I know about him."

As she speaks, she seems to get more and more vulnerable, at least in my eyes. I barely know her and yet I want to protect her. I watch her large eyes cloud, and I feel a wave of annoyance towards the aunt. "Your aunt doesn't sound very nice." I observe.

Her face tells me all I need to know. "Aunt

Josephine was … different." She says.

I nod. "So you went to boarding school?"

"Yes, when I was twelve." She smiles softly and shakes her head. "I didn't make a lot of friends, but we had a wonderful library."

"Of course." I chuckle. Books.

"That's all there is to me." She says, the small smile still on her lips. "I graduated, Aunt Josephine died, and I started working at the gift shop."

That doesn't tell me why she isn't going to college, like she should be. "So why no college?" I ask.

She frowns. "Maybe it's not for me." She says, "I'm moving to Bellevue to find a job."

The confidence in her tone can only be from the wine. She must be scared to consider doing something as drastic as moving away from the town where she grew up, without even the security of a job waiting for her, but she seems to be handling it well. "Why Bellevue?" I ask.

She looks deep in thought, and then she shrugs and doesn't say anything. I don't pursue it. I consider asking her to come to Seattle instead. I would get her a job, make sure she's all right. I watch as she licks her lips distractedly, and I know there's no way I would be able to keep my hands off her.

No, I should just leave her alone.

I notice a guy come into the restaurant with a brunette in tow. He doesn't take two steps before his eyes lock on Sophie. She has her back to him, so she can't see him. His expression turns to one of surprise, and he says something to his companion. As I watch, they begin to come towards us.

He looks young, closer to her age than me. A boyfriend maybe. Feeling unaccountably jealous, I wait as he approaches our table.

"Sophie?" The guy says when he is close enough for her to hear. Sophie frowns, her eyes still on me, then she turns around to see who it is. I watch her face, her reactions, wanting to see any sign that he means something to her.

"Hi Eddie." Her voice is friendly but not overly so.

"It's really nice to see you, Sophie." The guy, Eddie, says, his eyes leaving her face only for a second, to look at mine.

"It's nice to see you too, Eddie." Sophie replies, for a second she looks unsure what to do. "David, this is Eddie," She starts tentatively. "We were neighbors growing up."

I watch her face for any sign of another meaning in that statement, wondering at my sudden and unjustifiable possessiveness.

"Eddie, this is David Preston," she continues,

"he…" she stops and I watch the blush steal into her cheeks.

"I'm attending a conference here in town," I finish for her. "or I was. I'm heading back to Seattle in the morning."

My eyes don't leave Sophie's face as I speak, so I see the look of disappointment that immediately clouds her features. A small frown steals into her face. I feel an unfamiliar surge of concern. I try to pay attention while her friend introduces his companion.

"I'm sorry for your loss Sophie," he says to Sophie, giving her a smile that makes me want to give him a job somewhere very far away. "I'm sorry I haven't tried to see you before now." He adds.

"You were away at school," She replies, "and I'm okay."

He gives her another smile before moving away from our table. I watch him go, jealousy eating at me. "Old boyfriend?" I ask, turning back to Sophie, the coolness in my voice hiding the fact that I really need her to deny it.

"No," her eyes widen, and she shakes her head. "Of course not. I don't have any old boyfriends."

I'm almost ashamed of the relief I feel. "Young ones then?" I probe, looking intently at her.

She shakes her head, filling me with an insane and

inexplicable feeling of exultation.

"You didn't tell me you were leaving." She says in a small voice. The thought that she doesn't want me to go is selfishly elating. I lean back on my chair and watch her face.

"I was leaving this afternoon," I say with a small shrug, "and yet when I saw you, I stopped to ask you to dinner."

A blush steals into her cheeks. "Oh."

I smile ruefully. "But then I left anyway."

"I don't understand." She says, puzzlement creeping into her face, "You're here."

But I shouldn't be, if I had any sense I would be far away from her. I suppress the voice of reason. "I was going to call the shop and apologize to you, but I came back, and now here I am, back in Ashford, on a date with an eighteen year old."

For a moment, she looks incredibly sad. "I'm glad you changed your mind." She says finally, her voice intense.

The passion in her response surprises me. God, I want her. The desire I felt earlier has turned into an acute craving, I want to take her away from this godforsaken town and put a mark on her that'll make her unquestionably mine, but I know that I'm not what she needs. I'm no romantic hero, and if she's cast me in that role, I would only disappoint her expectations.

"Somebody should have warned you to stay away from men like me." I'm warning her now.

Her eyes never leave my face. She studies me intently, as if weighing me for my faults and surprisingly finding none. "What kind of man are you?" She asks.

I don't pause. "The type that's bad for you."

She ignores the warning in my voice. "I wouldn't have listened." She tells me, her eyes burning. I take a deep breath. Somehow, I know I'm already lost.

"I should take you home." I say, signaling for the bill.

She keeps looking at me. I would give a lot to know what she's thinking. "Let's go." I say, as soon as I've settled the bill. I help her out of her chair and lead her outside to the car. Silently, I open her door and then go over to my side.

"Will you come back here?" Her voice is barely higher than a murmur.

"I'm not sure." The sooner this is over, and she is safely at home, away from me, the better for all concerned. I shrug. "You'll be in Bellevue anyway."

Her silence gets to me. Her face is turned away, looking towards her lap. Regret washes over me. I wish I were a different man. I wish a lot of things.

"Are you okay?" I ask, placing my hand under her chin as I turn her face towards me. Her eyes are covered with a sheen of tears, and her lips are trembling. Everything in me, everything in my life suddenly takes second place to the need to take away those tears. I don't know what I'm doing. I just find myself leaning forward, and in the next moment, I'm kissing her.

Her skin smells delicious, and her lips are soft and warm, just like I knew they would be. I lose the ability to think, as I get lost in the taste and feel of her. She lets out a soft moan, opening her lips to me. I can't help myself. I plunge into the warm sweetness of her mouth, letting my tongue explore her.

I undo her seatbelt, needing to feel her against me. When she's free,I pull her towards me and feel the softness of her breasts against my chest. The ache in my groin intensifies, spreading all over my body, until I'm almost mad with the desire to touch every inch of her skin.

Still kissing her, I allow my fingers to explore the softness of her body, cupping a breast and finding a nipple through her dress. I rub it until it's swollen, clearly outlined through the fabric.

"Oh," her moan is one of surprise and arousal. I search her face, quelling the desire to take her lips again. The look in her eyes, the surprise in her reactions to my touch, tells me what I should have guessed.

She's never done this before.

The realization wars with my blinding urge to lay claim to her. I'm still struggling with myself when she lifts her face and kisses me. Once again, I'm lost. I dive readily into the pleasure of her lips. My hands find the hair tie holding her ponytail in place, and I free her hair, watching the waves cascade over her shoulders.

"Sophie…" I breathe. I feel bewitched. I ought to let her go, to do the right thing, but my hands are itching to touch her, my body is aching for her. I feel like a caveman. I want to throw her over my shoulders, take her somewhere, and mark her as mine. "I wanted to do that since I saw you outside the shop this afternoon," I say, striving for calm as I thread my fingers into her hair. I smile, "You don't know what you've done to me."

She takes a deep shuddering breath, but she doesn't say anything.

I release her with a small sigh. I have never been so frustrated in my life. "I'd better take you home." I say, even though it's the last thing I want to do.

Her expression of disappointment is my only consolation. She wants me too. I touch her soft lips, tracing a finger over the curve, "Sweetheart, I want you so much."

"I want you too." She whispers, her eyes on my face.

Frustration is making me mad, I think, as I run a hand through my hair, laughing softly at myself. I have to warn her, I think desperately. I have to let her know exactly what she's going into. Maybe if I did, she would reject me.

"I can't make any promises, Sophie." I say. "You don't deserve someone who will forget about you the moment he's out of town."

Her eyes widen, threatening to drown me in their green depths. "Will you forget me so quickly?"

I look away. I should say yes, and then maybe she would walk away. "I don't know." I say instead, because deep down, I don't want to go.

For a long time, she says nothing. In my mind, I imagine my lonely drive back to Seattle, a cold shower, a night spent working in my study. I can do that, I think, just send me on my way Sophie.

"What if I don't care?" She asks softly, her words piercing my brain and making it incapable of rational thought. "What if I want you anyway?"

Chapter Four

THE CAR IS SILENT EXCEPT FOR the sound of our breathing. I feel as if I'm drowning in the invitation in Sophie's eyes. God I want her, I want her so badly I've lost the ability to think clearly. I tear my gaze away from her face and start the car.

Driving as fast as I can, I clear the distance to her apartment in almost no time. I go over to her side to open the door, and as I take her hand I feel my palms burn where they touch her skin.

She looks up at me, her eyes questioning. Her lips parted invitingly. I want to claim them again, but I know that if I kiss her, I won't be able to stop myself from making love to her right here by the car. I almost groan as that particular image enters my mind. I'm already aching and swollen with arousal. I gesture for her to lead the way, barely restraining myself from grabbing her as she walks ahead of me on the stairs to her apartment.

Once inside, I can't contain my hunger. I reach for her, pulling her close and filling my senses with the fresh scent and taste of her skin. She rewards my touch with a sweet, soft moan, fanning the feverish flames heating my blood to a boiling point.

Her body is beautiful, soft, smooth, and so incredibly responsive. I undress her, devouring the sweetness of her lips and trailing my fingers over her firm curves. Soon I have her almost naked, her legs wrapped around my waist, her breast wondrously soft in my hands, my heavy, aching groin pressed against her moist panties. I want to plunge deep into her warmth. I want to feel the deepest parts of her. I'm going insane, and there's nothing I can do to stop myself.

She moans and rubs herself against me, causing an explosion to go off in my brain. And even though all I want is to turn her anticipation into the sweetest passion she's ever felt, I attempt to warn her again.

"I am going to make love to you now," I say thickly, trying to still my hungry hands, "so if you want me to stop, tell me."

She shakes her head, and that's all I need. I manage to tear off my clothes before I carry her in the direction of her room.

I want to make it good for her. So I hold myself back, pleasuring her body, tasting her, arousing her, making her come with my fingers and my tongue, and reveling in the pleasure of watching her lose herself with abandon.

When I finally press myself against her silky warmth, she is wet and ready. I want to go slow, but the pleasure is indescribable. It takes over my mind, and I lose control, plunging deep into her, and feeling every mind blowing sensation as her body closes and tightens around me.

Her cry of pain tears through the haze of my pleasure. I stop, but then she urges me to continue, moving her hips to let me know what she wants. I try to hold back the waves of sensations that have taken over my body. It's no use, when she starts to moan, her hips moving to meet mine, my brain switches off, and it's only her sweat slicked body under my own, her soft sounds of pleasure, her heaving breasts, and the sweetness between her legs.

My heart is beating like a drum. My hips flex, moving on their own accord as I thrust into her again and again. I groan, her warmth driving me over the edge. Her body stiffens, and she cries out. I thrust deeply into her one last time, helpless as my own body explodes in a peak of pleasure I've never experienced before.

I collapse on the bed, trying to keep my weight off her. There are no words to describe how I feel.

"You're beautiful." I whisper and I turn on my side and pull her to me. "You're so damn beautiful."

I wake up relaxed and sated. Beside me, Sophie is staring at my face, her lips curved in a shy smile.

"Good morning." She whispers. I watch her stretch, her naked body perfect in the morning light, reminding me of last night. My own body hardens in arousal, eager to pounce on her. I restrain myself. She looks okay, but I'm sure she must feel a little soreness.

"How are you feeling?" I ask her.

"Great." She smiles, clearly not unhappy, "A little sore." She adds with a shrug, as if it doesn't matter.

I nod. I should leave. I have to get back to the office, and she'll probably have to go to work.

"When do you have to leave for work?"

Her good mood seems to dissipate. It turns out that she doesn't have to leave anytime soon. "When are you leaving?" She asks me, her voice tiny.

"At noon." I ignore the sadness I can hear very

clearly in her voice. There's no point in trying to postpone the inevitable. I'll leave, and she'll forget about me. The thought is depressing, but I shrug off the unwelcome feeling as I get up to go to the bathroom.

The tiny bathroom has barely enough space to turn around in, but I manage as best as I can. I try not to imagine what life will be like for her in a new city. It's hard enough to find a job when you're qualified, for her it'll probably be hell. I explore different scenarios in my mind, trying to find one in which I can offer her my protection, but in each scenario I can't help taking, and taking everything she has to offer. Somehow, any assistance I can give her doesn't seem worth everything she'll give me in return.

When I leave the bathroom, Sophie's gone. I find my briefs on the floor, and pull them on. I'll have to stop by my apartment to shower and change before going to the office. The rest of my clothes are still in Sophie's tiny living room. As I leave the bedroom to find them, I hear the sound of the doorbell.

In the living room, Sophie is standing by the door in her robe, peering into the peephole. My clothes are lying on the couch. I start to pull them on, wondering who it is at the door.

The bell rings again. "Are you going to get that?" I

ask. Sophie turns around, looking surprised to find that that I've joined her. I want to see who it is. It's unreasonable how obsessively jealous I feel, but I can't help it. I had to have her, now I can't bear the thought of her with anyone else.

She waits, watching me put on my clothes, and then she turns back to the door, only opening it about an inch.

"Hey Sophie." I instantly recognize the voice of the person on the other side. It's Eddie, from last night at the restaurant.

"Hey Eddie." I hear her reply.

My chest expands as I take a deep breath. There's no overt friendliness in her voice. The knot in my stomach loosens a little.

He continues to talk, giving a long speech about wanting to make sure that she's all right. What's his deal? I'll bet he'd like for her to invite him in and allow him to show her how worried he really is.

I move from my position beside the couch until I'm standing behind Sophie, directly in his line of sight. He looks up, and I watch with satisfaction as his expression changes.

His boyish smile fades and his voice loses its light friendliness. "I see you have a guest." He says to Sophie.

She turns around to look at me, then back to Eddie. "I'm all right, Eddie," she says, firmly, "You have no reason to be worried about me."

That should have been enough to send him on his way, but he just had to try, one last time.

"Are you sure?" he asks her, his voice grating on my senses, "Because if there's anything you need, you should know that I would help."

The insinuation that she might not be safe with me is irritating, as is the assumption that she would turn to him for help. "She said she's fine." I tell him, my tone conveying my impatience with his presence. "She doesn't need you to take care of her."

"And she needs you?" His pleasant face turns into a sneer. "Don't pretend that you give a damn about her." He accuses. "We all know what happens now that you've had your fun, don't we?" He adds with a bitter laugh. "The rich playboy strikes again, too bad you couldn't find someone your own age."

He's only a boy. I tell myself as I rein in my annoyance. That's the only thing that prevents me from teaching him a lesson he wouldn't forget in a hurry. "You should go now." I tell him. "And try to remember that from now on nothing about Sophie is any of your concern or your responsibility."

I watch him weigh his options. Then he turns on his

heel and disappears.

Sophie shuts the door quickly, a frown on her face. "I've never seen him like that before." She says musingly.

"Really?" I ask, jealousy clouding my senses. The fact that he wants her is unmistakably clear to me, and the knowledge that when I'm gone, he'll find another excuse to come back and inveigle himself into her life is almost unbearable.

"Really." She replies with a frown.

"Really?" I ask again. She is still standing by the door, and I move towards her until she's backed up against the hard wood, and my body is so close to hers I can feel the heat of her skin. I place a finger under her chin and lift her face towards mine. "Because anybody can see that he's in love with you."

She looks nonplussed. "Why would he be in love with me?"

"You really have no idea, do you?" I sigh in equal parts exasperation and wonder. "Somebody should have told you how beautiful you are." I drop my hand from her chin. "I promise you that as soon as I'm gone he'll be back to offer you his 'help' again."

She takes a deep breath. "I don't want his help." She says, her voice low, with a little hint of stubbornness. Although it's what she doesn't say that I hear.

She would rather have me.

Her eyes are green pools of invitation. Desire flares in my brain. I slide my hand into her robe and up her smooth thighs. She parts her legs in an invitation I can't refuse, and my fingers move upwards. I let out a low groan when I find her hot and wet.

The only thing that stops me from spreading her legs and burying myself in her is the knowledge that it might be too soon for it not to be uncomfortable for her. I tease her with my fingers instead, watching as her face contorts in pleasure while the sweet ache of my arousal fills my pants. I concentrate on her, keeping a tight rein on myself as I stroke her pulsing core, bringing her body to a shuddering climax.

I cover her mouth with mine, swallowing her cry as she comes. I press her body against mine, unable to control the consuming desire to possess her in every way. I feel as if I have no control. She belongs to me, not to the Eddie Newtons of Ashford.

"Don't forget who made you feel like this." I whisper against her ear.

She trembles, "Take me with you." She says, taking me by surprise with the soft words.

At that moment, there is nothing I want more than to lose myself in the pleasure of her body again and again and again. I feel her stiffen in my arms, and I pull her closer, kissing her hair. I'm not usually impulsive, and on some level I know that what I'm about to do is absolutely crazy. My mind should be on my company, but at this moment, I don't care about Toby Felt, or Carole with her ultimatums... I'm not vindictive, but if I were going to teach Carole a lesson, what could be better than letting her know how little her demands mean to me.

"There's one way you can come with me." I say, almost amused by the rashness of the decision I'm about to make.

"How?"

I pause for only a brief moment, and then, I dive in. "How long does it take to get a marriage license in Ashford?"

Chapter Five

MARRIED.

I doubt that most people would believe it if I told them. I can hardly believe it myself, until I close my eyes and my nose fills with the soft fragrance of Sophie's skin, and I can almost see her beautiful body spread out under mine.

I have a meeting scheduled in five minutes, but I can't stop thinking about my wife, the soft moans that have become so familiar that I can replay them in my head. I'm going insane, I think, looking up as the door opens and Bobby Ayers walks into my office.

I turn away from the windows, gesturing for him to sit as I walk towards my desk. He's been tracking the sales of Preston Corp stock, and from our phone discussion of last night, a substantial percentage of my business has been acquired in a matter of weeks.

I already know what he's going to tell me. I did my own investigating last night, working well into the night even though Sophie was lying awake, waiting for me. By all indications, it's only a matter of time before Toby Felt makes a public offer for my company. With his minority interest, he could petition for a seat on the board, and if he buys Carole's shares, well, I don't even want to think about that.

As Bobby reveals what I've already discovered. My mind is only half on what he's saying. I have to play this very carefully. I have a plan, but I need time. If Carole discovers anything about Sophie now, there's no telling how vengeful she can get. She would sell to Felt just to punish me.

If my plan works, and it will, the last thing on Felt's mind would be buying Carole's shares.

Bobby is still telling me things I already know, while I finalize my plans in my head. Then I call my assistant and ask for my stockbroker. If I'm going to be fighting a takeover, then I'd rather be on the attack. Egomaniacs like Felt never expect to be attacked, so their defenses are never as impregnable as they should be, that's why I'm taking the fight to him.

I'm going to preempt him.

By the time he finds out what's hit him, he'll be begging me to buy back the Preston Corp stock he's already acquired.

I spend the whole day in meetings. Ironing out the details of my plan with my broker, and then meeting with Rick Cruzman and my marketing and branding team to decide how best to sell his software. Even with the high intensity mental activity, it's almost impossible to push the thoughts of Sophie from my mind. I'm helpless against the overwhelming and obsessive desire I feel for her, and I hate feeling helpless.

Finally, as the day wears on, I manage to convince myself that I can push her out of my mind and concentrate on work. Yet, by the time I arrive at the apartment, my anticipation has built up to a level that I can hardly wait see Sophie.

I find her lying on the window seat in the living room, her hair spilling out in a gold curtain, and immediately awareness and lust assaults my mind. I forget all about work, as she comes to me eagerly, and

I indulge my desire, burying my senses in her soft lips. If I'm going to lose everything because of her, then it will be worth it. I swear it will.

When I finally let go of her, she sways against me, her eyes looking dazed. "Are you hungry?" she asks breathlessly.

I grin. I'm definitely hungry, hungry for her. "I am." I reply, my eyes on her parted lips.

Her cheeks flush and I know she knows what I'm thinking. "Mrs. Daniels left something for dinner." She tells me.

"Oh that." I chuckle, releasing her. There are many things I would prefer to any dinner my housekeeper has prepared, but the night is long. I start towards the bedroom. "I'll be out in a minute." I tell Sophie.

While I'm taking off my clothes, a text comes into my phone. The short message from Carole, asking me if I've thought of her offer, totally ruins my good mood.

I should be working on making sure her threats come to nothing.

Immediately after dinner, I go to my study, ignoring Sophie and the hurt and disbelief on her face. I have too much at stake to be losing my head to any woman, even her.

I work till very late, but Sophie is still awake when I get to our room. She's lying on top of the covers, her legs and thighs bare in a hip-length T-shirt. She sits up when I enter the room, her wide eyes, cloudy and unhappy, and even though I know she has a thousand reasons to feel that way, I really don't want to deal with it right now.

"You left so early this morning." She says tentatively, as soon as I sit on the bed. Her words are hesitant, but I can already hear the other accusations coming.

The thing about commitment, I think, is how much of explaining you have to do. "I always leave early." I say wearily.

"You were gone all day." She persists.

I am trying to be patient, but something in me snaps. I know I'm being unfair to her, that I have no one but myself to blame for using her innocence is a tool to tie her to me, but I can't help myself. "Maybe in your imagination," I start, hearing the cruelty in my voice, but doing nothing to temper it, "being married means spending every single moment together, but real life isn't a fantasy, I have a business to run."

She flinches, and the pain in her eyes stirs a flood of regret inside me. When she speaks again, her voice is halting and uncertain. "I was just…" She stops, looking like she's searching for the right words, then she turns away from me.

I should apologize, but I'm tired, and the words don't come. "I had a hard day Sophie, I was incredibly busy." I get up and go into the bathroom, leaving her alone.

When I return, she's lying on her stomach, and I wonder if she's crying. I join her on the bed and stroke her back, feeling her tremble at my touch. I continue, raising her shirt and spreading her legs. Deep down, I know this is not enough, especially not for her, but at the moment, I have nothing else to offer.

I touch her with my tongue, tasting and teasing until she's bucking uncontrollably and crying out my name almost incoherently.

I don't intend for it to go farther than that, but when she starts to caress my chest, moving slowly down until she has me in her hands, then in her mouth, I feel as if I'm the one who has lost all control. I'm entirely under her power. Anything she asks me now, I wouldn't be able to refuse. I would give her my life, my heart…

Damn.

I grab her and pull her off me, moving her until her hips are spread and poised over my swollen erection. I push her down, pressing myself into her exquisitely tight, warm heat.

I lose myself in her. My senses reduced to nothing but the sweat induced slickness of her skin, her soft fragrance, the heat of her body so tight around me. My hands move feverishly, squeezing full breasts, spanning her slender waist, as I guide her up and down my full length. I want to touch every inch of her all at once. I grab unto her hips, thrusting deeper into the very depths of her body, feeling her pulse around me as her body urges the most intense pleasure out of me. When she loses control, her cries send me over the edge. I grip her hips tightly, holding her in place as I thrust faster, finally exploding with a helpless groan.

She collapses unto my chest. Her soft body draped over mine. I forget everything but her warmth, her sweetness, and how easy it would be to let everything go, and allow myself to sink into her, body and soul, completely, forever.

I hold her against me, listening as her breathing

slows and her skin cools, and then I also fall asleep.

I wake up later than usual. I'm lying on my side, with Sophie snuggled against my chest. It's surprising how well I've slept, considering that I have so much to worry about.

Sophie protests sleepily when I pull away from her, but she doesn't wake up.

I take a shower and start to get ready for work. I'm putting on my clothes when Sophie comes into the dressing room.

"Hey." I turn at the sound of her voice and find her standing at the door, watching me with a wistful expression. "I wish you wouldn't leave so early." She says.

I want to tell her that there's nothing I would prefer to a few carefree days with nothing to do but discover her body in every way. But I'm afraid that if I say the words out loud, I might make another impulsive decision. I turn away from her and walk toward the mirror, busying myself with knotting my tie. I'm on the verge of throwing everything away and taking her somewhere far away, where it'll be just the two of us…

"I know you're really busy…" her voice cuts into my thoughts, faltering, apologetic.

I leave what I'm doing and turn to her, if anyone should be apologizing, it should be me. "I'm sorry, Sophie." I take a deep breath. "Yes, I've been busy. I've had to deal with certain issues at work, issues that were there even before I met you, but that's no excuse."

She moves towards me. "I understand," She says earnestly, "really. I'm not complaining. I just wish we had a little more time for us." Her eyes are wide and hopeful. I feel like a bastard.

"Things will clear up soon," I hear myself saying, even though I have no assurance of that, "and then I'll make it up to you, I promise. We'll go somewhere that'll blow your mind."

"You blow my mind." Her words are shy, but they're enough to heat my blood. I smile, raising her face to look at mine. I'm about to lean down and kiss her, when she rises up on her toes and places her lips over mine. I kiss her back, my tongue delving into the sweet recesses of her mouth. Then she suddenly pushes me away and runs her hands down the front of my shirt dropping to her knees in front of me.

Her fingers flit over the front of my pants, and my body responds forcefully. I can hardly wait as she undoes my zipper and frees me from the constraints of my underwear. Then she takes me in her mouth.

The heat nearly sends me over the edge. Her hot lips, velvety tongue, the sweet moist pressure as she tightens her lips around me and takes me deeper into her mouth... It's driving me insane. I bury my fingers in her hair, my knees going weak as she moves her head back and forth, her tongue teasing me to madness. There's no technique to what she's doing. It's just her, lovely, sexy, and mine. She moans against me, and the sound pushes me over the edge. I come with a loud groan.

She swallows. Her lips are still tight around me as I pull out of her mouth. My legs are shaky, and I can't catch my breath, I drop to my knees beside her.

"You're a bag of surprises, aren't you?" I growl, taking her lips as my fingers delve under her t-shirt to feel how wet she is. She moans, rotating her hips around my fingers.

"You're ready for me." I whisper softly against her ear.

She nods.

I stroke her until she's shaking and moaning her desire, her hips bucking sweetly to my touch. When I know she can't take much more, I turn her around and enter her slowly from behind.

She's so tight and so responsive. Her body tightens around me, her low moan piercing my brain. I close my eyes and let my body take over, pushing myself deeper into her with each thrust. I find her breasts under her t-shirt and fill my hands with their exquisite softness, squeezing gently.

She loses all self-consciousness, shouting my name as her body contracts around me, pulsing with her climax. I pull out of her, still hard, and move her so that she's lying on her back. I kneel between her legs and lift her off the floor, pushing slowly, teasingly inside her core. She's shaking uncontrollably and moaning loudly, and I'm losing more and more of my mind. I feel as if I'm going to explode, and when I finally do, it's the most powerful thing I've ever felt.

I want to lie down there with her for as long as possible. I want a repeat. I want to take her to some secluded tropical island and have her for breakfast, lunch, and dinner.

I get up and start to adjust my clothes. Sophie looks up at me, her eyes heavy. "Have I made you late for work?" She asks.

I tear my eyes away from her. If I don't leave now, I probably never will. "Not really," I knot my tie, telling her about the appointments I've asked my assistant to make for her. Clothes and shopping should help to keep her occupied until I resolve the issues at work. At least I hope so.

Chapter Six

THE NEXT FEW DAYS ARE BOTH crazy and exciting.

I played Pac-Man when I was a kid. The ghosts would chase me around until I got a pellet and then I would turn around and chase then, eating them up. I've never done the Pac-Man move in business though. I've never had to, until now.

On the first day of my plan, we start with a Dawn Raid. As soon as the stock market opens in the morning, I purchase a substantial number of shares in Felt Enterprises. By the time Toby Felt realizes what's going on, I've already built a substantial stake in his company.

The next day I communicate my cash tender offer to his stockholders, offering a generous price over and above the market price.

By the next day, he's calling to negotiate.

I don't really want to buy Felt's company, but I can, and he knows it. He also knows that he cannot pursue my company and try to keep his own at the same time. I did my homework, so I know he's spread too thin.

By the time I'm done with him, the only thing that's left to deal with is Carole.

When I invite her to my office, I can tell from the sound of her voice on the phone that she thinks she has won. When she saunters into my office, her smile tells me that she believes I have no choice, but to capitulate to her demands.

"David darling," She breathes, rising on tiptoe to kiss me on each cheek.

I suffer her attentions, waiting until she steps away from me and takes a seat.

"So have you reconsidered my offer," She crosses her legs, a triumphant smile dancing on her lips. "I don't have forever, you know."

"If I remember correctly," I reply, "I made you an offer as well. I offered to buy your shares." I pause, "Have you considered my offer?"

Carole laughs. "How like you to take a hard line

even though you know I hold all the cards, David." She shrugs. "I've given you an easy way out. You can give me what I want, or I'll give Felt what he wants."

"And just to be clear Carole, What you want is marriage, to me?"

"Yes." She squares her shoulders, and then looks down at her fingers. "I want a ring David, no pre-nup of course, those are so unromantic." She pauses. "Give me your word and I'll tell Toby to go to hell."

I start to laugh. I can't help myself.

She springs up from the chair, her air of calmness and complacency gone in an instant and replaced by a barely disguised fury. "Unless of course," She says angrily, "it's true that you're married?"

I consider her face for a moment. Her eyes are narrowed, and her lips on the verge of a snarl. The precautions I took could not have kept my marriage quiet forever, but what does it matter now? She doesn't know it yet, but I have her in a corner.

"I am married." I lean back in my chair and watch as her face goes livid.

For a moment, I think she's going to attack me. She looks wild. Then she smiles and picks up her purse. "You can kiss your controlling interest goodbye David. Toby will buy my shares, and everybody else's you have your precious voting agreements with. I hope he cleans your name off everything that is Preston Corp."

I chuckle, even though amusement is the last thing I feel. I'm done with her threats. "He won't." I tell her coldly.

She stops to look at me, her eyes searching my face.

"Did you really think I was going to let you blackmail me into doing something so stupid as to tie myself to you Carole? Did you think that I would be so easily coerced?" I bite out the words, watching her flinch as she feels the whiplash of my annoyance. "You must have been taking lessons from your friend Enrique." I pause as her face turns in a frown. "Didn't you know?" I ask, "He also tried to blackmail me." I retrieve the drive with her video from my desk drawer and toss it towards her."

She picks it up. "What is this?"

"Socialite porn," I say with a shrug, "staring you, and your friend Enrique." I smile cruelly. "You didn't know he made a video did you? Apparently, you're not the only one who likes to have leverage."

She sniffs. "What are you saying? That if I sell to Toby, you're going to release this?"

I snort in disgust. "I'm not like you Carole, I let my brain do my business, and I don't resort to blackmail." She looks surprised. "That's the last copy," I tell her. "You can keep it. Whenever you run out of all the money you were lucky enough to get from your father, maybe you'll find someone willing to pay for it."

She quickly drops it into her purse. "Don't think that this changes anything." She says with a sneer, "Don't think I won't sell to Toby just because you gave me this. Your 'kindness' means nothing to me."

I shrug. "I didn't think it would."

"So you're just going to let go of Preston Corp?" Her voice is full of disbelief. "I hope the brat you married is worth it, for your sake."

Her reference to Sophie annoys me, but I keep my calm. "She is worth it, but I'm not losing control of my company. Carole. Toby Felt is not going to buy your shares."

"I don't believe you." I hear the worry in her voice, and I know that I've gotten to her.

"Believe what you want," I say. "Felt and I have come to an agreement. If you go to him now, he will refuse to buy your shares. However, when you leave this office, you'll find my broker waiting for you outside, with my offer for your shares, valid only for as long as you remain in this building. You'll find that it's a very generous offer Carole, so don't be foolish."

She looks on the verge of tears.

"I hate you." She says suddenly, vehemently, "I hate you, you cold-hearted bastard.

I shrug. "That means absolutely nothing to me."

After Carole leaves, my mind turns back to Sophie.

I instruct Linda to make dinner reservations for Sophie and me. While I've been attempting to retain control of my company, I haven't been very attentive to her. For obvious reasons, I tried to keep the news of our marriage quiet, but that's no longer necessary. Now that I have everything under control again, I can give her some of my attention.

I start making plans, Dinner tonight, then tomorrow, a trip somewhere I can have her to myself for a while, remove any lingering doubts from her mind, and make up for the time I've been spending at work.

She'd like that. At least, I hope she will.

Filled with a sudden urge to hear her voice, I dial her number on my cell, listening impatiently as the phone rings over and over. I'm beginning to think she won't pick up when I hear her voice.

"Sophie." I'm surprised at the relief I feel. "I hope you can go out tonight."

Her silence unnerves me, and I can't shake the feeling that something is wrong.

"You want us to go out together?" She says finally, an edge of incredulity in her voice.

I close my eyes. She somehow found out about the NDA, I realize, a sinking feeling in the pit of my stomach. She may be shy, reserved, but she's no fool. I can explain that I require a level of secrecy from most people whose services I use, from tailors to employees who work closely with me. It's standard practice, but in this case I have to admit an ulterior motive. I wanted to keep my marriage quiet because of Carole.

She's still waiting for me to say something. "Yes," I say in reply to her question.

There's some more silence from her end. "Where?" She asks finally.

I hear myself breathe. Long after the call I'm still thinking about the way she sounded. I should probably go home, surprise her, and find out what the problem is.

"Mr. Preston, your housekeeper called to leave a message." Linda's voice comes over the speakers of the intercom, interrupting my thoughts.

My heart almost stops. My first suspicion is that Sophie has left. Linda's next words turn my fear into irritation.

"She says that Mrs. Weber is in your apartment."

Just what I need to ruin my day. "Thank you,

Linda." I say, not bothering to ask if the message included any clue to what my mother wants. I know what she wants. She's been trying to insinuate herself into my life since her husband died, and now I can imagine that she's decided to go through Sophie. I don't want my mother anywhere near me, and I sure as hell don't want her anywhere near Sophie.

In only a few minutes, I arrive at the apartment. My mother can be charming, and there's no way for Sophie to see her for who she really is, to see her the way I see her, as someone who would betray her own son for money.

They both look surprised to see me when I step into the living room. I let my mother feel the full force of my anger. I let her see in my face, what I think of her presence in my apartment.

"I was just getting to know your mother." Sophie says with a sweet smile, getting up and walking towards me.

"Isn't that wonderful?" even though I'm relieved that there's no accusation in her eyes, I'm unable to keep the sarcasm out of my voice. "Well, now she's leaving."

"David..." They both speak at the same time.

I turn to my mother. "Why did you come here?" I ask her, disgusted with her continued attempts to act as if she wasn't the one who ruined our relationship so she could stay married to the bastard who abused her every day of their marriage.

She sighs dramatically. "David, my only son just got married, and I had no idea. I just wanted to meet Sophie."

"Well, I don't want you here." I ignore the pained expression on her face. I don't care how she feels. I'll never care again. I still remember very clearly, going out of my to protect her, because I cared, and I paid dearly for it. "The next time you persuade anyone into letting you in I will fire them."

"No, you won't." Sophie's interruption surprises me. "and you may not want her here, but I do." I turn to look at her, She doesn't understand, if she did, she wouldn't be defending my mother. Maybe, someday I'll tell her, but not right now. "Sophie..."

She interrupts me again, her voice rising. "No stop," She says, "Why don't you want her here? Is it because you want to continue keeping me a secret? Why don't you make her sign a non-disclosure agreement?"

I take a deep breath. "You don't know what you're saying."

"Don't I?" She looks fierce now, her eyes burning, and I can't take my eyes off her. "Didn't you make the beauty team, the personal shopper, every person I've spoken to in all the days you've kept me hidden in this apartment sign a document to prevent them for saying anything to anyone about me?"

God this can't be happening, not in front of my mother. I don't even realize how frustrated I am until I catch myself running my fingers through my hair. "You wouldn't understand." I tell Sophie.

Her eyes cloud as she looks at me, and I see the pain clearly in her eyes. I watch helplessly as she turns away and walks out of the room.

I turn to my mother, "I hope you're glad." I say, knowing that it's really not her fault. If it's anyone's fault, then it's mine. I should have resolved my problems before bringing Sophie into my life, I should have waited for God's sake, but I was too impatient to take what she didn't even know she was offering, and now I'm paying for it.

"I'm sorry." My mother says, with another of her elegant shrugs. "I had no idea."

"Well now you do."

She gets up from the couch, taking her purse. "An NDA does seem rather extreme for hairdressers and such," She says softly. "Does this have anything to do with Carole Banks?"

I ignore her, letting her know by my silence that it's time for her to leave. I have no intention of sharing my problems with her. She is a stranger for all I care. I follow her to the foyer and go ahead of her to press the button for the lift.

"David," she begins, as we wait for the doors to open, "I know you're angry with me..."

Whatever she has to say, I don't want to hear it.

"I'm not angry mother," I interrupt. "I stopped being angry with you a long time ago. What I feel now is disgust. I don't want to have anything to do with you. I hope you have a very happy life with Henry's money. You've earned it."

"Don't try to tell me that you don't care about money David," She retorts." You worked hard to make much more than your step-father ever had."

I sigh. "Yes I worked hard, and I'm proud of it. What did you do? You received every beating the bastard ever gave you, lied about it, and turned your back on me without a thought. You make me sick mother."

She doesn't look at me as she steps into the lift. "I'll never understand how you turned out to be so cruel," She says, her voice low.

"You haven't tried hard enough." I say unsympathetically, turning away before the doors close.

I panic when I can't find Sophie in our bedroom. I check all the rooms in the apartment, my heart racing. I finally think to look in my study and I find her, curled up on the couch, reading on her tablet. The relief I feel on seeing her temporarily weakens me.

"I've been looking for you." I don't mean for the words to be accusing, but they sound that way. Sophie only shrugs and turns back to her reading, ignoring me.

On the screen of the tablet, I can clearly see that she's reading what little about my relationship with Carole is available on the internet. "Nothing you find there has anything to do with me and you."

She looks at me, her eyes wide and glistening with a sheen of unshed tears. "Tell me about her."

Carole is nothing to me. That's the truth. We dated for a short time, and I tried to be a good friend to her, in spite of her shortcomings, especially after her father died, but now she's nothing more than a temporary inconvenience, one I've finally managed to overcome.

"There is nothing to tell." I say.

Sophie's eyes flare in anger, "Really? Because it's very clear here that she was your girlfriend only a short time ago."

"Don't believe everything you read in the papers Sophie." I say gently. "We saw each other on and off for a while, but it's been over for a long time."

"Do you love her?" She asks. "Is that why you're keeping me hidden, so that she won't find out about me?"

The idea that Carole can mean that much to me is laughable. I go to sit beside Sophie on the couch. "You don't need to concern yourself about Carole." I tell her, meaning every word, and hoping she can see the truth in my eyes.

"Her father invested a lot in your career." She murmurs.

"In return for a huge profit." I reply." It was good business, and he made money from Preston Corp every day we've been in existence."

She draws in a deep breath, and I can see that she wants to believe me. "All those pictures of the two of you…"

"Mean nothing," I insist, "We went to a lot of the same places, and people are used to mentioning our names together."

"Why don't you want anyone to know about me?" She asks with a small sniff.

Where do I start? I'd have to tell her everything about Carole, Toby Felt, and how I almost lost my company.

She gets up suddenly. "Fine, don't tell me," she says

angrily, walking away from me. I follow, stopping her at the door.

"Sophie." I take her hand. I don't want to fight. Carole is not important enough for us to fight about.

She turns around to face me, for a moment, I think she has relented, but then she pulls her hand away from mine. "Don't touch me." her voice is shaky, "Don't ever touch me again."

Now she's definitely overreacting. "Don't be childish Sophie."

She reacts as if I've slapped her. She turns and rushes away from me.

"Sophie, for God's sake." I follow as she runs to our room, catching up as she rushes into the walk-in closet.

She wants to leave.

I feel a knot tighten in my stomach. I reach out for her, gathering her into my arms. "Stop." I can hear the plea in my voice. "Stop."

She holds on to me, clutching me tightly. I bury my nose in her hair, breathing in the essence of her. This is what I want, to feel her like this, to know that she knows that she's mine.

I stroke her hair, listening as her breathing slows.

"Why did you marry me David?" She asks shakily.

I pull back so that I'm looking into her face.

"Because I wanted you," I say truthfully. "I wanted you the moment I saw you standing outside that little shop in that small town, looking so lost and alone. I wanted your innocence, your beauty," her lips are trembling. Distracted, I kiss her gently at the soft corner of her lips. "I wanted your body Sophie, I wanted to see your face when I make you scream my name."

She sways, her body pressing against me. "You didn't have to marry me," she says quietly, "You already had me."

As if once would ever be enough. "And then I wanted no one else to ever have the pleasure. Understand that Sophie, You are mine."

Her lips are parted, inviting me. My body responds without holding back. I kiss her, tasting the sweetness of her lips.

I undress her in a hurry, and tear off my clothes as fast as I can. The bed is too far away, so I carry her to one of the armchairs, kneeling between her parted legs. Then she takes me in her hand and guides me inside her slickness, her eyes closed, and her lips parted in an expression of ecstasy. My breath hisses out of my chest, and I almost explode. The fever of desire engulfs me, and I plunge in deep, going insanely, pleasurably mad with each thrust. Wanting her is like a fire in my blood, and it doesn't let go until I'm utterly spent, and barely able to carry her to the bed.

We lie side by side, her head resting on my shoulder while I stroke her hair. I have never felt like this with anyone else. It's crazy and scary at the same time.

"You know, I owe you a honeymoon." I say.

She turns to me and smiles. "Yes, somewhere that would 'blow my mind'."

"Is there anywhere in particular you would like to go?"

She sighs. "I'd go anywhere with you."

In that moment, I'm totally, irrevocably hers. I lean over and kiss her until I've tasted every corner of her mouth.

"I think I know just the place." I say when I pause for breath.

She smiles. "I thought we were going out for dinner?" She doesn't sound too eager.

My eyes skip to rosy nipples, erect and asking for my attention. What dinner?

"Forget dinner." I say decisively.

And then I make her forget.

Chapter Seven

"YOU'RE A CHANGED MAN, AND IT'S about time."

The memory of Carlo's words, spoken when his family spent an afternoon with Sophie and me in Florence, is accompanied by vivid memories of the two-week holiday, lazy days in the sun, making hot sweet love in every single room of my spacious villa, and just enjoying each other's company.

I turn to look at her, sitting beside me in the back of the car, Sophie looks beautiful, her figure perfect in a beautiful blue evening gown, and her face serene, showing no signs of the fact that we just made mind-blowing love in the apartment before setting out for the charity event we're attending. Around her slender neck, the stones in the necklace I had made from one of her designs sparkle fiercely, reminding me of the few instances when I've experienced her temper.

As if she can feel my eyes on her, she turns to look at me, wide green eyes drawing me into their depths.

For a second, I can't quite catch my breath.

I do feel like a changed man. I feel like I've been given something that I don't deserve. It's the best thing that's ever happened to me, and every single moment, I'm terrified by the fear that I'll lose it.

That I'll lose her.

I give her a small smile and turn away, busying myself with looking out of the windows on my side. Steve is driving, quiet as usual. I wonder what he would say if I told him that I'm afraid.

Afraid of falling in love with my wife.

Love is a weakness. I learned that the hard way. Love makes you risk everything, and gives you nothing but disappointment, scorn, and the lifelong scars of heartbreak in return. I know that from experience.

Experience I'd rather not repeat.

Regardless, I can feel my control slipping away. What began as an impulsive decision has become the defining event of my life.

And it's not just the sex, though that is phenomenal. I only have to close my eyes to relive the feeling of just a few minutes ago, my hard erection fully encased in her warm tightness, her long low moans as I drove deeper into her with each thrust, the blinding pleasure, the explosive release.

I take a deep breath and snap out of my erotic thoughts as Steve parks in front of the hotel where the event is taking place.

Inside, there is a crush of well-dressed people, eager to be seen and admired. I can't help thinking of the parties my mother and Henry Weber used to have, all glamour and no substance. This however is different, I remind myself, at least we're raising money for a cause.

Peggy Hart waylays me almost immediately. She's one of the richest women in the country, and she actively supports a whole lot of causes. I've always admired Peggy. Outside, she doesn't look like much, but she's relentless in getting what she wants. Today it's money for the Alliance for education, and from the smile on her face, I'm sure she's already raised a lot.

"David darling!" She kisses both my cheeks before turning to Sophie. "You must be the lovely Sophie." She says, "I've only recently heard about you, you know. David has been keeping you a terrible secret."

As if, we need anybody to remind us of that. Sophie doesn't seem offended at all, she's looking curiously at Peggy, who is laughing. "Aren't you a pretty thing though?" She tells Sophie.

Sophie turns to me, a small curious smile on her

lips. I remember my manners and introduce them. "Sophie sweetheart, this exceptionally beautiful lady is the incomparable Peggy Hart."

Sophie's eyes widen with comprehension. "I'm very honored to meet you." She says to Peggy.

Peggy dimples, obviously flattered. "Thank you darling." She tells Sophie, before turning to me with a snort. "I'm not even going to respond to your flattery."

She leads the way into the room, taking the time to tell me before she leaves us, that Carole has insisted on being seated at my table. Knowing Carole, that's her way of announcing to the world that she doesn't care that I'm married. I'm not really bothered. Carole and her antics are a thing of the past. She can't do any harm.

As the dinner progresses, I occupy myself with conversing with Leon Boise, a website entrepreneur who's seated beside me, while listening with half an ear to the speeches, and to Sophie talking with Rick Cruzman, whose software company is the latest addition to Preston Corp.

At least she's not bored. I know I am.

Everyone is clapping halfheartedly as another speech ends when I feel Sophie stiffen. I'm about to ask her what the problem is when I notice Carole and a companion I don't recognize, take the empty seats at our table.

I hear Leon Boise tell her how nice it is to see her. For me, that couldn't be farther from the truth. Sophie looks dismayed. Her eyes skip from Carole to me, and I cannot even imagine what she's thinking.

Leon turns to me. "I had forgotten to congratulate you David," he continues, "I read something about the attempted takeover," his gaze goes back to Carole. "I hear David has you to thank for retaining his control on the board."

Carole looks like she would gladly tear Leon to pieces with her teeth, then she transfers her angry glare to me. "Yes," She says, her voice like saccharine. "I sold him the shares of his company I got when my father died." Her face is expressionless, except for her eyes, which are dripping with venom as she looks at me. She laughs humorlessly and turns back to Leon. "Which means David Preston will always control Preston Corp."

"As he should." I say with a smile. I turn back to Sophie, noticing that she still looks uncomfortable. Carole and her barely hidden fangs would do that, I think. I place my hand over Sophie's on the table. "Have you met my wife?" I say, looking at Carole.

"No." Carole's voice is sweet, masking the rage in her eyes. "I don't believe I have had the pleasure."

I make the introductions, not so much because I'm taking any pleasure from riling Carole, more because I want Sophie to see that Carole means nothing to me.

Sophie's expression is hesitant. "Nice to meet you." She says politely.

Carole chuckles. Her voice has an unmistakably mocking ring to it. "The pleasure is mine."

Thankfully, the last speech ends, and I lead Sophie out to dance.

"What was that?" She asks as soon as we're alone.

"What was what?"

"What just happened at our table, with that woman?" She frowns, looking up at me.

I shrug. "Carole isn't too happy with the price she got for her shares, that's all."

Sophie gives me a curious look, "You didn't pay her as much as she wanted?"

"I couldn't." I say.

A puzzled frown creases her features. "Then how did you get her to sell them to you?"

"I have my ways."

"Wait," Sophie's frown deepens, "What did she want?"

"She wanted me," I shrug. "Either me or my destruction," I spin her around as she stares at me, open-mouthed.

"I don't understand." She says.

This isn't the time to explain all that, I decide, as I hand her over to Leon Boise, who's cutting in.

I spent the next few minutes in conversation with other business people. Finally, I end up on the balcony, eager for some fresh air.

The solitude is enjoyable. I breathe in the cool night air and enjoy the sight of the city all lit up in the night.

"I didn't take you for someone who's attracted to children." Carole's voice cuts into my thoughts.

I turn to find her standing beside me.

"Did you marry the first person who smiled at you just to teach me a lesson?" she continues.

"You think too much of yourself." I say drily.

"It's you who thinks too little of me." her voice is bitter. "It meant nothing to you that I was willing to stoop as low as blackmail just to be with you again. Did I always mean so little to you?"

"Carole," I say patiently, "Don't act like we ever had a real commitment. I'm surprised you keep hanging on to a brief fling that happened a long time ago."

"Well, I didn't forget how good it was between us." She states peevishly.

I start to shrug, but she steps towards me and pulls my face down towards her, kissing me. She's holding on tightly to me. I don't want to shove her, and it takes a while to extricate myself from her embrace.

I take a step back. "I don't know what you're trying to prove Carole, but it's not working."

She narrows her eyes. "Whatever, go back to that mewling baby you call a wife." She shrugs. "I don't care."

I leave her there, intent on finding Sophie and leaving. I don't expect to look for her everywhere and not find her. I don't expect to call her cell phone over and over and get no answer. I don't expect the fear that grips at my stomach when the guy at the front desk tells me he called a cab for someone who fits her description.

I can't get to the apartment fast enough. I don't know why Sophie's left but my worst fears are realized when I find her in the apartment, in our room, packing her bags, her face stained with tears.

She is really leaving me this time.

I feel like something is squeezing my chest. It's suddenly very difficult to breathe. I have been dreading this for weeks, with a certainty that one day she would decide that she made a mistake and leave.

One day. But not today, not so soon.

I want to beg her not to leave, desperation clouds my thoughts, and I feel like a little boy again, throwing myself at my mother, begging her not to leave.

I take a deep breath. "What are you doing?" I ask Sophie, my voice calm, masking the mounting apprehension beneath.

"What does it look like?" She doesn't even stop to look at me.

I swallow the angry words threatening to come out of my mouth. "I left you for a few moments at a party, and now you're leaving me?"

"You left me for far longer than a few minutes, to make out with your old girlfriend." Her voice catches as she speaks. She pauses and swallows, then goes back to her packing.

Silently I damn Carole and myself... mainly myself. This is all my fault. With the realization comes a blinding anguish.

"So now you're running off back to Ashford," I lash out before I can stop myself. "Tell me, is it Eddie Newton who's going to be picking up the pieces of your broken heart, or will it be somebody else?"

"What do you care?" She chokes out the words.

I care. I care so much I feel as if my senses are being obliterated. "For God's sake, Sophie!"

She steps away from me, as if I've threatened her. "Let me go." She whispers almost inaudibly. "I don't belong here, in this big apartment, or in your luxurious life, and we both know it."

"You don't know what you're saying."

She sniffs and looks up at me. "David, do you love me?"

I stiffen, looking from her face to the bags on the bed and back again, I don't want to deal with her question. I can't, not now, not yet.

"What's come over you?" I ask, eager to steer the conversation in another direction.

It doesn't work. "Do you love me, David?" She asks again.

I turn away from her. "What do you want from me?" I'm not a man who loves. I know what she's asking me. She's asking if I'm willing to open myself up to hurt, to betrayal.

I'm not.

"You don't love me do you?" She states softly, with the wounded expression of someone hearing the confirmation of something they already knew.

I scramble in my head for something to say. "Love isn't all it's cracked up to be Sophie." I say finally. "Other people would take what they have and be grateful for it."

"And what do I have?" She asks accusingly, "tell me the truth David. Why did you marry me?"

How could I not? How do I tell her about the lust that drove me to claim her body, the possessiveness that made me tie her to me, and the desire now to have not only that body, but also everything that comes with it?

She took my body prisoner that first day. There was no way I could have left her in Ashford. No matter the reasons I've given myself for marrying her, it was because I knew even then, that I wanted her forever.

And I still do.

I can't let her go.

I reach for her, my eyes never leaving hers as I run my fingers down her arm. Her lips tremble softly as she shivers.

She can't hide her reaction to my touch. "Because of that." I tell her. If we have nothing else, we have that. The pleasure we find in each other's arms.

I continue to explore her body, drawing out the reactions I know she can't conceal. Feeling her tremble beneath my fingers, I lean closer to whisper in her ear. "Because of this, Sophie. This is what we have between us."

"This is only sex." She says shakily. "We have nothing."

What we have is enough, and I'll be damned if I don't make her accept that.

I know how to make her light up, and as I touch her, I can feel her resistance crumbling.

"Is this nothing, Sophie?" I whisper, letting my breath warm her ear. I hear her ragged sigh, the shaky explosion of breath. "Don't you want this Sophie?" I continue, "Don't you want me to touch you? To make love to you, over and over again?" I kiss her neck exactly where I know she likes. "Isn't it enough?"

She shakes her head. "No."

"Don't lie to yourself? Sophie, what else is there?" My fingers are busy, undressing her. I let her dress fall to the ground, exposing her flushed skin. I continue to tease her, touching her lightly, until I know she is aching for more

She is begging me with her eyes and body to make love to her, but it's not enough. I want her complete capitulation. I want to hear her say it.

"What do you want Sophie?"

She doesn't reply. She's panting softly, her breasts heaving, her lips parted. She wants this. I squeeze her firm breasts through her bra, gently, the way I know she likes, and she lets out a soft moan.

"Isn't this enough?" I ask again.

She shakes her head again.

I sigh, undoing her bra and freeing her breasts. Deep down I know that what I'm doing is despicable, but I'm used to fighting with all my weapons, and I'm used to fighting to win.

I undress quickly. When I'm naked, I guide her hand to my aching erection. She gets on her knees, stroking me lightly with her fingers, then she takes me in her mouth. I groan, almost losing my head to the pleasure. But this is not what I want. I want to feel her tighten around me, I want to hear her moan from the pleasure I give her. I want her to lose her head. I want her to accept that she's mine, only mine.

I lift her up to her feet and position her over the bed, with her perfect backside facing me. I stroke her with eager fingers, feeling how wet she is through the silk of her panties.

She clenches around my fingers. "Please." Her voice is a plea. "Please David."

"Tell me what you want."

"Please," She moans.

"Tell me."

"I want you." She admits, her voice hoarse, telling me with words what her body is already saying very loudly.

"You want what?" I insist.

"I want you to make love to me. David, please."

Pulling down her panties, I spread her legs wider and enter her slowly, drawing out each movement, teasing her. She tightens around me, pulsing, hot and so incredible sweet. I hold on to her hips and drive in deep. She lets out a long sigh as I pull out and drive in again. I press her body to mine, thrusting in and out, over and over again, drawing my pleasure from the sounds of her moans, the heat of her skin, from her tightness clenched around me. When she comes, I can barely hold myself back.

"Isn't this enough?" I ask again as her body shudders, then stills.

She doesn't say anything. I want her to accept it, that what we have is more than any desire for love, or whatever she thinks she feels. Love is an illusion, a weakness.

She's still sensitive when I start to move again, her low moans fill the room, her body is shaking, slick with sweat. I feel her insides pulse around me again and again, but still I don't stop. I don't stop until she agrees that what we have is enough.

"Don't mistake what we have." I tell her, when I'm able to catch my breath, "and don't underestimate it either."

"And what about Carole?" She retorts, an edge of pain in her voice. "What do you two have?"

I have already inferred that she must have seen me with Carole on the balcony, but that can't be all. "Is that what this is all about? Carole? Did she say something to you?"

"You used her, just like you're using me." Her eyes are accusing. "You wanted the shares she had in your company."

"And she threatened to sell them to the man who wanted to take over my company, if I didn't marry her." I shrug. "A man she was sleeping with I might add, along with a few others."

She stares at me. No doubt, she has convinced herself that Carole is some innocent victim of my cruelty. "You're just saying that." She says finally.

I laugh humorlessly. "Maybe you should try to get your information accurate before you start throwing accusations."

"It doesn't make any difference." She says resolutely. "Even if she did all those things, it doesn't change the fact that you don't love me. I'm just the girl who was stupid enough to marry you so you could teach your ex-girlfriend a lesson." She gets up from the bed. "I can't take it David."

I watch her put on a robe and fasten the zippers of the bags she has packed. "What are you doing?" I ask, although I know, I know that I haven't managed to convince her to stay. Apparently, sex is not enough for her.

"I am leaving."

My throat thickens as I try to fight the desperation

rising like bile in my throat, "Don't threaten me." I say, getting off the bed.

"Why not?" She flings each word at me. "Will you marry someone else to teach me a lesson?"

"Don't test me Sophie." I reach for her. God! I want to beg, but somehow I can't find the words.

She ignores my touch.

"Fine." I turn away. "Do whatever you like. Go back to Ashford. I'm sure your little boyfriend will be more than eager to find you a place in his bed." I snort with derision. "But while you're at it, you might want to ask yourself why you married me."

She looks like she can't believe what I just said. "I love you." Her voice breaks on the words and my chest clenches.

She loves me. Even in her pain, she loves me.

I almost back down, but she's already cast me in the role of the villain, and that is a role I know how to play.

I laugh mockingly. "What love? Did you fall in love with some stranger you barely knew Sophie, just because he asked you out to dinner. Get real sweetheart, this has always been about sex."

"Not for me." She argues, tears in her eyes.

"Then you're a liar as well as a fool."

"I hate you," her voice is low but decisive. "I hope I

never have to see you again. Carole was right about you. You use people, and when you're done with them, you toss them away like rubbish. You're not worthy of my love."

Each word pierces me like a barb, because I know she's right. I turn away from her. "Do whatever you want Sophie."

I'm so angry, with her, with myself. I can't even bring myself to look at her, because I know I've just ruined the best thing that's ever happened in my miserable life.

I can't sleep. I spend the night in my study because I can't bear to sleep on our bed alone. I'm assaulted by unfamiliar emotions, loneliness, heartache, pain... I don't want her to leave. I won't be able to bear it. As soon as morning comes, I go to her. I'll do anything she wants, and if it's not enough, then I'll leave, if that's what she wants, if she hates me that much.

I open the door to the guest room where she spent the night, and see her body stiffen on the bed. She lies still, pretending to be asleep. Words fill my head, but I can't bring myself to say anything. After a few minutes, I leave her lying there. I've always known that I didn't deserve her. Now she knows it too.

I give Mrs. Daniels the day off, sure that Sophie would want to be alone to do whatever she's decided.

Downstairs, I instruct Steve to take her wherever she wants to go.

Leaving me is probably what's best for her. She deserves better than an empty carcass with a barely beating heart. She deserves a man who'll love her, everything about her, and never hesitate to announce it to her, and to the world.

I just wish I could be that man.

Sophie

Chapter Eight

I ALWAYS THOUGHT OF LOVE AS a beautiful feeling, and it is, when you're happy. When you're sad, it's a monster that tears at your insides, until the pain spreads to every part of you, until you just want to be numb, to lose the ability to feel, to ever feel again.

I have no clear idea where exactly I'm going when I leave the apartment. I just know that I can't stay there anymore. I feel humiliated and empty. Each memory of last night is like a raw wound in my mind. I remember every hurtful word David said to me as clearly as if I can still hear them. I can't believe that he would use my body's need for him to prove his point.

That our marriage is nothing, only sex.

How could I have been so stupid? I was so desperate for him to love me that I ignored all the signs that he didn't. I lied to myself because I wanted to belong to someone, to be happy for the first time in my life.

"Isn't this enough Sophie?"

His taunting words resound in my ears, and the memories of my easy capitulation make me cringe. I hate him, but I hate myself more.

Thankfully, Mrs. Daniels isn't in the apartment. I'm glad that I don't have to face her. I don't want to face anyone. I feel like a failure, a fraud who attempted to take something that didn't belong to her in the first place. I just want to go silently. I take the service elevator to the ground floor, leaving the building through the service entrance. This way there's no chance of running into Steve outside, or seeing the curious looks of the doorman.

The service entrance leads unto a side street. Outside it's clear and sunny. On the worst day of my life, the weather chooses to be perfect.

I walk along the street for a while, eventually, I find a bus station. I don't even know where the bus is going when I climb in, but as long as it will take me far away from David. It's fine with me.

Luckily, I'm in the right bus. After a couple of stops, it goes over the bridge to Bellevue. I make a few enquiries at the station and find a small hotel close to the main street. I intend to stay there only for a little while until I can find a small apartment and a job.

For the next two days, I scour the job listings and respond to ads. I only succeed in getting turned down for jobs as an office assistant, a receptionist, and even as a waitress. At night, alone in my room I succumb to the weariness, heartache, and the pain that thinking of David brings, but I can't stop thinking about him. I can't stop aching for him, wanting him, torturing myself with wondering if he cares that I'm gone.

After three days, I still haven't found a job. After exhausting all the leads from the job listings, I return to the hotel, tired and painfully aware that I have to find something really soon.

I haven't been in my room for five minutes when there is a knock on the door. I haven't ordered any room service, so even before I go to look through the peephole I already have a dreadful suspicion in the pit of my stomach. Yet the sight of David standing outside my room knocks the breath out of my chest. My stomach tightens as a mixture of feelings assault me, confusion, longing, regret, and an overwhelming desire.

I'm not going to open the door.

"Sophie." His voice is gentle, as if he knows I'm just on the other side.

I step back, heart pounding, desperate to get away

from the sound of his voice and the temptation that comes with it. What is he doing here, what does he want?

"Sophie, I know you're in there." He says. "Open the door."

I take a deep breath. I don't know why he's here, but it doesn't change anything. It's doesn't mean that his feelings about our relationship have changed. There's no reason to let myself get affected by his presence, and there's no reason to be afraid of talking to him.

I open the door.

And my heart tightens in my chest.

I love him.

Just looking at him. I want to cry. I want to forget everything that's happened and let him hold me. I devour the familiar planes and angles of his face, the piercing blue eyes, wavy black hair, sensual lips that I've kissed a hundred times.

This has always been about sex.

The memory of his words mock me, and I step back before I let myself be overwhelmed by my desire for him.

He steps inside the room, his tall frame dwarfing the small space. Compared to his apartment, it's little more than a shoebox, but it's not so different from my old apartment in Ashford.

His blue eyes turn in my direction, scorching my face, so intense, that I almost lose myself. His brow creases in a frown. "You can't keep staying here." He states.

I stare at him, barely able to process the fact that he's actually trying to dictate to me, even now. Anger overcomes any longing I feel for him.

"What are you doing here?" I ask, only managing to keep my emotions in check.

"I've been trying to find you for two days Sophie." He takes a deep breath. "Did you think I was going to let you just disappear? Steve was waiting outside to take you anywhere you wanted, but you never came out. I was worried. You weren't in the apartment..." He stops and runs a hand through his thick hair. "Why didn't you go back to Ashford?"

Go back to Ashford. I'm sure your little boyfriend will be more than eager to find you a place in his bed.

I close my eyes against the memory of his words. He really expected me to go back. Did he really believe that Eddie was waiting for me in Ashford, or did he say that just to be cruel?

As if, I could ever choose any other man over him.

I fold my arms over my chest in a defensive movement. "I always had plans to move here."

"Yes, I remember." the gentleness disappears from his voice, "but I didn't think you would do so even though you have no job, no friends, nothing waiting for you here."

"Why do you care?" I retort, "It's none of your business."

"On the contrary, it's very much my business." He sighs and draws in a deep breath. "You may have a very short memory, but let me remind you that you're still my wife."

For how long? I think mutinously. For all I know he's already working on dissolving our short marriage.

"Be reasonable Sophie." He continues more gently. "You can't stay here. It's a dump, and it's not safe."

I wish his voice didn't affect me so much. "Just leave me alone, David."

He moves until he's standing right in front of me, so close that my nose fills with his masculine scent, his cologne, the clean smell of his clothes. All my senses are screaming for more. "Is that what you want?" His tender voice assaults my ears. I look up at him, at the concern on his face. The temptation to shake my head and lean into his chest is so strong. I step back

"Yes." I lie, looking everywhere but at him, I'm not going to be trapped into thinking he cares about me again, and I can't be with him knowing that he doesn't love me. I love him too much for that.

He sighs and steps away from me. "You can have the apartment." He says tiredly, "I'll leave, You don't have to stay here."

As if I could go back there. The idea of living in that apartment, among all the memories of our time together, is not something I can contemplate.

"I don't want your apartment."

"Then what do you want? Tell me, Sophie, because I'm not going to leave you here at this third rate hotel for God's sake."

I close my eyes. Part of me wants him to leave, the other part want everything that's happened to go away, so I can go to him and take comfort in his touch.

"Look," he says when I don't say anything. "Let's be reasonable. You want to stay in Bellevue? Fine. I'll get you a place to live. I have the resources to do that."

I shake my head. "No."

"Don't argue." His tone takes an air of finality. "You are entitled to a lot from me, and I don't mean just because we're married. Much of what I have is yours now. Think about it. You can go to art school, design jewelry, do anything you want. Whatever you want, I won't fight you. You can have anything you want."

I want you to love me. The words are silent in my

head. That's all I want. It's all I ever wanted.

His jaw hardens, "In time we'll have to discuss some sort of settlement…"

It's the word 'settlement' that does it. I don't hear everything else that he says. The thought of lawyers, the finality of a divorce, it makes me want to curl up somewhere and weep. Maybe Aunt Josephine was right, maybe I'm weak, spineless, not worth the space I occupy. Maybe David can see that, maybe that's why he can't bring himself to love me. Desperation floods my stomach. I feel sick.

"I don't want your money," the words come out in a torrent. I feel the sting of tears in my eyes. "You can keep your settlement. I don't want anything from you. Just leave me alone and let me forget that I ever met you."

I hear his sharp intake of breath. "Sophie." He steps towards me, his voice so tender I can't bear it.

"Please David, just leave me alone." I whisper.

"That's the thing," he says, stopping just shy of touching me, "I can't."

I swallow, closing my eyes against the pain and the tears that are threatening to erupt. "It was all a mistake." I can hear my voice breaking, "I should never have left Ashford with you. I should never have…" I'm about to say that I should never have fallen in love with him, but I stop myself.

He takes my hands, and the sudden contact makes me start to tremble. I look up at him. "I'm sorry I've hurt you Sophie." He says, his voice a little rough. "But it wasn't a mistake, not for me. I'm not sorry I met you."

I look down at my hands, entwined in his. I hate that he's talking like this, playing with my emotions, turning me against myself. I pull my hands away. "Well I am. I meant everything I said before I left David. You've hurt me, humiliated me," I swallow the painful lump in my throat. "I never want to see you again."

His eyes close and I watch him take a deep breath, when he looks at me again the pain I see in his eyes is crushing. I have to try very hard to remember the hurtful things he said to me and the utter humiliation he made me feel.

I wait for him to go, but he doesn't move. For a moment, I think he doesn't believe me. We're standing so close, I can feel the heat from his body. I almost imagine that he's going to come towards me, to hold me. My skin heats up in all the places that anticipate his touch.

Finally, he steps back from me. "Just call me if you need anything," he says finally, his voice impersonal.

I nod and look away, waiting silently until he leaves.

Only then do I crumple onto the floor and burst into tears.

Surrender

A Dangerous Man #4

by

Serena Grey

Chapter One

THE PAINTING IS OIL ON CANVAS, _not very large,
but so distinct it stands out from all the other paintings in the
small museum, at least to me._

_Light pours into a small room from an open window, casting
a soft glow that highlights the rosy skin of the girl seated at the
edge of an unmade bed. Her naked back is exposed, and her face
is turned to the side, as if she was about to turn around, towards
the painter. Long gold hair falls in soft waves to the middle of her
back, and you can tell by the slight curve in her cheek, that she's
smiling._

_It's not remarkably beautiful or outstanding, but it's sweet
and sensual at the same time, and yet more than that, it reaches
out to something in me, something that's separate from my misery
and incessant loneliness, something that I can't explain or even
understand. I'm drawn to it. It makes me curious, and somehow
certain that it has the power to assuage my curiosity._

I stumbled across the small museum a few days after I finally found a job at Empathy Zone, a graphic T-shirt store where I process orders and manage deliveries. The museum was only a few blocks down the street from my new workplace, and it drew me in, promising perhaps a few moments respite from my constant dejection, and pathetic mental fixation on the man behind it, the man who broke my heart.

David.

As usual, as soon as his name enters my mind, I lose the ability to think of anything apart from the pain, the intense ache I still carry around with me, every minute of every day.

I force my thoughts my thoughts to return to the painting in front of me, banishing all thoughts of David from my mind. It's only temporary, I know. It's only a matter of time before he invades my thoughts again, making me helpless against the memories.

Blinking back the sudden aching moisture in my eyes, I concentrate on the small printed card below the frame, which displays the painter's name. Jonathan Cutler. I wonder if he's a local painter, or some well-known artist I've never heard of. I remind myself to find out more about him when I get the chance.

I'm so engrossed in my thoughts that I don't hear someone come up to stand beside me. "You're here again." A friendly voice says, startling me.

The voice belongs to Trey Welty, the curator. A middle-aged man with thinning brown hair that's liberally sprinkled with grey, and lively dark eyes that twinkle behind his thick dark glasses.

"Hi Trey." I reply, forcing a smile, even though I don't really feel like smiling. My smiles are probably languishing somewhere along with the pieces of my broken heart. I don't imagine that David's finding it as difficult to smile. In my mind, I can see his easy, relaxed grin directed at someone else. It hurts.

Oblivious to my thoughts, Trey grins at me, and I turn away, unable to stomach the friendliness. He likes to chat whenever I come in, and usually tells me about the paintings and the museum, which is private and non-profit, and funded by a bequest from a long dead heiress. It displays most of her personal collection, as well as some recent purchases.

"It's not our best piece." Trey states, his eyes following mine back to the painting. He gives me a quizzical look, which I ignore. It's not the first time he's commented on my obsession with this particular work of art. At first, he tried to get me interested in the 'treasures' of the museum's collection, but he's since given up.

"I know it's not." I admit with a shrug.

"But you're drawn to it anyway." He nods reflectively. "Sometimes art speaks to parts of our subconscious that we're not even aware of."

It does speak to me in some way, I agree silently. I can't stop looking at it. I can't stop wondering about the two people in the room. They weren't just a model and an artist. I'm sure of it.

Were they in love? Did their emotions rise to some stunning crescendo and then fall, leaving them shattered and heartbroken, like me?

"It has a story behind it." Trey says thoughtfully, interrupting my thoughts again. He glances towards me, waiting for me to indicate that I'm interested in the story, whatever it is.

I am interested. "I hope you'll tell me." I say, encouraging him to continue.

"Of course." He replies, obviously pleased to have an audience. "The painter was an art professor at one of the local colleges, who had some small success as a painter back when he was a young man, but he hadn't painted anything in years."

I nod, waiting for him to continue.

"Well, on their anniversary, about twenty years ago," Trey says, "his wife… she was a poet, I remember, moderately successful too… Well she makes a dinner reservation at a restaurant in Seattle, then she goes to pick him up from his office at the university and drives the car over a bridge with the both of them in it."

"Oh!" My eyes widen in shock. "Why?"

He shrugs. "Who knows? She didn't leave a note, but she did write a poem that day. It was found on her desk, handwritten on a plain sheet and held down with a paper weight, as if she wanted to make sure it would be found. I can't remember what it said, but it sort of pointed towards the fact that she knew what she was doing. One of those 'If I can't have you, no one else will' themes." He looks at me, "Gossip on campus was she found out he was having an affair with one of his students."

A small shudder runs up my spine as I turn back to the painting. There's a certain poignancy in every stroke of color, an aura of love and feeling. How sad! I think, imagining the kind of emotions that would have made the poor woman do what she did. And the painter, how did he feel in the end? Was he resigned, or desperate with the knowledge that he would never see the woman he loved again?

"The student…" I wonder out loud, "She was the girl in the painting."

"It was his first painting in about fifteen years, and it does fit the time." Trey smiles wryly. "The family gave it to the university after their deaths, and when it was auctioned a few years later, we bought it."

My eyes go back to the girl, naked except for a little crease in the bed sheet that covers the most intimate parts of her backside. I imagine her turning around and saying something to the painter, a light teasing smile on her face. "Who was she?" I ask.

"Who knows?" Trey replies, shaking his head, "Just another student who fell for her professor."

That night I dream about the painting, the unmade bed with the rumpled sheets. I imagine the painter, his eyes filled with desire as he sketches his lover. I imagine the girl, her smile turning into a laugh as she turns around, green eyes dancing, her *face as familiar to me as my own.*

I'm wearing a bright red t-shirt with the words 'Welcome to Empathy Zone' printed across the chest in a bright, yellow text, the same words I'm supposed to say with an upbeat cheery voice whenever anyone walks into the store.

My first few days, I kept the big, fake smile within reach, ready to hide the unhappiness I felt, as soon as anyone walked in. Not many people have walked in, thankfully. Well... thankfully for me, not for Jan Rippon and Larry Moss, my bosses, two middle-aged best friends who started the t-shirt company together back when they were still in college.

From what I've learned, the Empathy Zone t-shirts were very popular back in the day, with their signature quirky art and inspiring text. The business succeeded in making both my bosses very rich at a young age. Years later, it's less successful, with most of the new orders coming in from nostalgic old customers.

I suspect that even Larry and Jan don't do it for the money anymore. They're both divorced now, with grown children, and, I assume, investments they live on, because they hardly seem concerned about the lack of sales. Most days, they're content to sit in the back office playing video games while half-heartedly sketching new designs to display on the website.

My job is to process the online orders and forward them to the company that actually makes the t-shirts. I also track the deliveries to ensure our customers get their orders on time. Even though it sounds like a lot of work for just one person, based on the volume of customers, it isn't really. Right now, it's still morning, but I've already caught up on all the pending orders, so I actually have nothing to do.

Naturally, my thoughts return to David.

David.

Even thinking his name causes a hollow ache in my chest. How long will it feel like this? When will I be able to think about him and feel only a faint yearning, or even better, nothing at all?

I read somewhere that the real reason most people can't get over an ex is that they don't want to. Deep down they hold on to the hope that they'll get back together, and that hope prevents them from moving on. These days I can relate to that. The thought of moving on and leaving my feelings for David behind makes me unbearably depressed. The thought of David moving on, the idea of him happy with someone else, it causes a physical pain in my chest that feels like my heart is being torn apart.

He haunts me, day and night, like some part of him is still buried inside me. My memories possess me, keeping me in a state of painful longing. I have to force myself not to freeze whenever I see any random dark haired man with even the faintest resemblance to him. It takes all my will not to cry myself to sleep every night, not to succumb to the dreams where I'm not lonely, not heartbroken, where I'm still happy, and still with David.

Sometimes, my will is not strong enough.

My phone starts to vibrate on my desk, interrupting my thoughts. The silver and black plasticky device is a far cry from the sleek smartphone David bought me, but that was one of the things I left behind when I left him. The fewer things I have to remind me of that life, the better for me.

I'm not surprised to see Stacey's name flashing on the screen. She's been calling me almost every day since I finally told her about leaving David. Though she warned me at the beginning not to rush into marriage with a man I hardly knew, she hasn't given me any 'I told you so' speeches. She's just been incredibly supportive, and I'm very grateful for that.

"Hello." I inject as much cheerfulness into my voice as I can manage.

Stacey isn't fooled. "Hello dear," She replies, the old sound of worry back in her voice, "How're you doing?"

"Perfect." I tell her, still trying to be cheerful. She's been trying to convince me to move back to Ashford and take a job at the local grocery store. In her opinion, I won't be as lonely there as I am in Bellevue, but I know that's not true. I'll be lonely everywhere. I'll be lonely in a roomful of people, as long as David isn't there.

"You don't have to pretend with me Sophie," Stacey says kindly, "I know it's got to be hard."

It is hard. Every day is more painful than the last. I feel like an awful, yearning, mess inside, but I don't want to talk about it.

I don't want to talk about him.

David.

When I stay silent, she sighs. "I wish you'd consider coming back to Ashford."

"I can't." I tell her earnestly, "and it's not just that I don't want to, as soon as I have enough money saved I'm going to take some courses so I can get a job in jewelry design sometime in future." I pause, hoping that this time, she'll actually be convinced to drop it, "I have a better chance of doing all that here than back in Ashford."

"Oh well." She agrees reluctantly. "At least you have a plan. That's a good thing."

I sigh. "I hope so."

She is silent for a few moments. "Have you heard anything from David?" She asks softly.

Just the sound of his name and I feel as if I can't breathe. The permanent yearning ache in my heart intensifies, and I have a sudden desire to burst into tears.

I was so sure when I left him, that it was the right thing to do. When I told him I never wanted to see him again, it was because I was so sure that what I needed most was to start over, without him, that being alone was a better option than being with the man who declared that our marriage, our entire relationship, had always been only about sex.

Now I'm not so sure. After weeks of carrying my loneliness and my desire for him around with me, I'm not even sure how I feel about anything anymore.

Have I heard anything from him? Well no, and that's the part that hurts the most.

The last time I saw David, I told him I never wanted to see him again. He left, and even though I desperately hope that I'm wrong, I'm afraid that now, he has no intention of seeing me again either. I try not to think about how barren, how empty my life feels now, how the possibility of that barrenness stretching for eternity tortures me. I feel like I'm barely holding on, as if any moment I'll break, shatter into pieces that only David can put back together.

The day after I left the hotel and moved into my new apartment, Steve delivered two cases packed with some of my stuff from David's apartment. When the doorbell rang, my heart leapt with the hope that it would be David again, coming to insist that I return to Seattle with him, just like he had at the hotel. I'd been battling with anticipation and dread when I opened the door and saw Steve's bulky frame dwarfing the whole hallway.

"Good evening Mrs. Preston." He'd said, waiting for me to move aside before carrying the cases inside my apartment. If he saw the disappointment on my face, he didn't show it.

I didn't waste any time wondering how David knew that I had moved, and where to. It was David after all. I lingered at the door, looking down the hallway, unhappy at the dawning realization that Steve was alone.

"It's just me." I heard Steve say, his voice a little quieter, graver than I remembered.

I swallowed, embarrassed, then my eyes went to the cases he was still carrying, waiting for me to tell him where to put them.

"What are those?" I asked warily.

"I don't really know." Steve told me. "Mr. Preston wanted them brought here to you."

"I don't want them here." I said. I didn't care what they were. My yearning had already turned to resentment, at David, at myself, at how eager I was to see him again.

"I could take them back," Steve said quietly, "but Mr. Preston would just have me bring them back, or maybe bring them himself."

For a moment, I was tempted. I imagined David in my tiny apartment, beautiful and implacable, fiercely demanding that I listen to him. I flushed, my traitorous body reacting to the image in my mind. No, I decided, his presence would only break down my resolve and fill my mind with the knowledge of how much I want him, not how much he hurt me. I sighed. There's nothing as hard as wanting someone so much it's almost unbearable, and knowing that being with them would be so much worse.

"Just put them down Steve." I said, giving in.

He placed the cases on the floor in a corner of the living room, the largest part of the space that had been artfully split into a sleeping area, living area and a kitchen area. All together, it was still much smaller than any one of the three bedrooms in David's apartment.

Steve straightened. I waited, hoping pathetically that there would be something else, a message from David maybe. "Would you like something to drink?" I offered politely.

"Some water." He accepted, surprising me. I don't think I'd ever seen him eat or drink anything before. I went to the counter that marked the kitchen area and poured him a glass of water, gesturing for him to sit on one of the stools next to the counter. For some reason, I wasn't eager for him to go. Even though he wasn't the object of my obsession, his connection to David made his presence welcome.

"Have you been with David long?" I asked, trying not to be too obvious about the fact that I just wanted to keep talking about David with the first person I'd seen in a few days who knew him too, perhaps more than I did.

"You could say that." Steve replied with a small smile. "I used to drive him around when he was a boy."

I didn't know that, and my face betrayed my surprise. If Steve was surprised at my lack of knowledge about my husband, he didn't let it show.

"What was he like?" I asked, imagining a teenage David been driven around in a chauffeured car, even then he would have been beautiful to look at.

Steve contemplated my question for a few seconds, and then shrugged. "Clever, curious, and adventurous," He said, finishing his water, "Like most boys that age." He paused. "He was also the loneliest boy I'd ever met."

He looked almost sad for a moment, but his usual taciturn expression soon returned. "Mr. Preston also asked me to give this to you," he continued, digging into the inside pocket of his jacket and retrieving an envelope, which he placed on the kitchen counter. "Thanks for the water." He said, getting up.

After he left, I opened the envelope and found the cards for the expense account David had set up for me. I'd left behind in David's apartment for my own reasons. The cases contained some of the things I'd also left behind, clothes and jewelry, phone and tablet. I put the cards in one of the cases and left them all in a corner of my bedroom.

That was almost two months ago. Since then I've heard nothing from David. I've taken to scouring the news for any mention of him. The few articles I've managed to find about his work aren't nearly enough, but I devour them hungrily. Sadly, there's usually nothing about his personal life, nothing about our marriage or separation, nothing about us.

I may very well never have been a part of his life.

"Sophie?" Stacey's voice pulls me out of my thoughts.

"No, I haven't heard anything from him." I reply to her question. And I shouldn't care, I tell myself. In time, I will get over him. I will forget the short time I spent as a billionaire's wife. I will forget David Preston.

Even if I don't want to.

"Have you tried talking with him?" Stacey persists. Sometimes, I think that she imagines that my separation is just temporary, a little hitch waiting to be smoothed out, but she wasn't there, she didn't see the scorn on David's face when I told him that I loved him.

This has always been about sex.

"There's nothing to say." I tell her.

"That can't be true." Stacey urges. "He's still your husband." She reminds me. "Unless you mean to..." She stops talking abruptly, but already I know what she was about to say, unless I mean to get a divorce.

Heaven knows I should want that. I should want to do something about the fact that I'm still legally married to David. It's the clear first step to moving on with my life.

Except, I don't think I want to move on. At least, not right now, and not just yet.

I spend my evenings alone. Sometimes I read, trying to keep my mind occupied, but it doesn't always help. Everything I do ends up feeling like a temporary measure, a small pause until my mind goes back to David, and I start thinking about how much I miss him, how unclear my reasons for leaving him have become, even to me, and how much I wish things could be different.

My apartment is empty and lonely, almost as bare as it was when I first moved in. I took over the lease from Jan and Larry's former assistant who used to live there before he suddenly decided to go to New York to sell his paintings. It's not David's luxury apartment, but its fine. I could barely afford it with what was left of my savings, and although I could have gotten something bigger if I'd used even a fraction of the obscenely large amount of money David transferred to my account, I do not intend to touch his money, now or ever.

It's not his money that I want.

Have you tried talking with him?

It's scary how tempted I am. How willing I am to wrack my brain for excuses to hear his voice again. I close my eyes and remember the sound of my name on his lips, the feel of his breath against my ear when he would whisper something to me, so effortlessly seductive that all he had to do was look at me, and my body would go crazy with need.

Outside the only window, I can see the happy hour crowds walking along the sidewalk. I wish I were one of them. I wish I had nothing on my mind but the thought of a drink with friends at a bar somewhere. I wish I wasn't haunted by the man who broke my heart. I wish I could close my eyes without seeing his face, his sensual lips that I've kissed a thousand times.

I take a deep breath. My sketchpad is lying on the bedside table. Picking it up, I go to sit on my bed, keeping my eyes from going to the cases stacked in a corner the room. I was only tempted to open them once, and seeing the familiar things so well packed by Mrs. Daniels had brought a huge lump to my throat. Later, I'll decide what to do with them. I'll give them away, eventually.

I flick through the pages of the sketchpad, looking at the familiar drawings I've done over the years. Pencil drawings of jewelry, earrings, necklaces all worn by a woman with my mother's face, my mother's smile, the way I remember it from the pictures I've seen. Before David, doing the drawings used to make me feel less lonely, now it makes no difference.

I flip to the last drawing, a half completed one started in Italy, on a sunny afternoon by the pool with David lying beside me, his firmly muscled body gleaming from the sun. He'd caught me admiring him and put my sketchpad away, then we'd made love right there by the pool, our sun warmed skin sliding against each other, fitting perfectly together. Afterward, we'd gone into the pool and made love again in the water.

The memories are enough to make me feel hot, needy, and raw. I close my eyes and take a deep, shaky breath, putting the sketchpad away. It's no use. I haven't drawn anything since that day. I can't complete the drawing without being assaulted by my memories, and I can't move on to the next one.

Soon it's dark outside, another evening, another day gone. It takes a while to go to sleep, and when I finally drift away, my last thought is of the piercing blue eyes I love, and the face that will haunt me until the day I die.

Chapter Two

HAVE YOU TRIED TALKING WITH HIM?

The idea has taken root in my brain, growing and growing until I can hardly think of anything else. It's not as if I've not been tempted before, when the loneliness seems unbearable, to dial his number just to hear his voice again, but I've always been able to stop myself.

This time it's different. The need seems intensified, almost uncontrollable, so much that I'm almost sure I'm going to give in, that it's only a matter of time.

I have no reason to talk to him, I tell myself, trying to be sensible. What would I say? What would be the point? It's not as though the sound of my voice is some sort of catalyst that can change the fact that I mean nothing to him.

If he wanted to talk to me, he would have called me.

He would have come to me. David's not the kind of man to wait for opportunities. He creates them for himself. If he hasn't created an opportunity to see me or speak to me in two months, it must be because he doesn't want to.

So even though I'm dying to hear his voice, even though I want to know that he hasn't forgotten about me, even though I want the assurance that, between his work and his business trips, there's still a part of him that misses me the way I miss him, I'm not going to call him.

On my way out to the store, I run into Bea, the girl who lives in the apartment across the hallway from mine. She's a recent journalism grad who works part-time as a barista in the café down the street, and writes fiction the rest of the time. She introduced herself when we bumped into each other in the hallway the day I moved in, and now most mornings we walk down to the café together on my way to the store.

"Hey you," She greets me with a huge smile. She's striking, with cropped burgundy colored hair and Disney-big, blue eyes in an attractive pixie face. "Looking glum, as usual."

I chuckle despite myself. "Not everyone can be as cheerful as you Bea."

"It's a gift." She agrees, nodding her head sagely.

It really is. It's not as if she has nothing to be sad about. Both her parents died in a car crash during her sophomore year, leaving her alone without any close relatives. Once, when she was feeling talkative, she told me about Jet, the guy who used to live in my apartment. He broke her heart when he suddenly moved to New York. He didn't tell her he was leaving until the day before, even though they'd been dating for more than a year.

As we cross the street, she starts to tell me another detail about Leticia Morse, the British heroine of the Young Adult series she's currently writing, who solves mysterious crimes with her quick wits and intelligence, even though she's just a teenager. Bea hasn't had anything published yet, but she doesn't let the rejections get her down.

"I still think you need a vampire in there somewhere," I offer teasingly, as she explains yet another plot twist, "People love vampires."

"Yeah, right." Bea replies, giving the idea an emphatic thumb down. "Never."

The café where she works is on the ground floor of a building a little further down the street from ours. A charming sign hangs over the doorway with the image of a steaming cup of coffee. The same image is etched on the glass of the door, which Bea pushes open, letting out the welcome scent of freshly brewed coffee.

I step inside, inhaling deeply. A few customers are seated at the tables drinking from steaming cups of tea or coffee. Behind the counter, Bea's friend Luke is already wearing an apron and attending to a couple of customers on a queue. He's a tall guy, cute, with unruly blonde hair and serious looking grey eyes. He looks up when we enter, and his eyes immediately lock on Bea beside me. His face softens as it always does when he sees her.

"Hey Luke." I wave at him.

"Hey Soph." He replies with a quick smile, and then he turns back to Bea. "Hey Bea."

She says hi to him and quickly ducks under the counter, appearing almost immediately on the other side to pick up an apron hanging on the back wall, which she quickly puts on. I watch as Luke reluctantly tears his eyes away from her to go back to serving the people on the queue. He loves her. I realize suddenly, and she doesn't know, she's still stuck on Jet, who didn't love her enough.

What a group we are. I think as Bea makes my coffee. We're the walking wounded, all longing for something we don't have, and trying to conquer the ache that never goes away.

"Here you go." Bea says, handing me a Styrofoam

cup with a thick paper belt, "have fun."

I try not to roll my eyes. "I'm going to work, Bea."

"Then have fun at work." She says with a wink, unrepentant as usual.

I ignore her and wave goodbye to Luke before making my way to the door. I'm already reaching out to push it open when someone pulls from outside and steps in, almost bumping into me, and narrowly escaping a hot coffee bath. I start to apologize for almost scalding him before I realize that I know who it is.

His face is still boyish, but his brown hair is sporting a more grown up cut. He looks older and in his suit, more mature than I remember, but it's undoubtedly Eddie Newton.

He's looking at me, and I see a whole lot of expressions cross his face, a little embarrassment I think, and some pleasure.

"Sophie?" The exclamation is almost a question.

I smile awkwardly, remembering the last time I saw him, almost a lifetime ago. I'm still not sure why he came to my apartment that morning back in Ashford, right after David and I had made love for the first time. I remember the terse words he and David exchanged, and David's assumption that Eddie was in love with me.

Well, Eddie does look very pleased to see me, but that's not proof of love. Not that I know what counts as proof of love, I reason, if I had any idea I wouldn't have allowed myself to be fooled into thinking that David's passionate lovemaking had anything to do with love.

"What are you doing here?" Eddie asks, smiling widely as we move out of the path of the door to exchange an awkward hug.

I force a light-hearted smile and raise my cup. "Getting coffee?"

He laughs. "No, I know. I meant here, in Bellevue."

I knew what he meant. I just didn't feel up to answering his question. "I live here now," I say reluctantly, hoping that he wouldn't press further. I don't want to answer any questions, no matter how well meant, about my life or my failed marriage.

His brows lift questioningly, but he doesn't press it. "I work here too." He says, going on to tell me about his new job at an investment firm.

"It sounds interesting.' Eddie." I say when he's done. "I'm happy for you."

"Thanks." He nods. "It's really great to see you again." He adds earnestly.

Is it? Maybe there's something wrong with me, but it feels awkward to me. I can hear the questions he's not asking, and the last thing I want is to have to deal with them.

"I have to go." I tell him, smiling apologetically as I edge towards the door.

"Oh, right." He frowns and starts to follow me. "I guess I'll see you around?"

Ignoring the invitation in his statement, I just smile, wave, and leave him standing there. I'd rather not see him. I'd rather not wonder how long before he asks me what I'm doing in a tiny Bellevue café when I'm supposed to be married to David Preston.

The store is only a short, fifteen-minute walk from the café. Maybe it's because I ran into Eddie, but as I walk, I start thinking about David again, and that long ago morning back at my apartment in Ashford.

I wonder how things would have turned out if I had let him go, if I hadn't begged him to take me with him. Would I have forgotten about him in time, learned to remember him as no more than just the instrument of my sexual awakening? I remember the desperation I felt that morning, the knowledge that if he left, things would never be the same. Those feelings closely echo the yearning I feel now. There's no way I'd have easily forgotten about him, I realize, then or now.

I'm close to the store when my phone beeps the alert for a text. I reach inside my bag as I walk, and take a quick look, thinking it might be a message from Jan or Larry.

It's another alert from my bank. The first time David transferred money to me was right after he left me at the hotel. The next transfer came a month later. This is the third one for the same, needlessly large amount.

It should be obvious to him by now that I have no intention of spending his money. I haven't used the cards he had Steve deliver to me, and I haven't touched the money paid into my account either.

I feel a faint spurt of annoyance. Is the money his way of paying me off and assuaging his guilt over how he treated me? Does he think the money will ever mean enough for me to forget his cruelty?

The store is still empty when I enter. At my desk, I power on my computer and start to get ready for the day ahead. My movements are practiced and mechanical, my mind shut against the urge I have to pick up my phone and make the call I've been dying to make for too long, especially now that I have an excuse.

I manage to control myself. I process the new orders, reply to some of the posts on the Empathy Zone Facebook page, and drink my coffee, all the while thoroughly ignoring my phone.

Jan comes in after about an hour. He's a tall middle-aged man with a pleasant, slightly lined face, and a very long blond ponytail. He's the friendly, gregarious one of the duo, and while he waits for Larry to arrive, he spends some time telling me about the glory days of Empathy Zone, when the t-shirts they designed were worn by a couple of movie stars and famous musicians.

Larry arrives, and they both go into the back office. It's supposed to be their studio where they create intelligent and artistic graphics for new t-shirts, but I soon hear the tell-tale sounds of the video games they're both addicted to.

I try my best to focus on the things I have to do, and it helps for a while, but later in the day, when most of my work is done, and I have nothing to occupy my mind, it goes back to David, and even though my brain is warning me to control myself, I find my fingers reaching for the beckoning phone.

It's not only because I want to hear his voice, I tell myself as my fingers dial the familiar numbers on the keypad. It's not because I miss him. It's only because I need to tell him that I don't want his money. That is the only reason why I'm calling.

It suddenly occurs to me that he may not have my new number. What if he doesn't pick up? I think in panic as the phone starts to ring on the other side. My stomach knots expectantly. My fingers are clammy and trembling, and there's suddenly not enough air in the room. Maybe I really shouldn't be doing this, I think frantically, feeling weak as his phone continues to ring. I'm about to stop the call when I hear a small click, and then the voice I've been longing to hear for weeks, deep and sensual, just the way I remember, and yet somehow, more incredibly seductive.

"Sophie." That's all he says, but in that moment, I completely forget how to breathe.

It's the way he says my name. I think helplessly as my whole body starts to ache. It feels like a caress, moving from my ears to enfold me like smooth velvet. I feel paralyzed, overwhelmed by emotion. How can he make me feel like this with just one word? I should say something, but I can't seem to find anything in my head that makes sense, all I want is to hear his voice again.

"Sophie?" He says again. This time it's a question.

"Hello." I choke out with a voice that sounds nothing like my own. I'm desperately trying, and failing to get my thoughts and feelings in order. He is silent, but I can imagine him listening, waiting for me to say something. I can imagine the frown on his brow. I can imagine every inch of his beautiful face, his perfect body.

"Sophie, are you all right?"

I hate that he sounds so concerned, because it makes me want to believe that he cares about me. It makes me want to admit that I'm not all right, that I miss him, that I've missed him every moment since I walked away from him.

"I'm fine." I say through the sudden thickness in my throat. Somewhere in my brain, there's the knowledge that I had a reason for calling, but I can't seem to remember.

We're both silent. I search for words, desperate to say something, to communicate anything other than how affected I am just by the sound of his voice.

"I was just thinking about you." He says softly.

My chest suddenly feels too tight. I hate myself for how those words make me feel. I hate the hope that soars in my heart at the simple announcement, and the urge to convince myself that he wouldn't be thinking about me unless he cared.

"David..." I begin tentatively, unsure what I'm going to say. My emotions are all over the place. I've never been so confused. He has only said a few words, but he's already succeeded in stirring my memories, my body, and my heart.

Get real sweetheart, this has always been about sex.

The recollection of his cruel words pulls me out of my traitorous, yearning thoughts. I'm being a fool, I realize, in allowing myself to want him so much it colors my reasoning. Of course, he doesn't care about me. He doesn't love me. He told me so himself, and there no reason to assume otherwise just because he has a voice that sounds like temptation.

"You can't keep sending me money." I say abruptly, forcing all the yearning and desire from my mind. "I already told you I don't want anything from you." Except your love, I add silently.

When he replies, his voice is brusque. "I won't argue about this, Sophie," He says, "The money is yours."

"Why?" I retort, annoyed that he would dismiss my request so swiftly. "As I remember, our marriage was always about sex, according to you, and I'd rather not be paid for sex, David."

"And this is why I finally got a phone call from my darling wife," he says, with a hint of sarcasm, "to be accused of paying you for sex, in addition to all my other crimes."

I flinch at his tone. "I'm not accusing you of anything," I reply stubbornly. "All I'm saying is that I don't want your money."

"Then do whatever you want with it." He says dismissively, sounding annoyed. "You can burn it in the street if you like, along with everything else about me that you now find so distasteful."

"Maybe I will." I fling back.

"For God's sake!" He exclaims exasperatedly. I hear him take a deep breath. "Sophie," he starts calmly, the anger in his voice suddenly replaced by something else, something soft, and tempting, something I don't want… can't bear to hear.

"I shouldn't have called." I mutter into the phone, interrupting whatever it was he was going to say, "I don't know why I thought that anything I want would mean much to you. It never has and it obviously never will." I sigh. "Goodbye David."

I end the connection before he can reply.

All of a sudden, I feel tired, weak, and spent. If David can make me feel like this just from a phone conversation, I have to concede that there's no way I can be hopeful of my chances of getting over him anytime soon.

The rest of the evening is uneventful. I have ample time and opportunity to obsess about the phone call and every word we exchanged. I'm still going over it in my mind when Jan emerges from the back office with a stack of sheets and hands them to me.

They're all sketches for new designs. Sometimes, he or Larry would have a burst of inspiration and actually produce some new work, which they always ask me to look at.

"What do you think?" He asks as I look through the drawings. They're not bad, just a little old fashioned. We always put the new designs up on the website, but people hardly order them. Our sales are from people who remember how the old t-shirts made them feel a long time ago, and order the same ones to try to recapture the feeling.

People living in the past, like me.

"They're good." I tell Jan. "I like them."

"Oh well." He shrugs, looking skeptical. "So…" His tone turns friendly, "What're you doing tonight? Hot date?"

I almost laugh. "Not really, no." I say, shaking my head.

He tuts. "Honey," he says patiently, he calls everybody honey, even the pizza delivery guy, "You can't nurse a broken heart forever."

I frown. Is it so obvious then? Can everyone see the pain I'm feeling inside just from looking at me?

I take a deep breath, but before I can respond to what he said, I hear the sound of the door opening, and I look towards the entrance, ready to smile and say 'Welcome to Empathy Zone!' but the smile freezes on my face, and for the second time in one day, I lose the ability to breathe.

Chapter Three

I'M TREMBLING. I CAN HEAR the roar of blood rushing in my ears. My skin feels hot and cold at the same time, and my heart is hammering violently against my ribs. I can't think, and I can't stop looking at him.

David.

He's standing in the doorway, with the late afternoon sun spilling in behind him, framing his tall figure like some sort of godly aura.

My body reacts immediately, every inch of my skin drawn to him like he's some sort of magnet. I want to go to him. I want to touch him. I want to hold on to him and never let go.

I close my eyes and force some air into my chest. I must be imagining things. There's no way David is actually here, there's just no way. I know that if I open my eyes, he won't be standing at the door.

But he is, looking as unbelievably handsome as I remember. Every feature, from his thick, wavy black hair to his classic nose, sensual lips, and firm jaw, is achingly perfect. I'm staring helplessly, unable to control myself. He is just too devastating.

I hear an intrusive sound, and I reluctantly tear my eyes away from David, turning towards the source. Jan is looking pointedly at me. He clears his throat again.

I frown, confused, unable to get my thoughts in order.

He rolls his eyes. "Welcome to Empathy Zone." He says to David.

I turn back towards the door, where David is still standing, his eyebrows raised as he looks at me, his expression expectant and faintly amused.

Embarrassment heats my cheeks. "Welcome to Empathy Zone." I mutter.

He grins lazily and steps into the store, letting the door swing closed behind him. I find myself staring again. He's wearing a dark suit, with a snowy white shirt and a light blue tie. His face is leaner than I remember, but it works for him, making perfect features stand out even more. No man should look this good, I think, unable to tear my eyes away.

David's eyes never leave my face as he walks

towards me, his gaze like flames licking at my skin, and his steps easy and confident. Jan may well not be in the room at all. He doesn't stop until he's standing in front of my desk, so close that I can smell the subtle hint of his familiar masculine cologne.

I clench my hands together to try to stop them from shaking. I can't get my heart to stop pounding. I'm hot, sweaty, and confused. He's mesmerizing, and I'm mesmerized

"Hello Sophie."

His voice flows over me like a caress. His face is so close that if I just reach out, I can trace my fingers over every inch of skin I love so much. My mouth is so dry I can't even swallow. I want to look at him forever. I want to cry. I don't know what I want.

From the corner of my eye, I can see Jan looking from me to David, but I ignore him. I can't tear my eyes away from David's blue gaze, and I don't want to. Jan clears his throat again, and David turns to him, releasing me from the singular intensity of his stare.

"I take it you're not here for the T-shirts." Jan quips half-jokingly.

David smiles pleasantly. "No, not really." He says, turning back to me. "Sophie and I are …"

"Old friends." I say quickly, cutting him off.

One eyebrow goes up in an expression that's so

heart achingly familiar, I have to look away.

"Yes we're old friends." David agrees, amusement sounding in his voice. "I'm David Preston." He says, holding out a hand to Jan. "Sophie's old friend."

Jan takes it with a smile. "Jan Rippon."

The door to Larry and Jan's office opens and Larry steps out. He's the total opposite of Jan, short, portly, with none of Jan's gregariousness. Like Jan, he's dressed like a college boy, with an Empathy Zone t-shirt, jeans, and trendy sneakers.

"Hello?" He says questioningly, looking from me to Jan to David.

"This is Sophie's 'old friend'," Jan volunteers, "David Preston."

Larry frowns. "Preston Corp?"

There's only a short pause before David nods.

"I've heard of you." Larry says, "Good to meet you." I watch as they too shake hands. Maybe now they can all go inside the back office and bond over video games, I think sourly.

"So you and Sophie are old friends?" Larry asks.

"Yes actually." David smiles charmingly. "I was hoping you would let her leave early today," he says. "I'm planning to take her to dinner."

My jaw drops, but before I can say anything, Jan beams. "Of course!" He says, "Sophie never goes anywhere." He continues, turning to Larry, while I silently plot ways to murder him. "I'm sure we can manage for an evening?"

Larry nods enthusiastically. "That's if Sophie doesn't mind."

They all turn to look at me. I don't want to go anywhere with David. I don't.

Under the force of their combined stares, I cave in.

"I don't mind." I lie.

"Great!" David smiles at my bosses, who finally decide it's time for them to leave us alone together, and go back into their office.

David's eyes find mine again, and I take a deep breath. He's so close, every inch of my skin is tingling in anticipation. I'm assaulted by the memories of what it felt like to touch him, to feel his lips on mine, to feel his breath feathering across my skin.

"Aren't you going to say anything Sophie?" He asks, looking slightly amused. His eyes are gleaming dangerously, sensual and provocative. "Not even hello?"

I swallow, feeling my pulse start to flutter wildly. "What are you doing here?" I ask with bravado I don't feel.

He tilts his head slightly as he looks at me. "I believe we were having a conversation earlier," He says with a careless shrug, "One that we didn't finish."

I shake my head. "I shouldn't have called you." I say tensely. "Maybe you should forget that I did."

He turns away from me to look around the small store. I'm sure he's not really interested in anything Empathy Zone is selling. I wonder what he's thinking, what he's going to say.

He turns back to me. "What if I can't?" he asks suddenly, leaning forward on my desk. "I don't want to forget that you called. I want you to tell me everything that's on your mind."

His nearness is doing things to me. "I've told you everything I have to say." I retort, folding my arms across my chest in a gesture that's supposed to be defensive, but which I know would be useless against him. "I don't want to go anywhere with you either."

He bends forward, coming closer until our faces are only inches apart. "Well I haven't told you everything I have to say." He whispers. His eyes are suddenly dark and fierce, searing into me. He's not even touching me, yet I can feel him everywhere.

"How about 'get real sweetheart, this has always been about sex,'" I give him a challenging glare, "or 'you're a liar as well as a fool.'" I snort dismissively, "I'd say you've said enough."

He flinches, the expression almost imperceptible

and very fleeting. Straightening slowly, he moves away from me. "We need to talk Sophie," He says slowly, "I know you don't want to see me, but I'm sure you can bear just one evening."

If only he knew, I think as I shut down my computer and put on my jacket over my t-shirt, before following him outside. On the curb, Steve is standing by the black jaguar waiting for us. The familiarity of the whole scenario makes my heart ache.

Steve pulls the car door open for me. I smile at him, resisting the urge to tear up. "How are you Steve?"

His smile is warm as he replies. "Fine. Mrs. Preston."

How long had it been since someone called me that? So long that I'd almost forgotten how it sounded. I swallow my reaction. "It's nice to see you again." I say before I step into the car.

Once inside, I deliberately don't look at David. The car starts to move, and I struggle to conquer the tension gripping me as we sit side by side. He's so close, too close. Out of the corner of my eye, I can see his hands spread out on his thighs, palms facing downwards, his long, graceful fingers tapping a silent rhythm.

His face is turned away from me, looking out of the windows. I allow myself the luxury of looking at him, letting my eyes drift from his smooth brow to the shadowed hollows of his cheeks, and to the lips I'm dying to kiss again. I've missed looking at him. I've missed touching him. I've missed so many things. I'm so aware of him I can't focus on anything else.

My whole consciousness is fixed on the fact that he's right there beside me. That if I reach out, I can touch him, the way my fingers are aching to.

I sigh. It feels so familiar to be here with him. If I close my eyes I can easily imagine that things are back the way they were and that we're on our way to the apartment where he'll carry me to the bedroom, slowly undress me and make sweet love to me until my body is totally sated.

My body, but not my heart.

I force myself to stop looking at him. It's no use getting caught up in my feelings when they mean nothing to him. Steve soon pulls up in front of a glass-fronted restaurant with a wide awning over the sidewalk.

Stepping out of the car, I wait as David comes around the back to join me, and I catch myself admiring his beautiful body, shown to perfection in his tailored suit. As I watch, I realize that he's stretching out an arm and that he's going to put it around me, as if we're a regular couple, as if we haven't been apart for months. I stiffen, my stomach knotting tightly. There's no knowing how my body will react to his touch, and I'm not eager to make a fool of myself again, where he's concerned.

He must have seen something in my expression, because he pauses, cocking an eyebrow, as a dry smile curves his lips. He drops his hand and smiles wryly. "Shall we?" He says, gesturing towards the doors.

I follow him, silently wondering how I'm going to fit in an elegant restaurant with my jeans and 'Welcome to Empathy Zone t-shirt'. David however, doesn't seem to care. Once inside, the manager leads us through the main dining area to a curved stairway that leads to a private dining area upstairs. There's only one table for two, and a set of wide windows that look out to a small park. It's cozy and intimate, a room for a couple in love and eager for a romantic dinner alone. It's definitely not the sort of place where I should be alone with David.

The manager pulls out my chair, and I sit, listening with half an ear as he and David discuss wine. After he leaves, David turns his full attention to me.

"I hope you don't mind my picking this place," he says, looking at me intently. "I know it's a little... intimate, but I thought we should have some privacy."

I shrug, schooling my face into a false expression of

nonchalance. "I can't imagine why."

He lifts an eyebrow, then smiles patiently and leans back in his chair. "Because, as I said, we need to talk, and I'd rather not do that in a roomful of people."

"You must have been confident that I would agree to come with you," I observe, "reserving this place beforehand."

"I wouldn't say anything about confidence" He chuckles. "But I certainly hoped you would come."

I swallow and keep silent as I pick up a menu from the table, gazing halfheartedly at the options available. From under my lashes, I can see David doing the same. Finally, he presses a button on the table, and immediately a door opens and a waiter comes in to take our order.

We're both silent. The wine arrives, but I only take a sip of the mellow liquid, intent on keeping my senses about me while I'm in the same room with David. He looks relaxed, as if he has no care in the world. I'm far from relaxed, being so close to him is making me nervous.

"You said you wanted to talk." I say finally, breaking the silence.

"Yes." He nods. "But that can wait." He smiles at me, but I'm not deceived by the appearance of friendliness. He is dangerous to me, and I should be on my guard. "Tell me about you," he urges good-naturedly. "What you've been doing… work and all."

"You already know everything that's been going on in my life." I say, "You knew where I worked without asking me, you know where I live, and I'll bet you know everything I've done in the past two months."

He shrugs carelessly, and I know I'm right.

I sigh. "I really don't want the money David."

"We'll talk about that." He says firmly. There's a small hesitation before he speaks again. "There'll have to be at least some sort of settlement you're comfortable with."

Settlement. That word again.

I study his face, trying to read his expression, but as usual, there's nothing there. A knot of dread forms in my stomach. He wants to talk about a settlement, a permanent arrangement that will signify the reality of our separation and the beginning of a divorce.

I should welcome it, I think. The money aside, I should welcome a divorce, a chance to start again, but the idea fills me with anguish. I won't be able to bear it.

Get a hold of yourself Sophie, I tell myself as I take another sip of my wine. A divorce will hurt. It will break my heart all over again, but pain does not kill, and it won't kill me.

Pain does not kill.

Our food arrives, but I can hardly eat. My stomach is in knots as I wait for David to say something. Finally, he summons a waiter to clear the dishes and then it's just both of us again.

I close my eyes, waiting.

"Sophie." He starts, saying my name softly, almost as if he's not actually calling me, but saying it just to feel it on his lips, like a prayer. I force myself to look up at him.

"You said something about a settlement," I say, the words thick in my throat. "If you want a divorce, just give me the papers." I force my voice to be steady. "I'll sign them."

He looks taken aback, almost shaken, as his brow creases in a frown. For a long moment, he is silent. I realize that I'm gripping the edge of the table.

When he speaks, there's an edge to his voice. "Is that what you want?" He mutters, "A divorce?"

I should say yes. How can I let go of the past if I don't break the only thing still holding me captive to it? Yet I know that being married to David is not the only thing holding me captive to the past. A thousand divorces won't change the way I feel about him.

I look away from him, avoiding his question and the intensity of his gaze. I don't want to see the desire in his eyes. I don't want to hope, when hope will only lead to pain. "Isn't that what you want?" I whisper.

I feel, rather than see him lean forward. "No." He says intently. I look up at him, and the earnest expression on his face almost kills me. "I don't want a divorce, Sophie. I want you."

My heart starts to pound again. I close my eyes and let the words wash over me, letting out a shaky breath as I try to control the emotions rioting in my blood. How is it possible to feel such joy and such pain at the same time? All the feelings I've managed to keep at bay for months rise swiftly to the surface.

"I've tried to give you some space," He continues, his eyes on my face burning and almost wild, "I was still trying this morning, Sophie, because I thought that was what you wanted... needed." He lets out a breath. "Well I'm done trying." He says, his voice firm and determined as those blue eyes burn a hole through me. "I want you Sophie, and I want you back."

Please don't do this, I say silently, opening my eyes. He's still looking at me, waiting for me to say something. I want to tell him how much I've missed him. I want to tell him how thinking of him keeps me awake at night, how he haunts all my thoughts and my dreams. I want to tell him that I love him.

But what would be the point?

"You want me back in your bed," I say softly,

"That's the only place where I ever meant anything to you."

His jaw clenches visibly. "You're wrong." He says.

"Am I?" I counter, "I don't think so. You spent our marriage living a life you never shared with me, flirting with you ex-girlfriend…." My voice catches in my throat as the memory of him and Carole kissing on the hotel terrace tears at my heart. "You never shared anything about yourself, your work… What we have isn't a marriage, it's a one night stand gone on too long."

He chuckles darkly, shaking his head. "And what would you know about one night stands Sophie?" he says, his voice a sardonic lash. "You want to know about me? Maybe I should write a damn autobiography starting from the day I was born. Would that make you happy?" He doesn't wait for a response before going on. "You want to know about what I do? Maybe you'd like to join me at the office every day, or would weekly reports be fine for you?"

I recoil from the sting of his words. "It wouldn't." I say frankly, "Nothing you do would make me happy."

He swallows, then leans back and runs a hand through his hair, messing his already tousled locks. "That's not true." He says.

I stare at him. My eyes going from his beautiful face

to the powerful body barely curbed in his tailored suit. No, it's not true, I admit to myself. He could make me happy. He could make me happy if he loved me.

"You don't love me." I whisper.

He doesn't say anything, confirming the truth of my words by his silence.

I draw in a sharp breath. Of course, he doesn't love me. What did I expect? That he came to find me because he'd realized in my absence that he couldn't live without me?

"Isn't enough that I can't stop thinking about you Sophie?" he says, his voice low and persuasive. "What else do you want from me?"

Love, but that's always been too much.

"Nothing, David. I don't want anything from you." I get up and pick up my bag, making for the door, and my escape from the temptation that he is.

He springs up after me, his movements fast, yet undeniably graceful. "Sophie." He says, making me stop. "Please wait."

What's the distance between wanting and love? I think as I turn around. How can he claim to want me so much and yet find it so impossible to love me?

He was standing right behind me, so that when I turn, I'm directly facing him, and our bodies are only inches apart. I look up at his face. Somehow, I know he won't move closer unless I ask him to, even though the desire I can see in his eyes is so intense, I can feel it burning through my skin, heating my blood.

Suddenly, I know I don't want to go. I know I'll succumb to the desire that's been building up since I laid my eyes on him. I barely notice as my bag hits the floor. The only thing that matters is the anticipation coursing through me as I reach up and pull his face towards mine.

Chapter Four

I'M ON FIRE, FALLING APART, trembling, and so hungry for him. His lips move over mine, and I moan softly, inviting his tongue to delve deeper into my mouth. He groans, and his arms encircle me, so strong and muscular as they pull me to him, molding my body tightly against his. He feels so familiar, and yet so different, hungrier, his body claiming control of mine with more urgency than I remember.

I press my aching body tighter against him, losing the last remnants of my self-control, and offering myself to him. I pull at his clothes, all the while moaning my wild and uncontrollable need. I'm helpless against the longing, the desire, the feeling of exultation that fills my chest as his warm body presses against mine, the hard evidence of his arousal stiff against my thighs.

I don't care where we are. I don't care about the voice of reason in my head, telling me I'll regret this. All I care about is being closer to his raw heat. I want him to give my body the satisfaction only he knows how to give me. I don't care about what comes after. All that matters is now, the heat in my belly, the fire in my blood, the warm pool of desire gathering between my legs.

His hands are under my t-shirt, moving slowly over my heated skin. I groan as they move up to cup my breasts, finding my aching nipples through my bra.

"Do you know how much I've missed this?" He whispers huskily. "Do you have any idea how crazy you've been driving me?"

I can't find the words to tell him how much I've missed his touch. My eyes find his, and I beg him silently not to stop. As if he can hear my thoughts, he starts to knead my breasts while teasing my nipples with his thumbs. Desire throbs insistently between my legs. I've wanted him for too long. I want him now.

He claims my lips again, his tongue teasing mine boldly. I reach down and wrap my fingers around him, stroking his rigid arousal through the fabric of his trousers. I hear him groan harshly as he grows even harder against my fingers.

Suddenly his hands leave my breasts and find the

hem of my t-shirt, pulling it up and over my head. I help him, eager to return to touching him. He undoes my jeans and pulls them down, going down on his knees to pull them off totally. Once they're gone, his hands cup my butt and pull me close to him while he's still on his knees. I gasp when I feel his lips on me, warm through the lace of my panties, nuzzling and kissing me. It's so blatantly erotic my knees buckle, and only his firm hands keep me upright. I push closer to his delicious lips, grinding against him as warm, pulsing heat floods between my legs.

Impatiently, I reach for my panties and pull them down, baring myself to him. With a soft groan, he reaches for me again, pulling my hips closer to his face, and his tongue plunges between my legs.

My fingers are digging into his shoulders. I hear myself groaning, crying, and begging, as he teases me until I'm delirious with pleasure. His tongue moves expertly over the center of my arousal, licking and sucking me until my body is pulsing so madly I feel as if I'll explode. Then he stops and rises slowly back up on his feet, his lips trailing kisses up my body, and his hands supporting me so I don't collapse.

He unhooks my bra and pulls it off. I hear his sharp intake of breath as my breasts are bared to his eyes.

"You're so perfect." He says tenderly, his thumbs

finding the erect tips and squeezing each nipple gently, with just enough force to make me want more. "Did you miss this Sophie?" he asks.

"Yes." I whisper.

Then I'm moaning again as he bends his head to tongue each erect nipple, one, and then the other, until they're both swollen and aching sweetly.

He moves away from my breasts, and his lips find mine, hot and demanding. I dig my fingers unto his hair and pull him closer, feeling his hands enclose my thighs as he lifts me easily, pressing me against his straining arousal. I moan and wrap my legs around his waist, rubbing myself against him, eager to feel him deep inside me.

Still carrying me, he moves until I can feel the wall at my back, then his fingers find me, slipping into my wet core, rubbing and stroking the most sensitive part of me. I strain against him, my back arching as his fingers move slowly in and out of me.

I can't take it anymore. "David," I moan, reaching for his zipper, but he's there before me. I feel his trousers fall, and then his hands are around my waist, holding me still as he positions himself so I can feel the tip of his arousal pressing lusciously against me, then he grinds his hips forward, plunging inside me.

I gasp for breath, my body tightening as he goes so

deep inside. He's so hard, and so incredibly sweet I feel as if I'm losing my mind. My hips move, urging his hot length deeper inside me as my hands roam under his shirt, over the hard, sweat-slicked surface of his chest.

"David." I moan urgently.

He is shaking, his jaw clenched, and his body tense. His eyes meet mine, and they're dark and smoky with desire. He looks totally aroused, and incredibly beautiful.

"Please." I hear myself say.

Slowly he starts to move, stroking sweetly in and out of me, until my legs feel weak and boneless, until I can't feel anything, only him, only his slow, sweet, tortuous movements inside me.

I lose myself to the pleasure, pulsing and needy, moaning and panting as my body tightens around him. He groans, leaning his hands on the wall, as he starts to move faster, thrusting with sure, slick movements of his hips. I'm going to explode, I realize as my body bows and arches off the wall. I clutch his shoulders, my voice rising as my breath comes out in a long high moan. His lips cover mine, swallowing my scream as my body explodes around him, the same moment, I feel him stiffen and thrust hard one last time, his body shuddering fiercely as he groans out my name.

We stay there for a while, him still inside me, both

of us breathing deeply as we lean on the wall. He's still almost fully dressed, while I'm completely naked, my legs shaking and wrapped around his waist.

"Come home," He whispers against my ear, his voice rough.

Oh, I want to. I'd like to follow him wherever he goes. I want to give him anything he wants, and why wouldn't I, when he's just made me feel so good. He's still inside me, and where we're joined, I can still feel a sweet pulsing ache.

"Come home Sophie." He says again.

My eyes focus. My fingers are threaded in his hair, my breasts pressed against his chest. Right in front of me, I can see the door the waiters have been coming through. I know no one will come in while we're like this. No one will come in unless we ring the bell.

But still, we've just had sex in public, in a restaurant.

I pull back from him, pulling my fingers from his hair, and pushing against him until he lets me go. I ignore the aftershocks of pleasure that run through me as he slips out of me, trying to stop my trembling as he sets me on my feet.

Why does this feel so familiar?

It's hard, but not impossible to find the answer buried somewhere under the lingering cloud of arousal in my brain. This is David, and sex is his weapon.

He's standing in front of me, towering over me. I stare at his shirt, noticing that I pulled off at least three buttons. "I have to go." The words come out in a whisper.

"No, you don't."

I move away from him and start to dress, hurriedly pulling on my clothes. "I think I do." I hiss angrily. "You're obviously not…" I pause and take a deep breath. "You said you wanted to talk David," I accuse him, "but of course it's much easier for you to make me want you, and then make your demands when the last thing on my mind is saying no."

His face hardens. I watch as he starts to adjust his clothes, his movements swift and mechanical, but still so mouthwateringly graceful.

"Aren't you going to say anything?" I ask, as the silence stretches, "Aren't you going to at least try to explain why you brought me here telling me that you wanted to talk while all you wanted was to break me down the best way you know how?"

"What would you like me to say?" he mutters. "You think what just happened here was about me trying to coerce you into doing something you don't want? Well I wanted you, Sophie. I wanted you so much I wouldn't have cared if the whole restaurant could see us. How about considering that for a change? That all night I've wanted you, that I'd have eagerly taken you on the table, on the chair, anywhere in this room." He glares at me. "You want me to apologize for that? Well I'm not sorry."

Why am I suddenly trembling and needy, wanting him again? I take a deep, shuddering breath. "And it's always about what you want, isn't it?" I say, fighting to control my desires, "Well this is what I want David, I want you to leave me alone."

He doesn't say anything. He watches me silently as I pick up my bag and leave. Outside, the wind is strong and salty, mingling with the salt of the tears I'm trying, and failing to keep from falling as I hurry along the sidewalk.

Chapter Five

"AH! HERE'S YOUR CUTE FRIEND AGAIN." Bea says with a wink as she hands me my coffee. I've been silent all morning, though she doesn't let that bother her. Probably, as far as she's concerned it's just another dimension to my constant melancholy. I wonder what she would say if I told her about David, about last night.

I turn around, following the direction of her gaze. Sure enough, Eddie is walking into the café, coming towards us with a smile on his face. "Sophie." He greets cheerfully.

"Hey Eddie."

"Hey Eddie." Bea chips in with a sly wink in my direction.

I roll my eyes at her, but she ignores me, taking Eddie's order, while smiling cheerily at him. From the

327

other end of the counter, I notice Luke looking from Bea to Eddie with a curious expression.

Eddie turns to me, and his eyes fall on the front of my t-shirt, another variation of the 'Welcome to Empathy Zone' theme. "You work there?" he asks, gesturing towards the words on my chest.

I nod.

"Oh." He looks pleased, "It's right on my way," he says with a smile. "If you're on your way there right now, we can walk together,"

"I'm not ready to leave yet." I tell him, ignoring the obvious, fake choking sound Bea makes as she hands him his coffee.

Eddie looks hurt. "Okay." He turns to leave, then pauses. "I just hoped we could have a drink sometime." He says with a boyish, hopeful smile. "That's if you don't mind."

I start to tell him that I'd rather not, but I catch myself. Is this what I'll do for the rest of my life? Push people away because of David? After last night, I don't know where we stand, but I know all my efforts to get over him have been set back years, if not decades.

"I don't mind." I tell Eddie, forcing a bright smile onto my face. I watch his face lights up in response. "I'd love to have a drink sometime."

"Great!" he says, still smiling as I give him my

number. He enters it on his phone, and then waves awkwardly at Bea and me before leaving.

I watch him walk outside, suddenly not sure how I feel about going anywhere with him when just last night David and I were making love against the wall of a restaurant.

I snap out of my thoughts at the sound of Bea's voice. "What?"

"I said, he likes you." She repeats.

I shake my head. "You don't know that."

"I'm not blind." She says with a smirk. "If he likes you, you should give him a chance."

"Like you're giving Luke a chance?" I ask. Luke is serving the only customer on the queue, but that doesn't prevent his eyes from wandering over to Bea again and again. As soon as she turns to look at him, he looks away.

"Luke's my friend." She says dismissively, "and we've known each other for ages." She shrugs. "Plus I haven't gotten over Jet."

I frown, trying to imagine how it must have felt when she found out the man she's been dating for over a year was moving away without even factoring her into his plans. It must have been devastating.

I look over at Luke, and his eyes are on Bea again. No, I'm not mistaken about this. He wants her.

I turn back to Bea. "Just because you've known each other for ages, he can't be in love with you?"

She frowns. "He's not." She says firmly. "Hey, Luke." She turns towards him, her voice challenging. "Sophie thinks you're in love with me."

He stares at her, his speechlessness a slightly more embarrassed version of my own. His throat bobs as he swallows. "Of course not," He says thickly. "That would be ridiculous."

Bea turns back to me, her triumphant smile a little dim. "You see?"

"I... yeah." I turn an apologetic glance towards Luke. "I'm going now." I tell Bea.

She has a small frown on her brow. "Yeah... see you later." She says, without looking at me.

The day passes slowly. Larry isn't coming to the store, Jan tells me, because his son is graduating and giving the valedictory address.

"He's really going to ogle Stephanie," He adds with a laugh. "That's his ex-wife, and he's still crazy about her."

I frown, wondering what the right reply is to that particular bit of information. *I'm still in love with my estranged husband as well, only last night we had sex, in a restaurant, up against the wall.*

And it was amazing.

"I should be there too," Jan continues, oblivious to my thoughts. "But Jo - that's my ex – will probably be there and things never go well when we find ourselves in the same room."

"Are you still in love with her?" I ask boldly, thinking that perhaps we're all stuck in love.

"Hell no!" He barks out a laugh. "We hate each other's guts. You know, we went in expecting so much from each other, with neither of us prepared to give anything." He shakes his head, "That never works."

"What if you give everything you have," I ask contemplatively, "and the other person just isn't ready to give anything."

Jan shrugs. "I'm no expert." He says, "If I were, I'd still be married." He studies my face. "So how'd your date go last night?"

We had mind-blowing sex, in a restaurant, up against the wall.

I close my eyes against the memory. "It was okay." I tell Jan, forcing a small, lighthearted smile.

When I leave the store later in the day, I walk down to the small museum down the street. Inside, it's quiet as usual, with hardly anyone around. I make my way over to my painting, as I've come to think of it, the painting I always end up looking at.

It's still in the same position, and nothing has changed about it. The young woman is still half turned towards me, perpetually in motion, looking as if any moment she would turn completely around and I would see her face.

But I don't need to see it. I already know, without a doubt, whose face it is. It's the face I've been drawing all my life. It's my mother's face.

I try to imagine what she would have said when she turned fully towards the painter, her married professor. Would they have talked about his wife? How wrong their relationship was? Did they plan their future together, or did they decide to enjoy it for as long as they could and then let it go?

I've searched the name of the painter online. There's a small article on the university's website about his work there. I also found a few news articles about the murder-suicide, some of his wife's poems and the haunting last poem she wrote before she drove herself and her husband off a bridge.

> *Don't tell me love is not forever*
> *Mine will only die when we close our eyes*
> *One last time*

I remember Aunt Josephine's taunts. Her favorite

words to describe my parent's relationship had been "sordid affair" It's agonizing to think that she was right. That my mother was instrumental in shattering someone's heart to the point where her only recourse was to drive her car off a bridge.

And even then, my love will take root
Grow, and last for eternity

However, was it her only recourse? Is it right to hold on to a love that isn't returned? Aren't I better off letting go of my feelings for David instead of holding on to a love that never was, and never will be mine?

I close my eyes, and when I open them, the painting is still there, and just looking at it, I can't escape the aura of love, the feeling that there's some intense emotion in the room. No, it wasn't a sordid affair. It was much more than that. I wonder sadly if my mother knew then that she was pregnant. I wonder if my father would have wanted me.

I sigh. What does it matter? He died, and even though, unlike Modigliani's wife, my mother didn't throw herself out of a fifth floor window in grief, she'd still died and left me alone.

I'm still at the museum when Eddie calls me on my phone. As usual, I've spent so much time looking at the painting, that the day has gone and left me behind.

"How about today?" He asks.

"How about what today?"

"Our drink." He explains with a cheerful laugh.

"Okay…" I force a smile into my voice. "Where?"

The lounge he has chosen isn't too far away. It's a casual place with an extensive menu, which includes light food and drinks.

"So how long have you been in Bellevue?" Eddie asks when we sit. He looks curious and interested.

"A few months," I reply, trying to listen as he keeps on talking, and wondering why I can't get into the conversation, why half the words he's saying seem to blur into each other. He is charming and nice, recommending drinks he thinks I might like, dishes I should try, asking me if I like my food…

But he's not David.

Tell me, is it Eddie Newton who's going to be picking up the pieces of your broken heart, or will it be somebody else?

Another one of the cruel things David said to me. How he could imagine that I could ever contemplate leaving him for Eddie, I still don't know. I can't even get through an evening with the same Eddie without thoughts of David making it impossible for me to enjoy myself.

"So what happened?" Eddie has been talking, but I only hear the last three words. He's looking at me expectantly, like I'm supposed to say something

"Sorry." I say apologetically. "I wandered off."

He chuckles wryly, "Yes," he says, "You've been doing that."

I sigh. "Eddie…"

"No, it's fine." He shrugs. "I was saying... I heard that you'd married David Preston," he gives me a curious look. "So what happened?"

I frown and look down at the shrimp skewers on my plate. I haven't eaten much. I think about Eddie's question. What happened with my marriage? My husband didn't, doesn't love me, and I couldn't bear it?

"I'd rather not talk about that?" I reply quietly.

He nods sympathetically, "I understand." He says.

Afterwards, he insists on walking me home. I don't object, he must be a glutton for punishment, I think silently, if he wants more of my company.

"When was the last time you went to Ashford?" He asks conversationally, as we walk along the sidewalk.

"Not since I got ... Not since I left."

He looks thoughtful. "You must miss Mrs. Carver."

"I do." I smile, thinking if Stacy and her anxious, concerned phone calls, "but we talk on the phone."

We walk in silence the rest of the way. Eddie seems to have given up on drawing me into a real conversation. I wish I could put aside my thoughts and my memories and actually have a good evening with a guy who seems genuinely interested in me. But it's just not possible, especially not when, as I turn from the sidewalk unto the brick walkway in front of my building, I see the silver BMW parked down the street, glinting in the streetlamps.

My heart skips a beat as I study the familiar car. It's too far away so I can't know for sure. Still, it can't be him, can it?

I'm trying to stay calm, while Eddie, oblivious to the sudden change in me, walks beside me until we get to the door.

"Thanks for tonight." He says politely.

"Thanks for putting up with me." I say with a small smile, thinking of the car parked only a few feet away.

He shrugs. "I'm sorry about your marriage," He continues, "though I'm glad we could have this drink tonight."

I steal another glance at the silver BMW, but its dark inside and I can't see anything. "It was nice to hang out Eddie." I say distractedly.

He nods, his lips pressed together, as if he's deep in thought. "You know," he starts, "When we were kids, I used to watch you." He says, "I usually had to wait hours just for you to come out of the house. You hardly ever did, your aunt kept you pretty locked up most of the time.

I chuckle wryly. "Yes she did..."

"But I did get to see you a couple of times," Eddie says, an earnest look taking over his features. "I used to stare out of my window at you when I was supposed to be doing my homework." He smiles. "Even then I thought there was something enchanting about you."

I try to remember those days of being homeschooled by my reclusive aunt, escaping outside whenever I got a chance to draw on my sketchpad. If the popular kid who lived opposite had been watching me every day, I had been totally unaware of it.

I bite my lip, wondering what to say. What does one say to a declaration like that?

"I guess somehow, I always hoped that one day, you and me..." He laughs self mockingly and shakes his head. "I don't know."

"You hoped that we would be together?" I finish for him.

He nods, "But then you met David Preston and got swept off your feet, I guess."

I smile wryly. "I did, didn't I?"

"Yeah, you did." He pauses. "When I saw you here, in Bellevue, and well... I began to hope..."

I start to shake my head.

"I know." He says, "I don't know what happened with your marriage, but even I can see that your mind is far away from here, and I'm just a guy on the outside who can only look in."

"I..." I'm not sure what I'm going to say, which useless platitude to choose, so I just stay silent.

He smiles and starts to move closer, whether for a kiss or a hug I never get to find out. Out of the corner of my eye, I see an unmistakable figure emerge from the silver BMW and the door slams so loud, Eddie jumps.

I turn towards the street, and see David walking towards us. Eddie follows the direction of my gaze, and when he sees David, his expression turns into something that looks like alarm, and he steps back from me.

David's face is expressionless, but that doesn't do anything to temper the air of danger he's exuding. His long stride is loose and relaxed, but purposeful. I find myself thinking of a jungle cat, an extremely beautiful and dangerous jungle cat.

"Obviously," He says lazily, with a small, humorless smile in Eddie's direction, "You're not kissing my wife tonight." He turns towards me, "Hello Sophie." He says, cobalt eyes burning. I glare back at him.

"What are you doing here?" I ask.

"Checking on my wife, obviously," he replies, with a thorny smile that doesn't quite reach his eyes. He turns back to Eddie. "You were just leaving?" He asks, his dismissive tone indicating that it's not really a question.

Eddie turns me. He shrugs apologetically. "Goodnight Sophie." He says, then turns and walks past David to the sidewalk.

I watch him walk away, seething quietly. "Why did you do that?" I hiss at David, annoyed with his behavior, and with myself, because regardless of everything, I'm desperately happy to see him.

"Do what?" He looks at me, brows raised. "He was about to maul you and you didn't look particularly excited at the prospect..." He pauses and raises his perfect eyebrows. "Or was I mistaken?"

"You're mistaken in thinking I need your protection." I snap, "and he wasn't about to maul me, he was just saying goodnight."

"So I didn't actually interrupt anything did I?" David says with a shrug, "He still got to say goodnight."

"Whatever." I mutter, "Goodnight David."

"I came to apologize," He says quickly, the words stopping me from flouncing into the building. "I came to apologize for last night." He sighs. "Sophie, I don't want you to feel that all you mean to me is sex, because even though I can't seem to stop myself from wanting you so badly that it drives me crazy, you do mean a lot more to me."

I blink. Of all the things I expected him to say, I didn't expect this. It's not enough, of course, but it's something.

"What exactly?" I ask.

He frowns. "Excuse me?"

"What exactly do I mean to you?"

He runs a hand through his hair. "A lot."

I sigh, hating that even now he still can't give me what I want, hating that I almost don't care, hating that I want him so much, regardless. I'm a slave to my desires where he's concerned, and I hate it. I can't let this continue, I decide. I have to move on with my life, the one that doesn't include him.

"I want a divorce." I say, surprising even myself as I speak the words out loud.

He seems to freeze. His eyes pierce me, almost glacial in their intensity, but he doesn't say a word. The silence is heavy and oppressive. Immediately, I want to take the words back, to unsay them and wipe them from his memory, because I don't really want a divorce, I want him to tell me that he can't live without me, I want him to love me as much as I love him, helplessly, hopelessly and totally.

I watch his jaw tighten. When he finally speaks, his

voice is harsh. "Why?" He asks, his eyes dark and furious, "because of that little boy who was trying to kiss you a moment ago? Does he know where you were last night?" He snaps. "What you were doing, with me? Or doesn't he mind sharing as long as he gets a taste."

I close my eyes against his taunting words. "Stop it." I almost shout.

"Why should I?" he demands angrily. "Am I supposed to just disappear, make it easy for you to forget about me?"

"Well you had no problem disappearing before." I accuse. "I heard nothing from you for two months."

"Well that was because I listened to you when you told me to leave you alone, remember. But I'll be damned if I'm going to make the same mistake twice, because we both know you didn't really mean that," he says, his voice cutting, "You don't really want me to leave you alone, do you, Sophie."

I hate his mocking tone, and more than that, I hate the fact that he's right. "Why do you always have to do this?" I cry angrily, "Why do you always have to be so hateful?"

"Because I love you, Sophie," The words burst out of him, freezing me in place. He freezes too, and stares at me, his face panicked, looking as if he's only just realized what he said. My heart starts to race expectantly. I feel as if I've been doused in water that's both hot and cold, and my body is freezing and scalding at the same time. I step forward, towards him, my whole body attuned to the words that are now hanging in the air between us, heavy and full of meaning.

He takes a step back, and I watch, hope dying in my chest as his face shuts down, turning impassive as he retreats behind his wall. "I have to go." He says, his voice suddenly clipped and impersonal.

I don't try to stop him. My chest is aching strangely as I watch him stride to his car and drive away. I feel more confused than I've ever felt in my life.

I want to sit on the steps and cry my eyes out. I want to know why the thought that he could be in love with me is enough to make him shut down so totally. Sadly, I turn around and notice Bea standing just inside the door, her eyes wide open. She pushes the door open and steps out into the night.

"Who on earth was that hottie?" She asks incredulously, "and was I dreaming, or did I just hear him say that he's in love with you?"

I sigh. "He's my husband." I hear myself say.

Bea's eyes widen even more, looking as if they're about to burst out of her head. For the first time since I met her, she seems to have nothing to say.

"And he either said it," I continue wonderingly, "or we both just had the exact same dream."

Chapter Six

BEA DOESN'T LEAVE MY APARTMENT until I tell her everything, from the beginning.

"Wow." She keeps saying, over and over again.

"Sounds like you've both come a long way." She says finally, when I finish.

"Have we?" I shake my head. "I think we're still stuck in the same place, Bea. I love him so much, but he's so... he's so complicated."

"He obviously wants you back." She offers.

"Yes but..." I sigh. "I don't know if I can trust him. For him, it's all about sex."

"Honey," Bea chuckles, "A guy who looks like that doesn't have to drive thirty minutes for sex."

"So you think..." I don't say the words, they mean too much.

"Yeah, I think he does love you, a guy who's not

interested forgets about you as soon as he's out of the door." She says with a sniff, "Trust me, I know." She smiles reassuringly. "But give it some time, Sophie. Think about it, and maybe talk to him okay? Before you make any decisions."

The next day, I finish early from work and take a cab to David's office in Seattle. It occurs to me, as I stand on the sidewalk in front of the impressive building, that in the short time David and I were together, I never came here. I shake my head. On the surface, that's another argument for the fact that our marriage wasn't really a marriage at all, and even though I know now that the main reason why we never really went out together had to do with issues David was facing with his company at that time, it still feels odd.

The security guard directs me to the main reception, where I get some curious glances form the front desk personnel. I expect them to call, to confirm from someone in David's office that he would want to see me. However, the efficient looking girl in charge hands me an access card almost as soon as she hears my name, even though I used my maiden name.

"Why don't you show Mrs...Ah...Miss Bennett to the elevators?" She asks one of the security guards.

So they know who I am, I think as I follow the

guard to one of the elevators. Had David always anticipated that one day I'd come here wanting to see him, and taken steps to make himself accessible to me? I frown, more confused even than last night. When it comes to David, I don't know what to think anymore.

A pair of glass security doors slide open almost as soon as I step out of the elevator, and I walk into the large reception area. The receptionist smiles a greeting at me, but before I can talk to her, David's assistant, Linda Mays, emerges from behind another set of wide glass doors, impeccable as always in a white silk blouse and another beautiful pencil skirt.

"Hello, Mrs. Preston." She says, her smile almost managing to crack her efficient manner.

"Please," I shake my head. "Sophie."

She shrugs elegantly, "Well come in." She says, leading me inside the office floor. "Mr. Preston has been in a conference call, but it should be over in a few seconds," She gives me a look, "So he doesn't know you're here, yet."

I nod, wondering if David will be pleasantly surprised or whether he'll feel the opposite. I follow Linda to a door at the end of the floor, past an office where a guy in a suit and nerdy glasses is talking emphatically into an earpiece.

"That's Cole." Linda tells me, gesturing towards the

guy, "He's Mr. Preston's other assistant."

The guy looks up at us and smiles, but keeps talking into his earpiece.

We stop in front of an opaque glass door. Linda glances at her phone screen. "You can go in now." She says, surprising me with another small smile.

"Thanks."

She leaves me standing at the door. I take a deep breath and push it open, stepping into David's office.

It's larger than any office I've ever been in, with about three different seating areas each one larger than my living room. There's a huge screen with various news channels showing all at once, and a huge desk, which dominates the room from the center. It's an office for a successful man, a powerful one. A man who can have anything he wants, anyone he wants.

What am I doing here?

I step farther inside the office, letting the door swish shut behind me. David is seated behind the desk, his back to me, and his face turned towards the glass windows that look out onto the city.

"Yes Linda?" he says, not bothering to turn around. He sounds tired, and I get the feeling that he would rather be alone.

"It's me David."

He shoots out of his chair, turning to look at me,

his expression turning from surprise to wariness, before the shutters come down, and his face is unreadable again. "What are you doing here?" he asks.

Last night you said you love me, David, is that true?

The words are on the tip of my tongue, but I don't say them, instead, I shrug. "I wanted to talk." I say lightly, "and I thought it would be nice to see where you work."

"Did you?" He regards me coolly, his impassive mask already making him look distant, as if just yesterday he didn't say the three little words that made my heart almost explode.

I nod.

"Well now that you've seen where I work," He says, "What do you want to talk about?"

I move forward, towards the desk. "I'd like to know that this won't end like our 'talking' did at the restaurant."

His eyebrows go up, and he chuckles, eyes glinting dangerously. He seems so in control, so relaxed, while I'm still reeling from what he said last night. He leaves his place behind the desk and walks towards me until he's so close I can feel the heat from his body. I stiffen automatically. Being this close to him does things to me, things I shouldn't even be contemplating.

"I wouldn't touch you unless you ask." He says with

a shrug, turning to go back to his desk. "I was just about to leave." He continues. "So you should tell me whatever it is you want to say. Although," he pauses. "If it's another request for me to stay away from you, perhaps you shouldn't bother. I'm done banging my head against that particular wall."

I can't believe what he's saying. He can't mean that he's just going to let go, even after last night"

You said you love me David.

I swallow. "I…" Why am I stammering? "Where're you going?"

He shrugs indifferently. "Home." He replies, "Where did you think?" He gives me a look. "Perhaps there's something about being around you that exhausts me." He adds wearily. "I'd ask you to come with me, but I wouldn't want to scare you."

"I'm not scared." I reply. "You said you wouldn't touch me unless I asked."

"And you believe me?"

"Shouldn't I?"

He shrugs again.

"Well then… since I'm sure I won't ask, there's no reason why I should keep you here when we can talk at… your apartment." I smile at him.

Downstairs Steve is already waiting outside the front of the building. As soon as he sees us, he opens the door of a black SUV parked behind him on the sidewalk. I follow David inside, smiling in reply to Steve's greeting. I notice that when his eyes fall on David, his expression turns to one of concern.

Once we're inside the car, I turn to David, and notice that he's sweating.

Why is he sweating? I can't be having that much of an effect of him, can I?

"Are you all right?" I ask.

He turns to me, his eyes momentarily unfocused. "I'm fine." He says tersely.

The drive to the apartment is short. As I climb out of the car. I falter for a second, assaulted by the memories and emotions rising in my chest as I take in the familiar building.

David walks ahead of me, then stops and turns around. "Are you coming?" he asks.

I nod and follow him. He doesn't touch me, and I find myself missing the way his hand would linger at the small of my back when we walked together. It feels strange, being so close and yet so far.

The doorman beams at me, smiling as if I haven't been gone for months. I smile back at him, trying to keep up with David, who, as usual, makes straight for the elevators.

"How does it feel to be back, Mrs. Preston?" David

asks mockingly, as we start to ascend.

I shrug. "I'm not back." I say.

He smiles without humor and turns away from me. I notice that he's leaning on the metal railing and despite how cool it is, he still has a sheen of sweat on his skin.

"David..." I say, concerned. "What's wrong?"

He laughs bitterly. "Nothing." He says sharply, dismissing my question, "Everything is just perfect."

Upstairs, the familiar apartment is empty. I look around the familiar space, trying to keep my emotions in check. "Where's Mrs. Daniels?' I ask.

"It's her day off."

"Oh." I watch as he drops unto a couch in the living room and closes his eyes.

"Would you like something to eat?" I ask.

He opens his eyes and gives me a measuring look. "You're being such a dutiful little wife today, honey," he says drily, "So concerned for my welfare." He snorts. "How can I say no?"

I ignore his tone and go into the kitchen to find something for him to eat. Mrs. Daniels always has something in the fridge ready for the microwave. I find a dish wrapped in tinfoil with fish and some sort of sauce. Working fast, I warm it up and put it on a tray.

Back in the living room, David seems to have fallen

asleep.

I set the tray on the dining table, keeping one eye on him. He's breathing deeply, his chest rising and falling slowly. After I set the table, I go over to him. There's still a layer of moisture on his face, which looks drawn and tired. He's still wearing his tie and jacket, and for a second, I wonder if I should take them off him.

Of course I should, I decide, it's ridiculous to feel so nervous around a sick person.

As soon as I move closer and reach for his tie, his hands shoots up and grips mine, pulling me down until I'm sitting on his lap.

"What happened to not touching?" he asks roughly, his hands moving to my waist, holding me still so I can't get up. "Or are the rules different for you?"

"You looked uncomfortable." I explain, trying to stay calm, to ignore the raging tumult in my mind at the sudden, unexpected contact. "I was only going to loosen your tie."

He releases me with a sigh, and I get up quickly. His eyes follow the scent of food to the dining area and he grimaces. I watch as he gets ups, shrugging off his jacket and pulling at his tie as he walks over to the table. For a moment, he stares suspiciously at the food, as if he suspects me of trying to poison him. Then he sits and starts to eat, slowly, without any appetite. It's so unlike him that I'm tempted to call a doctor.

"Aren't you going to join me?" he asks.

I'm more interested in watching him, but I pick up a fork and take a few bites. I've missed Mrs. Daniel's cooking I realize, savoring the taste of the home cooked meal.

He pushes his plate away after a while and leans back in the chair.

"Maybe you should go lie down." I suggest.

"I thought you wanted to talk." He says. "Don't worry about my feelings, Sophie. I can take whatever it is you want to say."

What does he think I want to talk about? I frown. "It's not important." For now, I'm more concerned about his present state than whether he meant what he said last night "We'll talk some other time."

He doesn't argue. He sways a little as he gets up but waves me away when I try to help him. After he goes inside, I busy myself with cleaning up, unsure of what to do. I don't want to leave him while he's in such a state.

After I finish with the washing up, I go into the bedroom to find him. I can't help being assaulted by the memories as I walk along the familiar hallway and open the door to the room where we spent so much time making love.

David is lying across the bed, still clothed. He didn't even bother to remove his shoes. Worried, I hurry towards him. He is already asleep, but still sweating profusely. I touch his forehead and my fingers recoil in shock. His skin is burning.

I try to remember what I know of caring with someone with the flu or flu like symptoms. It's not very much. I take off his shoes and start on the rest of his clothes.

"Go away." he mutters.

"You're ill." I reply firmly.

"For God's sake just leave me alone." He mumbles, before drifting off again.

I try to make him as comfortable as I can before I search his emergency contact list for his doctor's number.

"I think it might be the flu that's been going around." The doctor says, when I describe the symptoms. "I'll be over shortly. If you can, just try to keep the fever down."

I ignore David's mutterings as much as I can while I mop the sweat off his forehead and neck with a damp cloth. I can't hear everything he's saying, but I hear stubborn and woman so many times that I'm sure he's talking about me.

When the doctor arrives, he confirms what he's

already said over the phone. "Make sure he has lots of fluids," He advises, "and he should be fine in a day or two. Call me if he has difficulty breathing, starts to vomit…" I listen as he reels off a list of symptoms.

After he leaves, I watch David sleep. He's tossing and turning, restless. I find myself wishing that there was more I could do for him. It surprises me, this urge to nurture, but maybe it shouldn't. I already know that I love him. It's only natural that I would want to take care of him.

I spend all night trying to keep the fever down, and it's almost morning before I fall into an exhausted sleep on one of the armchairs in the room.

When I wake up, I look around, disoriented for a moment before I remember where I am. My neck is aching cruelly from being cramped in the chair while I slept. I get up and stretch, realizing that it's already light outside and that David is no longer on the bed. I only wonder where he is for a moment before he emerges from the door that leads to the bathroom.

Naked. He's totally, completely, and perfectly naked.

I gulp, trying not to stare as my eyes rush up his body, past his perfectly sculpted muscles and all the way to his face, the only safe place to look. He still looks tired, less ill than yesterday, but nevertheless, devastatingly attractive.

"You look tired." He tells me.

I shrug. "I am, a little."

"Maybe you should rest," he mutters, walking over to sit at the edge of the bed, "I'm just going to lie down for a minute."

"Don't worry about me." I tell him, but he's already lying down again and falling asleep almost immediately. I look at my watch. It's only past seven. I should call his office and tell them not to expect him. I should call the store too and tell them that I won't be coming in. There's no way I can leave him like this.

In the living room, I make the first call to Linda, and tell her that David is ill and won't be coming to the office. While I'm making the second call to Larry, Mrs. Daniels walks into the living room.

"Mrs. Preston!" she exclaims in pleasant surprise. "You're back."

'No, I'm not.' I almost say, but I stop myself. "David is ill." I tell her, watching her face crease in concern. "He has the flu."

She shakes her head in an expression of wonder. I suppose that, like me, she has never seen him sick before.

"I'll make some soup." She offers.

I smile gratefully. "That would be perfect."

After I make my calls, I take a shower and find something to wear from my old clothes, which are still in the walk-in closet. When Mrs. Daniels brings in the soup, I wake David up to eat. He's so weak his fingers shake as he picks up the spoon.

"Let me." I say, taking the spoon from him. He doesn't object, but watches me suspiciously as I feed him.

"I'm sure I can feed myself." He says, without making any effort to take the spoon from me.

"I'm sure you can." I agree, hiding my smile.

Some hours later, he wakes up and asks for more soup. I feed it to him again, wondering at the half smile on his face.

"Why're you smiling?" I ask suspiciously.

"Nothing." He says with a chuckle.

"The fever must have fried your brain." I say teasingly, "If you're smiling for no reason."

He sighs, "My brain was fried the day I met you, Sophie." He replies cryptically.

I pause, and then force my hand to continue moving the spoon towards his mouth. *Don't say things like that!* I want to yell at him. *Don't say things that make me hope, because I don't want to hope. I want to know that you love me.*

Afterwards, he falls asleep again. I suppose he must

have been pushing himself very hard to fall so sick, so fast. With nothing else to do, I watch him sleep. Already he seems stronger, his breathing even. I should go, I think. There's no reason left for me to be here.

Yet I'm reluctant. I don't want to leave him. I remind myself that we never got a chance to talk. I should wait until he's strong enough, then I'll ask him whether he meant what he said outside my apartment.

And then what.

What if he says that I heard wrong, that he didn't really mean it. What if he rejects me all over again?

No, I should go, I decide. I'm only staying because I want to remain in the illusion that nothing is wrong, that we're still together. Sighing, I go to find my bag in the living room, and then go into the kitchen to tell Mrs. Daniels that I'm going.

She takes one look at my bag, and her motherly face falls. "You're leaving?" She asks. There is no censure in her voice, but disappointment is clear on her face.

"I... yes." Why do I feel the need to apologize? "David's much better now."

She nods slowly. "Of course."

"I think you should make him something a little more substantial than soup for dinner." I continue, eager to escape the feeling that I've somehow let her down. "I'll just go check on him before I leave."

David is sitting on the edge of the bed when I enter the room, his hair wet from the shower. He's pulled on a pair of pajama bottoms, but his chest is bare. His eyes are sharp and alert, all hint of tiredness gone. They rake me when I enter the room, taking in the bag I'm carrying.

"You're leaving." He states tersely.

"Yes." I say cautiously. Why am I the one feeling bad about leaving, when he's the one who pushed me away in the first place? I swallow. "You're obviously feeling better."

"And so you're leaving?" he repeats slowly.

I raise my shoulders in a defensive shrug. "I never intended to stay this long," I remind him, "We were only going to talk, remember?"

He gets up from the bed, his eyes glittering as he rises to his feet. "Apparently, it's not just me you find abhorrent," he says, "even being here is so unbearable to you that you can't wait to leave." He glares at me for a moment. "You should have left yesterday." He continues, "Why didn't you?"

I look away from the challenge in his eyes, distracted by his bare chest, the firmly defined muscles still gleaming from his shower. "You were ill, David." I say, "I couldn't leave you."

"Really?" He closes the space between us in one

swift movement. "Is that the only reason?"

He is right in front of me, his face less than an inch from mine. I breathe in the scent of him, his warmth. 'Yes, that's the only reason.' I want to lie, but my lips won't move. I'm still trying to get the words out, when suddenly, his lips are on mine, firm and insistent, and I don't care about talking any more.

The kiss is deep and demanding, his lips moving over mine as his tongue teases my lips apart. I let him in eagerly, glorying in each stroke of his tongue against mine. In only a few moments, I'm out of breath, my whole body humming with pleasure and shaking uncontrollably.

He guides me towards the bed, still kissing me as he lays me down on top of the covers. Dimly, I register what's happening, what we're about to do, but I don't care. I'll never get enough of him. I want him, and if he stops now I wouldn't be able to bear it.

He reaches down for the hem of the dress I rescued from the closet earlier, pulling it up until I'm bared to him except for my bra and panties. There is a queer expression on his face as he bends his heads and starts to kiss my stomach, each touch, light and tender as he moves downwards.

I grip his shoulders, my fingers running over his back, urging him back up to kiss me again. He obliges, his lips capturing mine while he trails his fingers down my body until they're between my legs, rubbing me through my panties. I can't bear it. I rub myself against them, eager for more.

How can I live without this? How is it even possible?

"Don't stop." I beg, "Don't stop."

"Never." He replies huskily.

I reach for him, running my fingers along the ridge of his arousal through the cotton pajama bottoms. Desperately I pull them down, freeing him. He groans, his eyes closed as I stroke along the length of him.

He reaches behind me and unhooks my bra, and as my breasts spill out, I see his eyes darken. He squeezes both breasts, lowering his head to lick at one nipple, then the other. I gasp at the pleasure, my body tightening, convulsing. I lift my hips and rub against him. I can't take it much longer.

He looks up into my face and smiles, "Easy," he says softly, before moving down between my legs to pull my panties off my hips. He doesn't wait to pull them all the way down before he covers me with his lips, torturing me with his tongue.

I groan loudly, my body thrashing as the first waves of pleasure hit me. He grabs hold of my thighs, spreading my legs wider as he licks, tongues and sucks me until I'm totally wrecked, sobbing and screaming incoherently.

Finally, when my body has stopped shaking, and I'm silent, he comes to lie beside me and pulls me to him, holding me against his body and stroking my hair.

"Don't leave." He whispers against my ear.

I don't say anything. I just lie there in his arms until he starts to breathe deeply.

It feels so good to be lying so close to him, held against his warm male strength, that it only takes a few moments for me to fall asleep, and I don't wake up until Mrs. Daniels knocks on the door and announces that she's bringing dinner.

She's too nice to do anything other than smile knowingly as she carries a tray into the room, placing it on the closest table beside the bed. I look away from her smile, a little embarrassed because I know that she knows that, under the covers, David and I are naked, that we've just made love, even though not long ago I told her I was leaving.

I wait for the door to close behind her, before I get off the bed to see what's in the dishes.

"This looks nice." I say turning to David, who's sitting up, and throwing the covers away from his glorious body.

"Yes it does." He agrees, his eyes never leaving me.

"You shouldn't wear clothes," he muses, eyes darkening with desire, "Not when you look so much better like this."

He only has to look at me like that and my heart accelerates.

"Come here." He says, holding out a hand to me.

"You need to eat." I tell him, trying to be sensible, ignoring the sudden warm ache between my legs.

"Yes I'm famished." He grins, and I know he's not talking about the food.

"Why don't you let me?" He gets off the bed in a fluid motion. I watch him admiringly as he loads a plate with food and motions for me to sit.

He insists on feeding me morsels with his fingers, which he allows to linger on my lips. It's so extremely sensual that each time I can't prevent myself from licking off the little bits of food from his fingers. He does the same to me when I feed him, his tongue teasing the tips of my fingers and sending small shocks up my arms and down my spine.

When we're done he kisses the middle of my palm, making me tremble.

"You're perfect." He tells me, pulling me close.

They're not the words I want to hear, but I don't care. I press my body closer to his and offer my lips for another kiss. He groans and pushes me gently back unto the bed, his lips still on mine, and his tongue in my mouth. His fingers move between my legs, stroking, caressing, and mimicking the movements of his tongue above.

I spread my legs wider, easing his way, moaning into his kiss. When I can't take it anymore, I reach for him, guiding him towards where my need for him is driving me crazy.

He covers me with his body, placing his weight on his elbows as he eases himself into me. I press my hips forward to accommodate him, moaning as he fills me totally.

My breath comes out in a long sigh, and I reach for him, running my hands down his tightly muscled arms. He grips my leg, lifting it to hook it around his waist, then he rocks backwards, and forward again, sliding slowly in and out of me. His eyes are on my face, locked on mine, and his lip are gently parted, his breath ragged and raw. His brow furrows in concentration as he thrusts, his arousal clearly visible on his face. I meet each thrust with my hips, matching his rhythm, my whole consciousness concentrated on his hard length moving in and out of me, stroking me so surely, so sweetly. I tighten my legs around him, pressing his hips closer to me, feeling his muscles flex as he drives into me again and again.

He starts to go faster, each thrust spreading the agonizing pleasure gathering where his body meets mine. I grip the sheets, screaming as my body tightens, and my back bows off the bed. He doesn't stop thrusting until my body shatters completely, then he stiffens and groans, his eyes closed, his body shuddering as he comes inside me.

I wake up sometime in the night. The room is dark except for the faint glow of the city lights from outside the windows. David's arms are wrapped around me, his head resting on my breasts.

My body is still singing with pleasure. I sigh. It would be so easy to lie here and pretend that everything is now all right, but how long will it last? We haven't resolved any of the problems that made me leave in the first place. It may feel different, but everything is still the same.

I can't imagine where we'll go from here, and it's hard to think, held so close to his body. I try to move, maybe if I put a little distance between us, I can concentrate on thinking of what I should do now.

"Don't leave me."

I look at David's face, he's still asleep, but his arms tighten around me. "Don't leave me." He murmurs again, his voice cloudy with sleep, but filled with a certain urgency and desperation. "Please."

I pull him closer, every reservation disappearing as he relaxes against me. "I'm not going anywhere." I whisper softly. "I'm not going anywhere."

Chapter Seven

WHEN I WAKE UP AGAIN, IT'S MORNING, and I'm alone on the bed. I wonder where David is, squelching the familiar feeling of having been abandoned. He isn't in the bathroom, and when I go out to look for him in the apartment, I only find Mrs. Daniels making coffee in the kitchen.

"Good morning." I say, hiding my disappointment. "Have you seen David?" I ask, already knowing the answer to my question.

"He was going out when I came in," she offers, a note of sympathy in her voice.

I nod. "Of course he was." I say, more to myself than to her. I turn back towards the bedroom, wondering why I'm so surprised and disappointed. I had fooled myself into thinking things were different, but they weren't. With David, it would always be like this.

I take a quick shower and dress mechanically, eager to leave. This time, I assure myself, I won't be coming back. I'm done with not knowing where I stand. I'm done with feeling as if I don't matter. If last night was only sex to him, like our marriage was, then I'll accept it. I'll take it as a spectacular end to what we had together, and it will be the end.

I leave the apartment, my journey down to the ground floor reminding me of another time, the first time I left. It's been two months, and yet the emotions running through me are almost identical. When it comes to David, I'm stuck in the same place, hopelessly in love, and hopelessly unloved.

I'm so preoccupied with my thoughts that I almost walk straight into the woman standing at the entrance of the building.

"Sophie!" she exclaims enthusiastically, her face lighting up in a smile that's so exactly like David's it makes me want to look away.

It's Marianne Weber, David's mother. Vaguely, I wonder what she's doing here at David's apartment building. The last time she came here, he made it very clear that he didn't want to see her.

"It's so nice to run into you here," She says,

something in her tone causing me to suspect that it wasn't coincidence. "You look distressed dear." She adds, placing a comforting hand on my shoulder. "Are you all right?"

"I'm fine." I force a smile. "I was just on my way home."

"Ah yes." She sighs sadly. "You don't live here anymore." She studies my face. "Darling, I wonder if I can interest you in having breakfast with me."

I would rather not sit across from her and have to look at the face that reminds me so much of David. I try to come up with an excuse, but I'm not fast enough.

"Please." She urges, her blue eyes full of silent entreaty.

"Okay." I say, giving in.

"We'll walk," She declares genially, waving her driver off and threading her arm through mine as we walk down the sidewalk.

"I was very distressed to hear that you'd left David." She says suddenly, without preamble. "I wanted to talk to you but there was no way to reach you."

"I changed my phone." I offer woodenly.

"Of course you did." She nods, stopping in front of a wide awning over a pair of glass doors just off the sidewalk. A doorman pulls the doors open, and we walk into large and busy café. "Well I didn't see you," She continues, "but I did see David, and he was very…" She searches for a word, "wretched."

"Yes, very wretched." I scoff, remembering the empty feeling of waking up alone in David's bed.

She sighs. "I don't know how much David's told you about his past…" She starts, as she slides gracefully into her seat.

I follow suit, sitting opposite her, "Enough to know that you neglected him." I tell her, too involved in my own misery to care whether I'm hurting her or not.

She raises a brow, and then sighs again. A waiter approaches our table, and we make our order, coffee and scones for me, tea and a croissant for her.

"I spent a lot of time with my husband," She says, "most of my time actually." She chuckles self mockingly. "Henry and David never got along, even when David was just a little boy." She shakes her head as she daintily butters her croissant, looking for all he word as if she's not talking about years of neglect of her only child. "Henry couldn't have children, so I guess he was a little bit jealous." She looks at me. "I wanted to be in love and happy, so I chose my husband over David again and again."

I shake my head in disbelief. "You didn't think David's happiness was more important than yours?" I ask. I never knew my mother, but I always imagined that if she had lived, she would have loved me more than anything else, including herself.

She looks down at her plate. "My first marriage was great, you know. Almost perfect." Her eyes cloud, and I imagine that she's remembering her first husband, David's father. "I wanted the same thing again, so I did everything that Henry wanted, trying to make him happy, so that we could be happy." She sighs. "I was a fool."

I agree silently.

She drops the croissant suddenly and looks at me, the mask of easy friendliness gone, and replaced by the pained expression of someone who realizes what she's thrown away and can never get back. "A lot of things happened when David was a child, that may have led him to close himself off emotionally, but please don't give up on him." Her eyes are glistening softly as she speaks, "He was a very loving little boy, and I'm sure that somewhere in there, if you look hard enough, you'll find a loving man."

I look away from the pain in her eyes. I don't need anybody to tell me to give David another chance. What I need, is to ignore the temptation to let him hurt me again. What I need is to forget about him, even if it destroys me.

"Think about what I said." She says with genuine feeling.

I shake my head, blaming her, for how much she ruined David's childhood and made him the man he is.

I get up from my chair. "I'm not hungry." I say abruptly, placing some money on the table and picking up my bag. "I have to go."

She doesn't try to stop me. I hurry out of the café and out onto the busy sidewalk.

At the store, neither Jan nor Larry has arrived. I go through the motions of doing my work while inside, my mind is churning, and my thoughts confused.

Don't leave me.

Why do I keep thinking of those words? His words. And why do they make me feel so confused? He didn't want me to leave, the way he held on to me, even in sleep... Well I didn't go, but he did, leaving me with nothing but the sick feeling of emptiness that's still in my stomach.

Did he assume that he had won me over, that he'd succeeded is making me helplessly his again, and that he could do whatever he wanted since I had willingly given myself to him again?

Somewhere in there, if you look hard enough, you'll find a loving man.

Would I? Oh, David can be loving. I've seen glimpses of him being loving at various times in our marriage, but is he a loving man? Is there a loving man somewhere inside the same David who used my body to subjugate me until I lost myself in his lovemaking and became pliant to his demands, the same David who threw my love back in my face and told me our marriage was only about sex?

He's not a loving man. He is hard, ruthless and dangerous.

And yet I love him.

Don't leave me.

I hear my phone ringing again in my bag, I ignore it. It's been ringing all morning. If it's David, I don't want to talk to him. If it isn't, I don't want to talk to anyone else either.

Larry arrives, then Jan. For some reason, neither of them tries to make conversation with me. Maybe my feelings of confusion and dejection are clear on my face, either way I'm soon left with only my continuously ringing phone and the familiar sounds of videogames for company.

Don't leave me.

The phone stops ringing, then starts again almost

immediately, I pull it out of my bag, thinking of switching it off, but when I see David's name flashing on the screen, I give in and answer the call.

"Sophie." I hear him breathe. "Where are you?" He says, with something like relief in his voice.

I swallow the lump in my throat. "I'm at work."

"You could have let me know you were leaving."

"Like you did before you left?" I retort sarcastically.

For a long moment, he doesn't say anything. "I had something to attend to." He says finally.

"You always do." I reply.

He sighs, "Look Sophie, I need to see you."

I shake my head. "Please David, there's nothing more…"

"I'm on my way," he continues, interrupting me.

"Don't come here." I protest.

At first, he doesn't reply, but when he does, his voice is firm and determined. "Try and stop me." he says, before he cuts the connection.

I consider leaving before David arrives. I still feel too raw to talk to him. How do I tell him that I've had enough, that we're over, when I feel like any moment I'll shatter into a million tiny pieces.

He must have been driving really fast, because in less than thirty minutes, I see a black car I don't recognize park on the sidewalk in front of the store, and the next moment, David is striding through the doors.

I expected him to be dressed for work, but he's wearing casual clothes, jeans, a white shirt, and a black jacket. For a second, I allow myself to be distracted by how beautiful he is. From his perfectly sensual face to his athletic body and long, long legs.

This is the man I love, I realize. This is the man I'll always love.

"Can we talk?" he asks, gesturing towards the door to Jan and Larry's office.

Can I refuse? I wonder. If I say no, would he walk out of the door and out of my life? I don't think so.

I nod.

"About this morning..."

There's something about the sound of his voice. The tenderness is pulling at my heart, and suddenly I can't bear it anymore.

"Don't tell me." I say, stopping him, "Please David. This morning I..." I swallow as my voice catches in my throat. "Nothing has changed David. I'm always going to be the girl who loves you even though she shouldn't, and you're always going to be that man to whom love means nothing."

"Sophie…"

"No wait." I continue. "I spoke to your mother this morning."

His body stiffens and a shuttered expression comes over his face. "What?"

"I bumped into her when I was leaving this morning," I tell him, "and she asked me to join her for breakfast so we could talk."

"And what did she have to say?" He asks coolly, his tone betraying that whatever his mother has to say means little to him.

"She explained that she may have hurt you by putting your stepfather's needs ahead of yours." I say. "I think she was trying to say that she hurt you then, and that you're still hurting because of that."

He snorts bitterly. "Is that what she said?" He laughs harshly. "Well beneath those pretty words Sophie, the truth is this. I never got along with my stepfather. He hated me from the first, and I grew to hate him too. He mocked me, belittled me, and verbally abused me any chance he got. But my mother never saw that, all she wanted was to be his wife, to travel the world with him and attend parties, play the socialite.

David pauses and takes a deep breath. "He used to

hit her." He says with a deep frown. "She'd have a bruise and tell everyone that she fell or something, I didn't even know until I saw him hit her when I was fourteen."

I close my eyes, feeling his pain. "What did you do?" I ask gently.

"I didn't know what to do." He says, looking into my face, his eyes searching mine, as if looking for some confirmation that there was nothing he could have done. "When I begged her to leave Henry, she laughed and said I was imagining things because I hated him so much." He laughs mirthlessly. "It went on like that till I was about seventeen, then one day he lost his temper and hit her, right in front of me. He kept hitting her, and when I tried to pull him off, he started to hit me too. Well I fought back, and I beat him up really badly. I didn't know what my mother would think. But I didn't expect her to stand beside Henry when he had me arrested, and say nothing in my defense."

"She didn't explain why you hit him?"

David shakes his head. "Henry told the police that I was prone to violent fits, and she agreed with him, she agreed with everything he said. I spent a week in a facility for troubled teens, and he hired a psychiatrist who agreed with what they said. I was going to be transferred to a home because he had everybody convinced that I was crazy.

"I'm so sorry David."

He turns away, pacing away from my desk before coming right back, a frown marring his brow. "Do you know why my mother agreed with him, Sophie?" he asks, "because she signed a pre-nup before they got married. In the event of a divorce, she'd have gotten nothing. That's why she threw me over for him again and again, because losing the money and status meant more than her son's life."

I sigh, "She said she was in love with him, that she just wanted to make him happy."

"I'm sure she did." David scoffs, "She's very good at telling herself what she wants to believe."

"What happened after?" I ask, "How did you get out?"

"I don't know." He shrugs. "One day, I was released, all the charges were dropped, and my record wiped clean. Steve picked me up and took me to the house. When we got there both Henry and my mother had gone on another one of their trips. I left, and never went back, and I never heard from my mother until after Henry died."

I shake my head. "I didn't know." I say, my heart breaking for him.

"Well, you couldn't have." He frowns. "The next

time she tries to make you feel some sympathy for her and tells you that she 'hurt' me when I was a child, at least you'll know what she did."

I nod. At least now I know why he never lets anyone in, why he couldn't let me in. He's been hurt by someone he loved, at the time when it could make the most impression, and now he'll never expose himself to that kind of pain again.

I'll never hurt him, but what does it matter? He doesn't trust anyone enough to let them in, not even me.

"David," I get up and go around my desk to where he's standing. "I'd like to show you something."

He looks wary. "What is it?"

"You'll have to come with me." I tell him with a gentle smile. He waits while I interrupt the tournament going on in the back office to tell Jan and Larry that I have to step out for a while. They wave me off, more concerned about finishing their game than about me.

"About this morning..." David starts again, his voice strangely hesitant. I look at his face, confused by the uncertain expression I find there. What is he going to say?

"Wait." I tell him, leading him outside. "You can tell me later."

Surprisingly, he obeys, and follows me down the

street to the museum, as he holds one of the swing doors open for me to step inside, there's a quizzical look on his face, but he doesn't ask any questions.

Trey smiles and waves at me, but when he sees David, he doesn't come over to talk.

I lead David to the painting, faltering as we approach it. I've been so certain about it for so long, but now I wonder if maybe I'm wrong. What if David doesn't believe me? What if he can't see what I see when I look at it.

It's hanging in its usual place, everything about it the same as when I first saw it.

David stares at the painting for a while, and then reads the name at the bottom. "Jonathan Cutler," he says at last. "I've never heard of him." He looks at me, his eyes searching. "Does it mean something to you?"

"Yes." I sigh, "When I first started working at the store I used to come here just to look at this." I pause. "It just drew me, somehow."

David nods, his eyes encouraging me to continue.

"Then I learned that the painter was a professor at one of the local colleges, and that he had an affair with one of his students. When his wife found out, she drove her car over a bridge with him in it."

David gives the painting another searching look. "And this was the student?"

I nod. "He loved her." I say. "That's what I see when I look at this painting. That even though it was wrong, and even tough ultimately, it destroyed all their lives, he loved her."

"All their lives?" he frowns at me, I can almost see his mind working, "She... The student...You don't think...?"

I nod silently, answering his question. He remembers, I think in wonder, he remembers our first real conversation when I told him about my mother. It seems like ages ago, but he didn't forget, surely that means something.

"Are you sure?" He looks from me to the painting and back again.

"Yes," I smile sadly. "She was pregnant, and he was dead. That's why she left school, came home, and had me."

"And then she died." He looks sad. "I'm sorry Sophie."

"It doesn't matter now." I say. I look up into his face, searching his eyes, "David, I know that love can be destructive. I know it can hurt, and God knows I've been a victim, I grew up a victim of what love can cause when it's wrong, but I'm not ready to never be in love again, to never be loved again. Because without love, life doesn't mean as much as it should." I pause.

"You think that because you've been hurt by someone you loved, you shouldn't love anyone ever again."

"Sophie," David interrupts, "You're wrong, if you think I can't…won't love you because of my childhood, because of my mother and stepfather," he breathes, "Well you're wrong."

My breath hitches in my throat. Then why is it? I wonder, am I just unworthy then, unlovable in some way that I don't know. Am I good only for sex?

"You're wrong, Sophie," he continues emphatically, his eyes intense, "Because I love you."

I feel my breath leave my chest.

His eyes are searching mine, and when he speaks, there's a desperate edge to his voice. "I think may have loved you from the first time I saw you."

There is a lump in my throat. This is not the same as his outburst in Bellevue, only a few days ago. He is in control of himself, and he's telling me that he loves me.

"I love you, Sophie." He says again.

I close my eyes as his words wash over me, wanting so much to believe him. "Do you mean that?" I ask, "Or are you only saying it because you think it's what I want to hear?"

"No, I mean every word." He frowns, shaking his head. "I've spent my life avoiding close relationships. I think Steve may have been the closest person to me, before you. But everything I thought I was changed when I met you." He moves forward and takes my hands in his, "That day you left, I would have lain at your feet and begged you to stay, even then I knew I didn't want to … I knew I couldn't live without you." He sighs, his eyes imploring me to believe him. "But I was afraid, jealous, confused…" he shakes his head. "It's been hell since you left Sophie. Nothing is the same."

I want to cry. "But this morning…"

"About that…" he turns to look at the painting, and when he looks back at me he has a strange smile on his face. "This morning I went to get you something."

I search his face. "What?"

I watch, stupefied, as he gets down on one knee. "I love you, Sophie Bennett – Preston," He says, producing a ring from his pocket, "and if you give me another chance, I promise to do it right this time, to spend the rest of my life proving just how much I love you."

I want to scream, to let out the incredible rush of joy in my heart. I can't breathe. I'm crying, and I'm just so happy.

"Oh, David!" I say, wrapping my arms around him as tears start to fall down my face. "I love you so much."

He gets up, lifting me with him. "So you'll come home?" he asks, his face relaxing into a relieved smile.

I laugh happily and proceed to cover his face with kisses. "Nothing can keep me away."

Epilogue

I'M SCARED.

There's a storm, and it sounds really bad. I pull my blankie closer and try not to hear the scary noise outside. Mommy says it's just the wind whistling, but I know it's ghosts screaming, bad ghosts who haven't gone to heaven like my Dad.

I miss my Dad.

I want to cry, but I try my best not to, Henry, my new step-father, says only weak little boys cry. The night I woke up and ran around the big house looking for my Dad, he called me a sissy.

And mommy didn't say anything.

It's so dark in my room. I miss my old room in our old house, where me and mommy and my dad lived together. Henry's house is big and scary, even during the day. I hate it here, but mommy says I shouldn't say that.

Suddenly the room is very bright, and then it goes dark again. I cover my ears because I know there'll be thunder soon. My dad said that was only because light travels faster than sound even though they both happen at the same time. That doesn't stop it from being scary.

I don't hear anything, so I remove my hands from my ears. Then the thunder comes, and it's so scary because it's loud and I can hear it inside my head. I close my eyes, and the noise doesn't stop. The room is shaking like an earthquake.

I scream and run outside, down the long dark hallway to the big room where mommy and Henry sleep together now. I open the door and run inside.

Mommy is alone on the bed, so I climb up on her side.

"Mommy?"

"Sweetheart." Her voice is sleepy. It sounds like back in our real house, when I used to climb into the bed with her and my dad. She doesn't call me sweetheart anymore now, not when Henry is around.

"I'm scared."

She sits up and hugs me. "It's just a storm baby, an itty bitty storm."

I hug her back tightly. "I want it to stop."

"It will, soon."

I don't feel so scared anymore. I close my eyes and imagine that we're back at home, and my Dad is still alive. She'll sing something funny, and I'll laugh with my dad and then fall asleep on their bed.

"Sing something Mommy."

She looks towards the bathroom, and then she closes her eyes. She almost starts to sing, but then the door to the bathroom opens, and Henry comes into the room wearing a robe.

He stops when he sees me. Immediately I start to feel scared again.

"What's he doing here?" He asks my mom.

"There's a storm. Henry."

He doesn't say anything, but he's looking at my mom and he looks a little mad. She sighs and gets up from the bed. "Come on David." She says, walking ahead of me, out of the room.

I follow her, turning to look at Henry before I leave the room. Another flash of lightning comes from the window behind him, and it makes him look scary, like a monster. I scream and run out of the door, bumping into my mommy's legs.

She doesn't look at me until we reach my room. She puts me back to bed, her face looking sad. She didn't used to look sad when my dad was alive.

"Don't go back mommy." I tell her.

"Go to sleep.' She whispers.

There's another flash of lightning and before long the thunder comes again.

"Don't go mummy." I beg.

"David." She sighs and gets up. "It's only a storm."

But it's scary. I want to cry, even though I'm trying my best not to. "Don't go." I say, but she continues to walk towards the door.

"Don't leave me."

"David."

"Don't leave me."

Arms tighten around me, my nose fills with the sweet scent that's all her. I pull her closer, filling my senses with her.

"I won't leave you."

I sigh, relief flooding me even in my sleep. Opening my eyes, I see Sophie looking at me, her beautiful green eyes right in front of my face.

"I love you." I tell her, and I mean every word. My heart is full to the point of bursting from having her so close to me. "I love you."

She giggles. "We love you too." She says softly.

My hand drifts down to the smooth roundness of her stomach, where our child is growing. It's the most wondrous thing I've ever felt. "I love you." I say again. No matter how many times I say it, it wouldn't be enough. I have to tell her as often as possible, and not just with words, because she is my life, the end of my nightmares. My love.

Forever.

About The Author

Serena Grey discovered her first love when she was a child, and that love, reading, has been her constant companion since then.

She still loves to read, but now she also writes, because the stories in her head won't leave her in peace otherwise. Even though she loves all kinds of fiction, she has a soft spot for love and romance, and that flush of pleasure that can only be found at the end of a beautiful love story.

When she's not reading and writing, she enjoys cocktails, coffee, the Vampire Diaries, Smash, and constantly drools over Gabriel Macht as Harvey Spector in Suits.

From The Author

Thank you all so much for sticking with me to the end of this series. Even though I'm soooo happy to have completed my first series. I feel a little sad, knowing that my time with David and Sophie is over. Hopefully, I'll be able to create new characters before too long, that will also capture your hearts and keep you entertained.

If you enjoyed this book, please consider leaving a review. I would love to know what you think.

Come check out my website at www.serenagrey.com, or hang out at my Facebook page www.facebook.com/authorserenagrey.

If you would like to receive an email alert whenever I have a new release, then subscribe at www.serenagrey.com/alerts.

Thank you for reading.

Love,

Serena Grey

CPSIA information can be obtained at www.ICGtesting.com
Printed in the USA
BVOW05s1628310714

361209BV00003B/3/P